SIMON SAYS

Simon, Lord Launceston and Judith had agreed to make Antonia jealous, so that Simon might win Antonia back. Thus Judith could not protest when Simon said, "It's time we gave Antonia something to think about," and pulled Judith into his arms and bent over for a kiss.

Judith gasped. But she could not prevent her arms from sliding around Simon's neck, nor stop herself from straining up against him, responding to his kiss with every iota of desire that she had ever suppressed.

What Simon said was one thing . . . what Simon had just done was another . . . as Judith realized that what was make-believe love for him had turned real for her. . . .

MARY JO PUTNEY graduated from Syracuse University with degrees in eighteenth-century British literature and industrial design. She lived in California and England before settling in Baltimore, Maryland, where she was a freelance graphic designer before becoming a full-time writer.

Carousel of Hearts

by

Mary Jo Putney

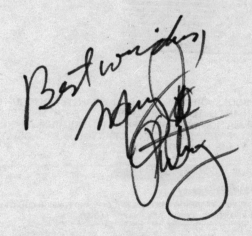

Best wishes,
Mary Jo Putney

A SIGNET BOOK

NEW AMERICAN LIBRARY

A DIVISION OF PENGUIN BOOKS USA INC.

Copyright © 1989 by Mary Jo Putney

SIGNET, SIGNET CLASSIC, MENTOR, ONYX, PLUME, MERIDIAN
and NAL BOOKS are published by New American Library,
a division of Penguin Books USA Inc.,
1633 Broadway, New York, New York 10019

First Printing, November, 1989

1 2 3 4 5 6 7 8 9

PRINTED IN THE UNITED STATES OF AMERICA

To Ruth Cohen,
who is everything
an agent should be,
and more.

Prologue

With a qualm that would have amazed the polite world, the dowager Lady Forrester drew a deep breath, then announced, "Since you refuse to engage a companion, I've done it for you."

Lady Antonia Thornton had been carefully darkening her brows, but at the statement she whipped her bright head around to stare at her aunt. "You did *what*?" she asked in a dangerous tone.

Strong men had been known to crumble under the beautiful Lady Antonia's cinnamon-brown gaze, but her aunt was made of sterner stuff. Lady Forrester had deliberately chosen to approach her niece in the young woman's boudoir, hoping that the informal setting might make the girl more malleable. It had been a very slim hope. "I have engaged a companion for you. It is bad enough that you insist on setting up your own establishment now that your father is dead, but it is unthinkable that you should live alone."

Antonia swiveled around on the chair to face her aunt. "I am twenty-four years old, the daughter of the ninth Earl of Spenston, a baroness in my own right, and the mistress of my own indecently large fortune," she said in a precise, controlled voice. "Why the devil should I have to tolerate the vagaries of some insipid, bantling-brained female?"

"Because you are a part of society, no matter how much you choose to think otherwise," Lady Forrester snapped. "Even birth and wealth will not allow you unlimited license, and you already had a reputation as a bluestocking and an eccentric even before you jilted Lord Ramsay. What would your father say if he were alive?''

Antonia stood, drawing herself up to her full, impressive height. ''My father would have encouraged me to do what I thought best. He abhorred missishness and was the one who taught me how foolish most social rules are.''

The dowager realized that it had been a mistake to invoke Antonia's father; the late earl had been a politician noted for his radical beliefs. Since the fool man had not seen fit to teach his daughter that females could not expect the same freedom as males. Lady Forrester tried a more conciliatory tack. ''I won't deny that many of society's strictures are foolish, but paying lip service can make your life much simpler and will give you more freedom to do what you wish. Your father would have been the first to recommend holding your fire for the battles that matter most.''

Seeing that her words were having some effect, she continued, ''I know better than to engage a companion who is, as you so vulgarly put it, 'bantling-brained.' Judith Winslow is a young widow, a connection of my husband's family. She's only a couple of years older than you, very intelligent, and no more missish than you are. I think you would deal extremely well together.''

''I don't care if she's a Fellow of the Royal Society,'' Antonia said in exasperation. ''I don't want a companion, and that's final. Go foist your poor relation off on someone else.''

The door to Lady Antonia's boudoir was open, and every word of the battling ladyships carried clearly to the slight young woman who sat in the adjoining sitting room, her hands folded in her lap, her expression carefully blank. Judith Winslow was used to being unwanted: as an orphan she had been shuttled between the homes of various relations, treated as something between a charity girl and a nursery maid.

Judith had learned early that to be noticed by men invited trouble, and for safety's sake she had developed a drab mode of dressing that rendered her effectively invisible. Dowdiness had served her well, and the only person who had ever shown serious interest in her was the curate who had briefly been her husband. She rather thought that Edwin Winslow's real wish had been to acquire a nurse for the fatal illness he had concealed when he proposed, but at least his attentions had been honorable.

In spite of her appearance of calm, the hand that Judith raised to subdue a strand of chestnut hair trembled slightly. She had known this journey was a mistake, but Lady Forrester had been insistent, and the dowager was not an easy woman to withstand. Well, in a few minutes it would be over and they could leave. Doubtless Lady Forrester would let Judith stay at her own town house for a few weeks while the poor relation searched the London agencies for a situation. Judith had had quite enough of being passed around the Forrester family like a parcel of worn clothes; it was time to find a position on merit. Perhaps, if she was very lucky, she would find an employer who wished his daughters to be well-educated in natural philosophy as well as embroidery and sketching.

She listened to the raised voices critically. Her situation had made her expert in judging other people's moods, and it was clear that Lady Antonia was not amused by her aunt's presumption. Lady Forrester appeared to have given up the fight. With resignation she said, "Very well, if you won't have Mrs. Winslow, tell her yourself. She's waiting in your sitting room."

"What!" Lady Antonia's rich contralto rose to a new level of outrage. "You dragged that poor woman over here and left her where she would hear us brangling? I've known you to do some cow-handed things, Aunt Lettie, but this is the outside of enough. How could you?"

The statement was accompanied by the sound of swift footsteps, and Judith was already rising to her feet when Lady Antonia swept into the sitting room. Judith was hard-pressed not to gasp. She had heard that Lady Antonia was beautiful and had taken the evaluation with a grain of salt; by definition, all heiresses are beautiful, and her ladyship's forceful, intemperate language had implied a masculine sort of female.

There was nothing the least bit masculine about the

dazzling young woman in front of her. Lady Antonia had a perfection of form and feature that mere money could never have achieved. She was above average height, with a splendid figure and a glowing vitality that illuminated the sitting room. Her most striking feature was a cascade of hair that was neither red nor gold, but a shimmering color somewhere in between, a molten shade reminiscent of apricots and sunsets. Her wide, direct eyes were a warm brown with cinnamon depths, and her mobile, high-cheekboned face looked better suited to laughter than tears. Even mourning could not dim her sparkle; indeed, she looked magnificent in black.

With weary resignation, Judith's eyes met Lady Antonia's across the width of the room. In the face of such splendor, Judith drew in on herself, unconsciously raising her chin as she waited to be sent away. She had survived worse than this; it had not been her idea to come, and she had no reason to feel humiliation at being rejected.

The moment stretched as the young women's gazes locked and held. Though her aunt had said the proposed companion was young, Antonia was still surprised at the widow's youthfulness. Mrs. Winslow looked scarcely old enough to have been married, much less widowed. She was small-boned and fragile of build, her thick chestnut hair pulled severely back, her fair complexion drained of color by the mourning blacks she wore. Her face would have been more than attractive under other circumstances, but today her translucent skin was stark and tight over the delicate bones.

Clothing was a mere detail; what struck Antonia was the fine gray eyes that returned Antonia's gaze with bleak bravery. In a flash of intuition, Antonia sensed a lifetime of forced patience, of poverty, of hopelessness, the life of an outsider who lives on the sufferance of others. Yet Judith Winslow was not defeated. There was strength and courage in those clear eyes that refused to drop, and Antonia responded to those qualities, wondering if she herself would be equally brave under such circumstances. "I'm sorry that you heard that, Mrs. Winslow. You'll have gathered that I find the idea of a companion quite insupportable."

The widow lifted her small chin as if bracing for a blow,

and the gallantry of her gesture triggered one of Antonia's impulsive decisions. "I don't need a companion or a slave, but one can always use more friends." She crossed the room and offered her hand. "Shall we see if we can be friends?"

The expressive gray eyes registered shock, then a rush of emotion that came perilously near tears. Antonia saw and understood the other woman's struggle for composure; when one is hurting, kindness can be harder to accept than cruelty.

Mastering herself, Judith Winslow accepted Antonia's hand. "I should like that very much," she said in a soft, cultured voice. "Very much indeed."

Though Antonia did not know it then, the casual, unthinking generosity that was the despair and delight of her intimates had just won her a lifetime's loyalty.

1

Antonia gazed at the book in her lap and realized that her eyes had traversed the page three times, yet she couldn't remember a single word. In fact, she didn't even remember what the book was. A novel, apparently. She raised her head and glanced across the sitting room to Judith. "Do you think Adam will be here soon? It must be almost noon."

Curled up in the window seat with her embroidery, Judith offered a sympathetic smile. "It is now five minutes later than the last time you asked that question, and midday won't be here for some time yet."

Antonia wrinkled her nose ruefully and gave up on her book, setting it on a table before standing and pacing the sitting room with long impatient strides. For the hundredth time since receiving her cousin's letter the month before, she fretted, "If I had known what ship he was arriving on, I could have met him."

As she had on numerous other occasions, Judith patiently replied, "I'm sure that is exactly why he didn't tell you. Even though you haven't seen each other in eight years, obviously your cousin remembers you very well. He must have known you would go rushing down to the port in person, and the Isle of Dogs is hardly the place for a lady to wait."

"Don't you dare be logical," Antonia exclaimed, laughing in spite of herself. She went back to pacing the sitting room, where the two women spent much of their time when they were in London. Less formal than the drawing room, it commanded a fine view of Grosvenor Square. The furniture was chosen more for comfort than for style, and books, periodicals, and musical instruments gave the room a friendly air.

It was not as good as being at her estate, Thornleigh, but it was the most welcoming spot in the house. Absently plucking the strings of Judith's harp, she said, "You're quite right, even after eight years Adam knows me better than anyone else."

Adam Yorke was not a near relation, only her second cousin, but they had been raised together. Three years older than Antonia, he was the brother she had never had. When they were young, he had been the most important person in her world; she had even once thought . . . She cut the thought off sharply. What mattered was that he was her best friend. Antonia shot Judith a quick, guilty glance. Well, Adam was her best male friend; one can be close to friends in different ways. Certainly Judith was the closest female friend Antonia had ever had.

As she had done approximately once a day for over two years, Antonia blessed the chance that had brought Judith into her life. Though the women appeared very different on the surface, their minds, opinions, and humor matched beautifully. Judith was the best of companions, while at the same time respecting Antonia's need for privacy, because Judith herself needed time alone. Aunt Lettie still preened herself on the success of her meddling and took considerable pleasure in the fact that Judith's calm good sense checked some of Antonia's wilder starts.

In return, Judith had blossomed in an atmosphere where she was not only encouraged, but required, to speak her mind. The pale little widow was gone forever. Now she was a quietly lovely young woman, her rich chestnut hair falling in gentle waves around a delicate face that looked younger than her twenty-eight years. The two women had emerged from mourning about the same time, and Antonia had taken the occasion to coax her companion into a new wardrobe, arguing that it was Judith's duty to be in her best looks, since Antonia was the one required to see her. Judith would have balked if she had known how much her elegantly simple clothing cost, but the bills were a secret between Antonia and the fashionable modiste both women patronized.

Abandoning the harp, Antonia crossed to the mantel and lifted a graceful wood sculpture of a peregrine falcon resting on a branch, its head cocked to one side, as if recalling the joy of flight. Adam had carved the falcon when he was fifteen, giving it to her for her twelfth birthday. She stroked the polished wood lovingly. It was beautifully made; her cousin had always been clever with his hands. As children, they had roamed the hills hunting nests together, taking care not to frighten the parent birds so the eggs and babies wouldn't be neglected.

As Antonia set the sculpture back on the mantel, Judith said slowly, "I probably shouldn't even suggest this, but have you considered how much your cousin might have changed over the years? He was scarcely twenty-one when he went to the East Indies. He's a man now. Things might not be the same."

"Nonsense!" Antonia caressed the satiny wood again. "With all the letters we've exchanged over the years, I would have noticed if Adam had suddenly become someone else. He'll have changed some, of course—who doesn't change in eight years?—but he'll still be Adam."

A slight frown was forming between her brows, and Antonia consciously smoothed it out. She had never understood why Adam had left England the way he did. Her father had intended to buy Adam a commission in the army when he came down from Cambridge. Then, abruptly, Adam was gone, leaving only a hastily scribbled note that he had decided to enter the East India Company instead, and he must catch a ship immediately. He had apologized for not saying a proper good-bye and had written faithfully over the years since, but had never once explained why he had not discussed such an important decision with her.

Antonia repressed a sigh. Perhaps Adam had known she would have tried to talk him out of leaving. His cavalier departure had been a tremendous shock, making Antonia understand how much she had misjudged his feelings. She shrugged, impatient with her thoughts. What mattered now was that he was back, and the bonds of blood and friendship were more powerful than romantic dreams had ever been.

Judith watched Antonia sympathetically. Judith herself was

almost as impatient for Adam Yorke's arrival as her mistress was. She had been hearing about Adam for over two years, had listened to lengthy excerpts from his letters, and had a mental image of an intelligent man with a kind heart and a ready sense of humor. She quite looked forward to meeting him.

Sometimes Judith wondered if there was anything romantic in Antonia's attachment to her cousin, but had seen no sign of that. In fact, Judith had never seen Antonia show even the faintest of *tendres* for anyone, in spite of the swarms of men who buzzed hopefully around when they were in London. Her employer was something of an enigma: Antonia was warm and demonstrative by nature, and she could be very outgoing, talking and flirting with her admirers, but there was a restless side to her, the side that needed the wide-open spaces and freedom of her estate in the Peak District. Because of her stunning beauty, she had few close friends; most women resented her and most men desired her, leaving little room for the relaxed pleasures of friendship.

Perhaps Judith's mistress would spend the rest of her days as a happy headstrong spinster. Antonia had no need to marry for either fortune or status, and considering how poorly many marriages turned out, Judith couldn't fault her friend for avoiding the state. Why marry unless one was sure it would be an improvement? And even then, a woman could easily be wrong; Judith had been. But perhaps Antonia just hadn't found the right man; sometimes Judith suspected that her friend had a secret romantic streak. Judith shrugged and returned to her embroidery. If Antonia ever decided to marry, there would be no lack of candidates for her hand.

As Judith concentrated on her tiny, exquisite stitches, she hoped that Adam Yorke would arrive soon; when her mistress was in this mood, it was like sharing a cage with a tiger. Admittedly Antonia was an amiable tiger, but the situation was not restful.

Some time passed while Judith stitched and Antonia played passionately on the pianoforte, nobly refraining from asking the time again. It was nearly noon when Judith straightened up in her window seat and stretched, glancing down into Grosvenor Square as she did. A hackney was stopping, and her gaze sharpened as a man stepped down and looked up at Antonia's house.

Surely this must be Adam Yorke, and for a moment Judith studied him as he in turn scanned the marble facade. The sun was coming at an angle that prevented the new arrival from seeing inside, but his uncertain expression was clearly visible to Judith. While Antonia might not think the time that had passed made a difference, apparently her cousin was not so sure. Perhaps eight years building a fortune at the other end of the world were longer than eight years moving through the timeless cycles of English society.

Dismissing the fanciful thought, Judith said casually, as if this was not a much-anticipated event, "I suspect that your cousin has arrived. At any rate, a gentleman carrying a package is about to knock at the door."

The pianoforte stopped abruptly, leaving a crashing silence. "What does he look like?" Antonia demanded.

"Sun-browned, solidly built. I can't see his hair under his hat," Judith reported. Before she could say more Antonia was gone, leaving an open door and a rapidly fading sound of footsteps. Even on her most restrained days Antonia was impetuous, and in her present mood she was neither to hold nor to bind. Amused, Judith rose and followed with more dignity.

Standing at the top of the stairs that swept down into the entry hall, Judith had a perfect view of the scene below her. The newcomer was handing both hat and package to the butler, revealing light-brown hair streaked by the sun. Somewhere in his travels he had found a notable tailor, but even Weston could not have rendered that broad, powerful frame elegant. Judith guessed that Adam Yorke was too muscular, too vital, to be fashionable. He looked like a man who knew a great deal about hard work, and work was very unfashionable indeed.

Antonia was wasting no time in analysis. Instead, she pelted down the steps, her apricot curls flaring behind her as she cried out, "Adam!"

Her cousin gazed up at the sound of her voice, and Judith got a clear view of him. His wide-boned features were pleasant rather than handsome, and for a moment Judith saw the same uncertainty she had noticed when he was outside. Then his face lit up at the sight of Antonia's headlong rush.

Two steps above the bottom of the stairs, Antonia launched herself out toward her cousin. It said much for Adam Yorke's reflexes and strength that he was able to catch her in midair, the force of her leap whirling him halfway around. He gave Antonia a comprehensive hug before setting her down on the marble floor. The cousins' laughter joined and floated up, Adam exclaiming in a deep, rich baritone, "Good Lord, Lady Hoyden, haven't you grown up yet?"

"Of course not!" Antonia's arms were linked around his neck as she beamed up into his face. "Wouldn't you be dreadfully disappointed if I had?"

"I expect I would."

Adam touched a gentle hand to his cousin's bright hair as Judith watched, and she felt embarrassed to observe the intimacy between them. Reminding herself that the butler was also an interested spectator, Judith descended the stairs at a much slower rate than her employer had. Antonia might think of Adam as her brother, but the world at large would consider her raptures unseemly, and part of Judith's job was to protect her employer from censure. That meant making her presence known now.

As she reached the bottom of the staircase, Antonia glanced up with a vivid smile. "Judith, you will have gathered that this is my prodigal cousin, Adam Yorke. Adam, this is my companion, Mrs. Winslow."

As the newcomer turned to her, Judith saw that Adam was only a little over average height, but his broad frame made him seem larger. His eyes were the changeable kind, gray-green with flecks of brown, and as they fell on her, she saw surprise in them. Then his expression warmed to amusement as he bowed very correctly over Judith's hand. His fingers clasped hers with the practiced gentleness of a man who must be careful of using too much strength, but she still felt power in his touch.

"A pleasure to meet you, Mrs. Winslow. If I look startled, it is because Tony has been systematically misleading me for the last two years." He glanced at his cousin. "So this is the ferocious widow that Lady Forrester foisted on you. I thought there was something smoky about that tale—I couldn't imagine you accepting foisting from anyone."

Antonia laughed. "I assure you, she is the veriest dragon. Say something in dragon, Judith."

Perfectly straight-faced, Judith said, "Most improper, Lady Antonia. That is the outside of enough, Lady Antonia." She had the exact inflection of Lady Forrester at her most top-lofty, and as she ended with "Deplorable what modern manners are coming to, Lady Antonia," her listeners succumbed to appreciative laughter.

"I am convinced. Mrs. Winslow is clearly ferocious." Retrieving his package from the butler, Adam suggested, "Shall we adjourn to the drawing room? In the best traveler's tradition, I have brought back bits of trumpery from the ends of the earth."

They went to the more informal sitting room, where Adam produced marvelous gifts that could hardly be called trumpery. There was an exquisite cloisonné pendant, smooth ivory figurines, even a crystal scent bottle from China with elegant goldfish painted on the inside surface. Antonia unplugged the bottle and sniffed, her eyes closed. "M-m-m, how wonderful. It smells so un-English. I can fancy myself in an Oriental bazaar."

As Antonia passed the bottle to Judith to test, Adam said cheerfully, "The Orient has its share of less appealing odors, but this particular perfume is said to be the favorite of the Emperor of China's chief concubine." He stopped, then laughed ruefully. "Now that I am back in England, I expect I shouldn't mention such a thing to an unmarried lady."

"Don't you dare get missish on me," Antonia said, her voice stern but with laughter shining through. Having Adam within touching distance still seemed to good to be true. As she studied her cousin hungrily, she felt a curious kind of duality; though his open, laugh-lined face seemed more familiar than her own, at the same time she felt the span of years that lay between them. His warm eyes were the same, as was his teasing half-smile, but years of sun and wind had weathered his complexion, making him look older and more authoritative. Antonia knew that Adam had done rather well with his business ventures and that he had had experiences she could never really understand. It was easy to imagine him as a formidable adversary, but he still felt like her cousin and favorite relation, not like a stranger.

While she had been thinking, Adam produced a length of brilliant silk and laid it in her arms. Antonia gasped at its incredible lightness, and the shimmering, ever-changing colors defied description. Certainly one of the rich shades that the sunlight struck from the material was the same apricot as her hair. There was also a broad border of gold embroidery along one edge, but beyond that . . . Words failed her. She lifted a length of the fragile shining stuff in her hands, admiring its softness and the sensual way it flowed. "This is the most beautiful fabric I've ever seen, Adam. Where is it from?"

"India. It's a sari, the garment Indian women wear." He reached inside his coat for an envelope, then handed it to her. "No mere male could begin to describe how it is worn, but a woman I knew in Bombay wrote down directions for the correct way to fold it. You'll probably want to have the fabric made into a dress, but I was sure that you would want to try it Indian-style at least once."

"Of course." Her arms full of silk, Antonia impulsively leaned across to give Adam a kiss on the cheek. "As usual, you think of everything. Thank you."

She felt her cousin tense slightly at her touch. Though he was clean-shaven, her lips registered the faint, barely perceptible prickle of whiskers as they pressed against his cheek. It was a masculine texture; more clearly than words, the contact reminded her that Adam was a man, not a boy. Disconcerted, she drew back from the contact quickly.

Perhaps she imagined the slight pause before Adam smiled and dug out one last item. "And this is for you, Mrs. Winslow."

Judith had been doing her considerable best to efface

herself to invisibility, and she was startled when Adam Yorke held the gift out to her. For most of her life she had been an onlooker, the one who had no right to expect presents or special favors, and the thoughtfulness of the gesture made her voice catch when she tried to speak. "You shouldn't have brought me anything, Mr. Yorke. Why, you don't even know me."

"True, but I wanted to turn Antonia's companion up sweet," he said, using the slang with the utmost gravity. "I thought that a box for medications would be a suitable choice for an aging widow of uncertain temper."

As Judith gazed into the warm, changeable eyes, she realized without question that Adam Yorke also knew much about being an outsider. For the first time, she wondered exactly why he had been raised with Antonia and what had become of his parents. But of course it was none of her business. Quickly she bent her head to examine the wooden box he placed in her hands.

"It's made from sandalwood," he added.

The box was inlaid with ivory and exquisitely carved in a rich pattern of flowers and leaves. A faint spicy scent was noticeable when Judith raised the lid; the inside was divided into a number of velvet-lined compartments of different sizes. Surely it had been expensive, and it was a thoughtfully chosen gift that would be useful to any female, of any age or disposition.

"It is the loveliest thing I have ever had," Judith said softly as she glanced up. If she had been Adam's cousin, she would have kissed him, too, but she contented herself with a smile. "Thank you. I shall cherish it always." Then, teasingly, "It will be perfect for my pills and nostrums."

They all laughed, then Judith withdrew to the window seat to resume her embroidery, leaving the cousins talking in the kind of half-completed sentences that close relatives or very good friends use. Judith also rang for the butler and gave a discreet order setting the midday meal back, on the assumption that Antonia and Adam would need to talk the first effusions out before they could think of food.

After an hour of nonstop dialogue, Antonia asked the question that had been prominent in her mind ever since her cousin had written that he was returning to England. "How long will you be staying, Adam? At least a few months, I hope."

He cocked a quizzical eyebrow. "Will you be hopelessly cast down if I say that I am back for good?"

"That's wonderful!" Antonia almost bounced in her chair. She seemed to be talking exclusively in exclamation points today. Fortunate that Aunt Lettie wasn't around. "What are your plans?"

His eyes intent on hers, Adam hesitated for a very long moment before shaking his head. "It's too soon to say. I need time to become reacquainted with England." He smiled. "What about you, Tony? I spent most of a year thinking that you were a respectably married lady, only to have you write that you had sent Lord Ramsay to the rightabout. Have you brought anyone else up to scratch yet?"

"Such vulgarity, cousin." She made a face. "I've had no shortage of proposals, but none worth accepting."

His voice serious, Adam asked, "What happened with Ramsay? You just said that you had called things off, but you never gave a reason. Did he behave badly?"

"No need to look so protective, Adam. Lord Ramsay was a perfect gentleman." Antonia smiled wryly and toyed with the Chinese scent bottle. "That was the problem. I had decided that it was time I accepted somebody, and Ramsay was the best of the lot—handsome, wealthy, titled, good-natured . . . and a complete bore. I was dragging my feet, and he finally gave me an ultimatum; set a wedding date or the betrothal was off." She chuckled. "You would not believe the alacrity with which I called things off."

"Minx."

"By that time, I think he was as relieved as I was," Antonia said a trifle defensively.

"Are you determined never to marry, Tony?"

Antonia considered her answer. Even to Adam, she would not reveal her foolish romanticism, her desire to fall totally in love. Especially not to Adam. "I would like to marry," she said slowly, "but I also would like to feel something more than mild affection for my husband."

"As romantic as ever, I see." Adam gave her his warmest smile. "Well, you can always marry me. I rather fancy the idea of settling down, and you're the only woman I know in England."

After another silence that lasted too long, Antonia laughed. "Be careful what you say, Adam. Think how appalled you would be if I accepted."

"I was prepared to accept the consequences," he said easily.

Across the room, Judith caught a note in Adam Yorke's voice that made her glance up. Perhaps it took a stranger to see that he was speaking in dead earnest, though her employer seemed oblivious to that fact. Antonia may think of Adam as a brother, but clearly he did not see his beautiful cousin as a sister. Judith returned to her needlework, embarrassed at seeing more than she should. It was an unfortunate situation; fond though Antonia was of Adam, she would never see him in a romantic light. For Adam's sake, Judith hoped that he would not pine after what he could never have. Far better that he seek a female who would return his affections. Such a woman would be very lucky.

The butler entered and made the discreet throat-clearing noise he used to gain attention. "Lady Fairbourne, shall I direct that the midday meal be served?"

Antonia glanced guiltily at the clock. "Lord, look at the time, I'll wager Cook is furious. We'll be down in ten minutes."

After Burton had withdrawn, she turned to find Adam staring at her with puzzlement. "Lady Fairbourne?"

Antonia cocked her head to one side. "Didn't I ever write you about that?"

"As I recall, Fairbourne was one of your father's minor titles, but surely your cousin Spenston holds that now."

Antonia straightened up in the sofa and said loftily, "I, sir, am Baroness Fairbourne in my own right." Then her

dignity dissolved into chuckles. "It is the
It wasn't until Papa died and the solicitors w
the legal aspects that someone noticed that
title is a barony by writ. Such baronies go b
times, and they can be inherited by a female
of male heirs. A barony by writ can be submerged in higher titles, then liberated when there is a female heir but no male one. The rest of Papa's titles and the entailed property went to Cousin Roger when he became Earl of Spenston, but Fairbourne stayed with me."

Warming to her topic, she continued, "Papa's lawyer told me that the de Ros barony, which is thought to be the oldest peerage in England, has gone through eight or nine families. It's dreadfully complicated. If I had sisters, we would be co-heirs to the title, and none of us would be called Lady Fairbourne. The title would be in abeyance, and it would stay that way until all of the claims were concentrated in one person again—for example, if one sister had a child, and the other sisters didn't. Some baronies by writ have been in abeyance for centuries."

Seeing Adam's bemused expression, she said kindly, "It's all right if you don't understand. It took the lawyer ages to explain to me."

"I can understand why," Adam said dryly. "So, which are you, Lady Antonia or Lady Fairbourne?"

"That's where the fun comes in." Antonia smiled wickedly. "In one sense, as the daughter of an earl, I am of a higher rank than a mere baron, but Lady Antonia is a courtesy title, where the barony makes me a peer in my own right—one of perhaps a dozen women in England of whom that can be said. My old friends and servants usually call me Lady Antonia, but Lady Fairbourne is more correct. Burton hasn't been with me long and is most dreadfully proper, so he always calls me Lady Fairbourne."

"Which do you prefer, your ladyship?"

"Don't you dare call me your ladyship, Adam, or I'll—I'll . . ." She halted, unable to think of a suitable punishment.

am rose and offered his arm. "Or you'll what?" he
ased.

"I'll think of something," she said darkly.

"Something wet and slithery, if memory serves me
correctly."

Antonia squeezed her cousin's arm, then glanced over to
the window seat. "Judith, you will join us?"

"Are you sure that you want me to be playing
gooseberry?" her companion asked. "You must have a
thousand things to say to one another."

Adam looked Judith up and down very carefully. "Not
green, not furry. You don't look in the least like a gooseberry
to me." He offered his other arm. "Do join us, unless you
think our reminiscences will be too tedious."

Judith laughed, then rose and took his arm to go downstairs. During the leisurely meal that followed, she
appreciated Adam Yorke's efforts to include her in the
mealtime conversation. He might adore his cousin, but when
he looked at Judith, she felt that he truly saw her and listened
seriously to what she said. He really was a most attractive
man, far more interesting than any of the London gentlemen
who had been pursuing Antonia. Even to an observer as
partisan as Judith Winslow, it seemed as if Mr. Yorke was
good enough for the Baroness Fairbourne.

A bowl of fruit from the Thornleigh forcing houses was
being served when Antonia asked, "By the way, where is
your luggage, Adam? Shall I send someone to pick it up at
the port?"

He shook his head. "I'm staying at the Clarendon."

Antonia stared at him. "How ridiculous! Of course you're
staying here."

"Tony, even with the ferocious chaperonage of Mrs.
Winslow, that would be inappropriate."

"But you're family!" She bit her lip suddenly,
remembering that he now had a life that she was not a part
of. Adam might consider it rather slow to be staying with
his cousin. "I'm sorry, I know I shouldn't press you. It's
just that I had assumed you would stay with me."

"I would like to," he admitted, "but we are not children anymore, and we are not that nearly related. Besides, there are any number of reasons why too-close association with me would do your reputation no good."

Antonia fixed him with a steely glance. "Don't be ridiculous," she said. "You make too much of something that is of no importance."

"I only wish that were true," Adam murmured.

Judith watched as the two cousins' gazes caught and held, feeling the tension between them, as if an old argument were being revived. She wondered what they were talking about, but again, it was none of her business. "No one would deny that London delights in gossip," Judith interposed, "but we will be removing to Thornleigh very shortly, and even the highest stickler would not look askance at Mr. Yorke visiting us there."

"What a wonderful idea," Antonia said, sunny again. "I was going to stay in London as long as you were here, Adam, but going to Thornleigh would be better if you could come with us. Surely you can take some time off before returning to work again."

Adam hesitated. "I would like to, but a friend of mine, Lord Launceston, returned to England on the same ship. You may recall my mentioning him in letters. Simon is visiting his mother in Kent now, but in a fortnight or so we had tentative plans to take a holiday together, perhaps to the Lake District."

"Of course I remember his name. Unless Lord Launceston is the sort of gentleman you wouldn't introduce to a respectable female relation, stop awhile with us. Derbyshire is on your way," Antonia suggested.

"Oh, Simon is most presentable, even though he has been out of the country for years. If you're sure you don't mind being landed with a stranger, I'll invite him to Thornleigh."

Much, much later, Antonia would look back at this moment in amazement that something begun so casually would have such unforeseen, long-reaching consequences.

2

The second morning at Thornleigh, Judith knocked on the door of Antonia's chamber, then entered at her friend's invitation. Antonia was curled up on a sofa by the window, her knees drawn up with her arms linked around them as she gazed outside. On a daily basis it was easy to become accustomed to her beauty, but Judith experienced one of those moments when she was sharply aware of how breathtakingly lovely Antonia was. The early-morning sun illuminated the golden skin and dreamy expression, and her shimmering apricot hair cascaded over her blue robe like molten gold.

Antonia gave a smile of welcome, then returned to admiring the rugged grandeur of the Peak District. "I read somewhere that one never thinks of oneself as being happy—that it is only something one realizes when looking back, 'I was happy then,' " she mused. "But that's not true. I'm happy now, and I know it. I'm at Thornleigh with my best friends, the sun is shining, and I haven't a care in the world. What more does happiness require?"

"Nothing." Judith sat down in a deep chair, content to share her friend's mood. "Your gift is that you know that." And that quality in Antonia was surely a gift. Cynics might say that anyone with her ladyship's wealth, position, and beauty had no reason to be miserable, but Judith had met many people with similar blessings who did not have Antonia's talent for enjoyment. Her employer had given Judith friendship and security, among many other things, but most of all she had provided a zestful example of how to be happy. Judith had known little of happiness in her earlier years; it had taken time for her to learn to recognize it.

Antonia rested her chin on her crossed arms. "I'm almost sorry that Lord Launceston will be arriving today. I'm sure he is a very good fellow or he wouldn't be Adam's friend, but he is a stranger. It won't be quite the same."

"He won't be a stranger for long," Judith pointed out reasonably. "By the way, do you know where he and Adam met?"

"Yes, in the East India Company observatory in Bombay, of all places, where Launceston was doing astronomical observations. Apparently he's a natural philosopher of some note."

"Really!" Judith, who took a more-than-casual interest in the natural world herself, was intrigued. "What does he study?"

"A variety of things." Antonia's brow furrowed as she tried to remember. "He doesn't share your interest in botany, but he's a founder of the new Geological Society as well as a member of the Royal Society and the Astronomical Society."

"Impressive. No wonder he and Adam are friends. Your cousin seems to be interested in everything."

"He always has been," Antonia agreed. She cocked her head to one side and surveyed her companion. "What do you think of Adam now that you've had a chance to get acquainted?"

Judith considered the matter. "If I was a cat, I should want to jump into his lap and purr."

Antonia chuckled. "Well-put. He has the same effect on me." She was grateful that her two best friends got on well; it would have been most awkward if they had taken each other in dislike. Uncoiling herself from the window seat, Antonia rang for her maid. "I had better dress, or I'll be late. Adam and I are going to ride up to the high country this morning. Will you join us?"

Judith shook her head. "No. The housekeeper and I are going to have a discussion about the state of the linens. That will take much longer than it should, but Mrs. Heaver doesn't like to be rushed."

"You needn't do that, Judith. You're my companion, not some sort of superior servant."

"It makes me feel useful." Judith smiled as she withdrew. Antonia's excellent managerial talents were concentrated on the estate, not the household. Even the best of housekeepers needed to know that someone was keeping an interested eye on her, and at Thornleigh, that someone was Judith Winslow.

An hour later, Antonia pulled off her riding hat and laughed in sheer exuberance, letting the wind tear apart her carefully arranged coiffure. The manor house was set in a dale, the fertile area that surrounds a small river, and she and Adam had ridden up the dale to the high country. At the top they had reached one of the great "edges," the Derbyshire name for the stone ridges that tower above the valleys. To the south the spa of Buxton was visible, while north lay the heights of Kinder Scout, the highest point in the Peak District. Far above them, a hawk drifted in the wind with graceful majesty. "Surely, Adam, India had nothing to match this."

Effortlessly controlling his restive horse, Adam glanced across at her with a smile. He had always been a superb rider, and the years had not changed that. "Every land has its own special beauties that can't be compared to any other, and the Peaks are one of the glories of England." His gaze returned to the dramatic, treeless green hills, where the bones of the earth occasionally showed through, adding softly, "And they are home."

Antonia's father had decided to leave Thornleigh to his daughter as soon as she was born, but it had been Adam's home every bit as much as hers, and she was glad that he still felt the same way about the land that she did. Through the years of her childhood, Antonia and Adam had explored the Derbyshire hills and dales together, sometimes taking food and disappearing for the whole day, returning wind-burned and content as darkness fell.

As they ambled their horses along the spine of the ridge, Antonia asked, "Could you afford to buy an estate in this area? I understand that quite a nice property on the other side of Buxton will be coming on the market soon."

At his inquiring glance, she looked stricken. "Sorry, I forgot that I shouldn't say anything that hints at money."

He laughed. Like her, he rode hatless, and the breeze ruffled his sun-streaked brown hair. "It is many years too late to begin standing on ceremony with me, Tony. In fact, I am something of a nabob, but as I said before, it is a little too soon to know exactly what I will do."

The trail narrowed and Adam concentrated on guiding his horse safely between the stones. "I intend to continue in the India trade. It looks like the East India Company will not have its monopoly renewed when the original charter expires in a few years, and that will open all sorts of possibilities. But I'm also interested in investing closer to home."

"What kind of investments?" Antonia asked as the path widened enough so they could ride abreast again.

"Steam engines," he answered promptly. "Steam is still in its infancy, but it has been powering mining machinery for years, and now ships are being driven with it as well. Soon there will be steam-powered land vehicles. There's a notable engineer working over in Macclesfield, and I intend to call on him soon. I never knew an inventor who didn't need more money for his work, and a businessman to show him how to get the most out of his ideas."

Antonia was startled. "Do you think horses will no longer be needed?" She gave her mare's glossy neck a protective pat. "I can't believe that."

"My guess is that long-distance travel will become much easier with steam-powered vehicles, probably ones designed to run along tracks, but such engines will be expensive, connecting only major cities," Adam said reassuringly. "We'll still need horses for travel in the local areas and to get to where the steam carriages run."

"All these new mechanisms fascinate you, don't they?"

"They are the future, Tony, and it is better to be fascinated by the future than frightened by it." A dry note entered his voice. "Of course, most members of your class prefer to stay in a protected world, ignoring what is happening among the common folk of Britain."

"Adam, how dare you refer to 'my class' like that,"

Antonia said with shocked disbelief, tugging at her reins so sharply that her mount whickered as it stopped. "I am no different than you."

His face serious for once, Adam pulled his horse to a halt next to hers. "We are different in a thousand important ways, Tony. It is to your credit that you ignore such distinctions, but the rest of the world notices them. You are an aristocrat, born to wealth and privilege. I am a merchant at best, an unfortunate blot on the family escutcheon at worst."

As Adam's wry gray-green eyes met hers, Antonia was reminded again that they were children no longer and that her cousin had been struggling to make his way in a world very different from her own cushioned existence. "You are what you have made of yourself," she said quietly. "Has it been so very bad?"

"I don't want your pity," he said, his deep voice harsher than she had ever heard it.

"Then what do you want?"

It was a perfect opportunity, but as he looked at Antonia, her cinnamon eyes earnest with the desire to understand, her bright hair a nimbus around her exquisite face, Adam lost the courage to speak. "I suppose I want the world to be different than it is," he said slowly. It was the truth, but his wishes were far more specific than that general statement.

"The world, like British weather, is constantly changing," Antonia said, her face relaxing into a mischievous smile. "If you don't like the way it is now, wait a few minutes. It will be different, and possibly better."

"But at the very least, different," he agreed, his lips quirking into an answering smile.

"Do you remember how to ride a wild-goose chase?"

Adam chuckled, remembering the mad races of their youth. In a wild-goose chase whichever rider was ahead set the course, while the followers tried to pass and take over the lead. "Of course! A miracle neither of us was killed."

"I hope that doesn't mean that you have gotten too respectable to run one. Catch me if you can!" With a flick of her whip, Antonia and her mount went tearing down the steep hill like a wind from Hades.

For just a moment, the practical businessman that Adam had become thought of badger holes and loose rocks and the risk Antonia ran of breaking her lovely neck. Then he laughed. Both of them knew and understood this country, minimizing the risks. Besides, who wanted to live forever? Kicking his mount, he charged recklessly after her.

As he bent over his horse's neck, urging the gelding to its best speed, he comforted himself with the reflection that it was early yet, too soon to speak of serious things.

Adam didn't know that time was about to run out.

Simon Launceston, fifth Baron Launceston, arrived that afternoon. Like all great events, Lord Launceston's arrival was ever after indelibly etched in Judith's memory. When he was announced, they were taking tea in the small parlor, which commanded a splendid view of the lush gardens. In the distance the green Peaks floated. The afternoon sun was softly bright, illuminating the rich colors of the Persian carpet with unnatural clarity, causing Antonia's apricot hair to glow like a living thing as she laughed and poured tea for the others.

Then Burton entered, intoning solemnly, "Lord Launceston."

All three of them looked up, Adam with pleasure that his friend had arrived, the two women welcoming.

At the sight of the man in the doorway, Judith drew in her breath, her eyes widening and her mouth forming a silent "O" of shock. Time seemed to freeze, as still and motionless as pollen suspended in the sun-drenched air. Next to her on the sofa, Antonia had gone rigid with the same awestruck reaction that Judith was experiencing.

Simon Launceston was, quite simply, the most beautiful man Judith had ever seen or dreamed of. His superbly tailored clothing would have drawn the eye in a lesser man, but for Lord Launceston clothing was no more than a foil for his height and perfect proportions. Though he had wide shoulders and an elegant figure, what one noticed first was his eyes, deeply and magnetically blue. Then his face, the planes and lines shaped with a perfection that a Greek sculptor could only yearn for, a faint in his cleft chin adding charm to a countenance that might otherwise have been too flawless to be approachable.

Judith's first thought was of Apollo, but Lord Launceston's beauty was of a Celtic kind; surely the sun god would be golden, while the newcomer's hair was the shining black of obsidian, all the darker for the contrast with his fair skin. But Launceston was more than just handsome; he was the very image of the parfit gentil knight Judith had dreamed of when she was still young enough to dream. Even now, after a lifetime's knowledge that no handsome prince would appear to fulfill her fantasies, she felt a moment of irrational belief that her dream lover had found her.

Then common sense returned. Judith ruthlessly suppressed the absurd longing that coursed through her veins, telling herself that what she felt was simply admiration such as any woman must feel at the sight of such an attractive man.

While Judith worked on her rationalizations, Launceston paused on the threshold, his face cool and remote until his gaze fell on Adam. Then he smiled with a quiet charm that could have melted the heart of Medusa. Adam rose and greeted his friend, then performed the introductions after the men had shaken hands.

The new arrival took Judith's hand in his and bowed over it, speaking politely as his deep-blue eyes met hers. Judith barely comprehended his words as she struggled to act like a rational being; her real desire was to stare at him with her mouth open. His lordship's slow soft tenor was as wonderful as his face.

When she released his hand, Judith thought dazedly that it was brave for his lordship to put any part of himself in a female's grasp; surely there was the risk that it would not be returned. If even a practical, unromantic woman like herself went weak and butter-kneed at the sight of Lord Launceston, it must be dangerous for the poor man to walk the streets.

Lord Launceston turned to Antonia, getting his first clear

look at his hostess. He clasped her hand, then time stopped again as he simply held it, forgetting to bow, as mesmerized by her beauty as she was by his. Antonia was in her best looks today, her hair shimmering like sunset, her vitality drawing the eye, her splendid figure the stuff of male dreams.

Rallying more quickly than Judith had, Antonia said, "Welcome to Thornleigh," in her husky contralto. Then her eyes met his and her next words caught in her throat. The two stared at each other, still hand-fast, the energy pulsing between them like a storm.

Though Judith had heard of love at first sight, she had not believed in it. But then, she had never seen anything like this. The beautiful of both sexes are not like the rest of the human race; Judith had never seen two people who were more obviously born for each other. There was something shockingly intrusive about witnessing their silent interchange, and she turned her head away.

As she did, her gaze fell on Adam, and the sight of the vivid, inarticulate pain on his face pulled her out of her disordered thoughts. Judith had guessed from the first that Adam Yorke was in love with Antonia. Now he faced the devastating knowledge that bringing his friend and his cousin together was disastrous for his hopes, and Judith ached for him.

"Would you care for some tea, Lord Launceston?" she asked, her pragmatic question shattering the spell that lay over the room.

Hastily releasing Antonia's hand, he said, "That would be very welcome." A faint flush colored his fair skin.

The four people sat down and exchanged commonplaces as if that strange, lightning-struck moment had not occurred. Lord Launceston commented on the geological history of the Peak District, Antonia mentioned how old the manor house of Thornleigh was, Judith asked about his lordship's studies.

Adam Yorke said nothing at all, merely drank his tea, that strange, blinded expression on his face. Judith was acutely aware of the crosscurrents, of the way Antonia and Lord Launceston were making love to each other with every word and gesture, and finally she could bear no more. She needed to escape before she succumbed to a wicked envy of her best friend. Equally important, Adam should be taken away.

Standing, Judith said, "I think I'll take a turn in the garden. Adam, will you join me for some fresh air?"

"Of course," he responded with numb politeness. She took his arm rather forcefully, guiding him through the French doors into the slanting late-afternoon sun. Antonia and Lord Launceston scarcely noticed when their companions left.

Judith drew the refreshing air into her lungs, grateful for its head-clearing qualities after so much pulsating emotion. Adam had no preference about the direction, so she steered them through the parterre and into the informal walk, trying to get as far away as possible. When the house was no longer visible among the trees, she said quietly, "I'm sorry."

Adam's muscular arm tensed under her clasp, but he made no attempt to pretend that he didn't understand. His voice was surprisingly steady when he said, "I should have realized that this might happen, but I've known Simon long enough that I'd forgotten what an impact the first sight of him makes."

"Being a male doesn't help," Judith pointed out. "You don't see him the same way a female does."

"True." He managed a smile. "I remember thinking when I met him that it must be a nuisance to be so strikingly good-looking that people ignore more important qualities, like character and intelligence, which he has in abundance."

"I know what you mean, but it is hard to be indifferent to such beauty," she agreed. "It is the same with Antonia. Admiring her is like enjoying a perfect rose, but she is so much more than her appearance, dazzling though that is." After a moment's hesitation, she said, "You've always loved her?"

"Always." They reached the stream that ran the length of the dale, and by mutual consent they sat on a bench over-looking the clear, chuckling water. Adam leaned forward, head bent, his elbows resting on his knees, his hands loosely clasped.

Judith studied his large, powerful hands, thinking it remarkable that they had the delicacy to carve the lovely wood sculptures he had made for Antonia when they were young. Though he had the strength of an athlete or a peasant, he must also have the soul of an artist.

Staring unseeing at his interlaced fingers, Adam chose his words with great care. "There are many kinds of love. My feelings for Tony are a mixture of friendship and gratitude and admiration. I don't suppose that that is the same as romantic love—it would be more accurate to say that I am in the habit of fancying myself in love with her.

"If she and Simon ran off to Gretna Green tomorrow, Tony and I would still love each other in the ways that matter most. Romantic love might ruin that." He shrugged, his russet coat straining across his broad shoulders. "Perhaps it is better this way. Simon is honorable, intelligent, and superlatively eligible. I could not hope for Tony to find a better husband, and it would be a waste of her warmth and love if she never married."

Judith did not bother to say that their speculations were premature; anyone who had been in the room when Antonia met Simon Launceston must think the result a foregone conclusion. She studied Adam's profile, the strong chin and the powerful body, and wondered if he truly believed what he had just said. In her experience, platonic love was a female ideal; when a man loved a beautiful woman, romance and passion were an inextricable part of the emotion.

She thought it likely that Adam was trying to make himself believe that his feelings for Antonia were not romantic in order to save his sanity. He could have been furious or bitter at the shattering of all his hopes; instead, he was acting with gallant and painful generosity, and Judith admired him enormously.

Hoping to distract him from his pain, she asked, "What were the circumstances that led you to grow up in the Spenston household? Antonia has never told me."

"No, she would not have mentioned," he said. Without looking at his companion, he continued, "I'm baseborn."

Judith's eyes widened, understanding now a conversation heard right after Adam had arrived, when he had said that close association with him would do Antonia's reputation no good. His cousin had replied tartly that no one cared about such things. Now Judith understood what was meant, and unfortunately, Adam was right: there were those who would condemn Antonia for treating a bastard connection with such familiarity.

Adam seemed to need to talk. "My father was a loose-screw cousin of Antonia's father, some kind of political radical. He ran off with the daughter of a Nonconformist minister, and they lived together in London." Adam's gaze rested unseeing on the clear water rushing past in the brook as his words came haltingly. "He was too radical to believe in marriage, even when his mistress bore a child. Both families cast them off.

"When I was two, he was killed in a carriage accident, leaving my mother to fend for both of us. She worked as a seamstress. I can remember her sewing by the light of a single candle, her eyes red, wearing cotton gloves so that the chilblains on her hands wouldn't damage the fine ladies' fabrics." He released his breath in a sigh. "By the time I was seven, she was dying, and she knew it. When she asked her father for help, he invited her to burn in hell for eternity, so she wrote to Lord Spenston, whom my father had said was the most approachable of his relations.

"By the time my mother's letter reached Spenston, she was dead, and the landlady of the house where we lived had sold me to a chimney sweep to be a climbing boy."

Judith gasped in outrage. "How could she do such a thing?"

"Very easily," Adam replied dryly. "My mother was unable to work at the end, and our rent was in arrears. The landlady felt entitled to what she could get for the dead woman's possessions, which included me. And perhaps she thought I was better-off with the sweeper, since the alternatives were the parish or living in the streets. At least the sweeper fed his boys, though not much—bad for business if we grew too quickly.

"Lord Spenston had never been close to my father, but he felt some sense of obligation to his cousin's son. His agents located the sweeper, and Spenston came and bought me after I'd been there about three months. I believe I cost him three pounds, which represented a good profit to the sweeper, who had paid only thirty shillings to the landlady."

Judith's mouth tightened at the reality concealed by the flat words. The treatment of climbing boys was a disgrace; most of them did not live to grow up. It was a form of slavery in the heart of Britain, but in spite of calls for reform, legislation to correct abuses had yet to pass Parliament.

Adam's tone was unnaturally detached; perhaps that was essential when speaking of such a past. "The earl took me back to Spenston House. He was going to deposit me in the nursery for the maids to clean up, but it was Tony's birthday, and a party was in progress in the schoolroom. When he brought me in, two dozen perfectly scrubbed, perfectly dressed little sons and daughters of the nobility turned to stare at me. I'll remember the expressions on their faces until the day I die. They reacted as if I were a rat just crawled from the gutter."

Judith could imagine the scene perfectly and was not sure if it was the thought of his hurt that caused her throat to tighten, or memories of her own; she was all too familiar with being scrutinized by those who had been born knowing that they belonged. Her voice uneven, she asked, "What happened then?"

"Antonia walked up to me. She looked like a princess, wearing an immaculate white dress and with that incredible hair tied up with blue ribbons. She said, 'You must be my cousin Adam. I'm so glad you came in time for my party.'

"Then, even though I was covered with soot, fit only for a chimney or a washtub, she kissed me on the cheek, introduced me to every other child in the room, giving the ones who weren't polite a killing glare, and ended by asking if I wanted an ice. I think her father's plan had been to clean me up and place me in a foster home or a modest school, but Tony wanted to keep me, as if I were a puppy that had wandered in. So I became part of the household." He finally turned to Judith, his eyes intent. "It should be obvious why I've loved her ever since."

"Antonia does inspire loyalty," Judith said softly. "She took me in also, when I was newly widowed, penniless, adrift in the world. And she made me not a servant, but a friend, and that is what we have been ever since."

At her words, Adam understood how he had come to confide his deepest feelings to Judith Winslow. Her understanding was a healing balm. She, too, loved Antonia; more than that, she had suffered loss, knew what it was to be an outsider.

He had liked Judith from the first time he had met her, but until now he had not realized how attractive she was. He had had eyes only for Antonia, and this moment of unexpected intimacy was like seeing Judith for the first time. The afternoon sun burnished her thick chestnut hair with auburn highlights. Her slim figure was graceful and feminine, and her delicate features perfectly formed. Strange that he had not noticed her exquisite complexion, so clear it was almost translucent. The fact that she was easily overlooked was a function of her quiet personality. Yet she was not shy; there was no lack of confidence in her fine gray eyes. "You've been a widow for two years?"

"A bit more than that." She sighed and turned away to watch the clear water. "To say I am a widow is to engage more sympathy than I deserve. It wasn't much of a marriage."

"Your husband was unkind to you?"

"Not really, but he was ill even before we married. I was little more than a servant, except that a servant can give notice. A wife can't."

There was a wealth of implications in those words; it was unnecessary for her to say more.

"He left you unprovided for?"

"He was a curate, with only his stipend." She smiled wryly. "I had been acting as an unpaid governess for some cousins. Like you, I had no close family. I was simply a poor relation, an obligation that could be put to work in return for room and board. Mr. Winslow was the curate of the parish church. A pleasant-enough man, at least before his illness overcame him. When he asked me to marry him, I thought it would be an improvement.''

''But it wasn't.''

Her gray eyes met his, her smile more genuine. ''If I hadn't married Mr. Winslow and been widowed, I would still be a governess and Lady Forrester would never have foisted me onto Antonia. Since the last two years have been the most rewarding of my life, it is fair to say that everything worked out for the best. In the long run, most things do.''

Adam thought of Antonia and Simon together, and the pain was instant and fierce, stabbing deep inside to where he kept his most secret dreams. But he had never truly believed that Tony could ever be his; she had always been too far above him, both by birth and by her own glorious nature.

In that sense, Simon's arrival was for the best; God only knew how long Adam would have hovered near Antonia, fearing to speak, waiting for the right moment that would never come. It was time to stop living for an unattainable dream; far better to try to match Judith Winslow's calm good sense. He wondered briefly how he would have responded to Judith if he had never known Tony, and the answer was very clear; he would have thought her lovely and would have wanted to know her better. He was comfortable with Judith in a way that he had experienced with no other woman save his cousin.

There was nothing to prevent him from furthering his acquaintance with Judith. Her marriage might not have been a good one, but she did not seem embittered. He liked the fact that she was a woman of his own age, who had experienced some of life's highs and lows. He would have found it impossible to open his heart to a vapid chit from the schoolroom.

Adam stood and offered his hand to assist Judith to her feet. She came up lightly, her small hand trusting within his clasp. ''Thank you for listening,'' he said quietly, hoping his tone conveyed just how much he meant by the words.

Her smile was gentle and grave. "I am glad I could be here with you. It has been good for both of us."

Between them lay a **faint**, sweet sense of possibilities.

3

Unmindful of his immaculate riding breeches, Lord Launceston knelt on one knee and poked in the scree of loose stones lying at the base of the cliff. Knowing of his interest in geology, Antonia had brought him to this spot, where she and Adam had found fossils when they were children. Now, while Simon examined the scree, she was free to admire Simon. Even though it had been a week since his arrival and they had spent almost every waking hour together, she could not get enough of the sight of him.

"We're in luck," he said triumphantly, rising and showing his prize to her.

"How lovely!" Antonia reached out and took the fossil from his hand, feeling a quick tingle of pleasure as their fingers touched. The limestone had shattered along a flat plane, leaving a perfect print of a fern, the delicate tracery of fronds dark against the pale stone. "Once Adam found one similar to this, but it was chipped and weathered, in nowhere near as good condition." Thinking back, she added, "The best fossil I ever found here showed part of a skelton. A fish neck, I think."

"Fish don't have necks," Simon said seriously.

Antonia was unable to resist saying with perfect gravity, "Then why do they sell cravats for fish?"

When Simon stared at her, she colored. "I'm sorry, that was an absurd thing to say. My sense of humor is quite deplorable."

Lord Launceston gave her one of his slow, charming smiles. "The problem is not your sense of humor, but mine. When I am thinking scholarly thoughts, I become most bor-

ingly literal.'' He glanced down at the fossil in his hand.
''This is such a fine specimen that it overwhelmed my ability
to appreciate wit.'' He then cast an appreciative glance over
the crumbling cliff face and the rubble of rocks. ''This place
is a geologist's dream.''

Just as Simon was a maiden's dream. Savoring his chiseled
profile and the inviting way strands of black hair curled on
his neck, Antonia found herself smiling. She knew that she
was acting like a besotted fool, and she did not mind in the
least. She was twenty-six years old and in love for the first
time in her life. As a child she had vaguely assumed that
she and Adam would marry someday, but that had been sheer
lack of imagination on her part. Later she ahd had the usual
girlish infatuations, but had never felt that the objects of her
fervor were destined to become her life's companion. Instead,
she had cherished a secret belief that there would be one
special man for her, a man worth waiting for, who would
love her as deeply as she loved him.

But as the years went by, she lost that certainty; realizing
that girls were raised to be bird-witted romantics, she came
to believe that she had been deluding herself. In a burst of
pragmatism, she had accepted an offer from Lord Ramsay,
then jilted him under the growing conviction that marriage
to that particular man would be a disastrous error.

As the years passed with ever-increasing speed, she had
begun to worry that she had waited too long, that her foolish
fantasy would keep her a childless spinster. And then Simon
had appeared and her life had snapped into focus. The
moment she saw him, she had known that she had been right
to wait. What if she had married Adam, then Simon had come
to visit them? To meet the love of her life when she was
married to another man for whom she cared deeply . . .The
mere thought of such a tragedy caused her to shudder.

Simon caught her involuntary movement out of the corner
of his eye. ''Are you cold? I'm a selfish beast for keeping
you out here in the wind.''

She smiled sunnily. ''I'm not cold in the least. In fact, my
guilty secret is that I'm as tough as a cavalryman, without
a trace of female delicacy, either mental or physical.''

He looked disconcerted at her words, then returned her smile, his blue eyes humorous. "You make it hard for me to admit what a frail fellow I am, Lady Antonia. Will I be utterly sunk in your opinion if I suggest that it is time we ate and that that stone wall should protect my feeble bones from the wind?"

Antonia laughed at how neatly he had maneuvered her to a warmer spot; she had to admit that the breeze was a trifle overfresh. Lifting the skirts of her navy-blue riding habit, she went to her horse for their al fresco meal. One of the things she loved about Simon was his quiet, self-deprecating humor. Any other man so handsome would be unbearably conceited, but he seemed oblivious to the effect he had on women. Instead, he was almost diffident in the way he treated her, as if not quite believing that she welcomed his attentions.

The protected spot by the stone wall was sunny and warm, and commanded a spectacular view north to the rugged hills of the high Peak country. There was a delightful intimacy in sitting so close together on a blanket, sharing wine, pâté, cheese, and fresh crusty bread.

After hunger was appeased, Simon leaned back against the stone wall, his long legs crossed at the ankle, a glass of red wine loosely clasped in one hand. "Is one of those hills *the* Peak?"

She shook her head. "No, in spite of the name, there isn't any one peak. Even Kinder Scout isn't a real mountain, though it is the highest point in the district. This country is more like the Scottish Highlands or the Yorkshire moors." She studied the prospect, trying to imagine how it looked to someone who had never seen it before. "Some parts are too barren even for grazing, fit only for grouse-hunting. I know it looks bleak to some people, but I find it beautiful, even though almost half of Thornleigh isn't arable."

"It *is* beautiful, and dramatic as well." Simon had a slow, quiet manner of speaking, every syllable clear and considered. "Once this land lay beneath the sea. Marine creatures lived and died, leaving their intricate forms for us to marvel at. Later the seas retreated and there were plants like the ferns, perhaps an exotic tropical jungle with creatures we can't even imagine. Later the earth lifted, the layers of stone folding over on themselves like lengths of velvet.''

He gestured at the valley, his blue eyes dreamy with inner visions. ''Powerful forces that we have only the barest inkling of shaped the earth. Now rivers run through the fertile valleys and fields fill the dales, but the peaks still lift their defiant heads to the sky, and the earth still changes, slowly but inexorably.'' Then he stopped, giving her an apologetic smile. ''Please stop me when I get carried away like that. I shouldn't be boring you with such dry stuff.''

''You aren't boring me,'' Antonia said softly, mesmerized by the images he created of her beloved land, and how close his shoulder was to hers. ''You make it sound like poetry. In fact,'' she confessed in a moment of candor, ''I love the way you speak, so slow and thoughtful. I would enjoy listening to you read the most boring sermon ever written.''

''I guess that is a compliment,'' he said with amusement, ''but one I don't deserve. I speak the way I do because I had a terrible stutter as a boy, and the only way I could speak at all was to do so slowly. It took years to get the knack of it.''

''How dreadful for you!'' Antonia had some idea of just how difficult such an affliction could be; she had gone to school with a girl who had a mild stutter, and had suffered vicarious agonies of embarrassment when her friend couldn't manage to get her words out. ''I suppose you were teased unmercifully.''

''Schoolboys can be horrid little beasts,'' he allowed. ''I spent much of my childhood buried in books, because then I didn't have to say anything.''

Antonia didn't reply for a moment, realizing that Simon had just told her something very important about what made him the way he was. It was easy to imagine him as a shy, sensitive boy turning to books because they wouldn't taunt him, growing more comfortable with things than people. That lack of confidence must have been what saved him from the arrogance of beauty. The thought increased her tenderness. ''Books proved good friends. Adam says you are considered a brilliant scholar.''

"Adam flatters me," he demurred. "I've written a few articles, but I've produced no earth-shattering discoveries or theories." He lifted his glass for a sip of wine, and with fascination she watched the muscles of his throat flex as he swallowed. "Actually, Adam is the one who is brilliant. He has a great breadth of knowledge; he seems to know something about every topic imaginable. More than that, he can take a theory and see the practical applications of it."

Antonia drew her legs underneath her, demurely tucking the dark fabric into place. "How did you two meet each other? Adam said something about an observatory."

"Yes, the East India Company maintains several observatories. I was doing some studies at the one in Bombay when Adam wandered in one night. He had never used a telescope and was curious to examine the heavens. I let him do some viewing and we started talking." Simon gave his self-deprecatory smile. "If I had realized who he was, I might have been shy about talking to him, but fortunately I didn't."

"Knew who he was? What do you mean?"

"Why, every Briton in India has heard of Adam Yorke." He gave her a surprised look. "He was known as one of the cleverest and most daring merchants in the East, someone who drove a hard bargain but was always impeccably fair. His youth and the speed with which he built his fortune made him something of a legend."

"My cousin Adam?" she asked incredulously.

"None other." Simon reflected for a moment. "I suppose he's too modest to have boasted of his accomplishments in his letters to you."

Antonia nodded, trying to absorb this new information. "I got the impression that he was doing rather well, but he never hinted at being a legend." She picked a sprig of ragwort, saying absently, "Judith makes the most exquisite drawings of plants like these." Brooding at the yellow blossom, she added, "How exasperating of Adam not to hint how well he was doing. I shall have to ring a peal over him."

"Don't do that. My bringing such a dire fate on his head would be a poor return after all Adam has done for me."

Lord Launceston's deep-blue eyes met hers earnestly. "If he hadn't helped me when I inherited the title, I would have been in dire straits."

At Antonia's inquiring glance, he elaborated. "I hadn't expected to inherit, so I was ill-informed about the family holdings. More than that, I have no head for business. Then my father and older brother died unexpectedly of a fever. The Launceston finances were in such a shambles that the family man of business, a lawyer, came all the way to Bombay to break the news and force me to make some quick decisions. My brother had been gambling heavily and the estates were badly encumbered. The lawyer thought I should dispose of most of the property to cover the debts. I would have been left with a modest independence, but nothing more."

He grimaced. "I've always been rather vague about money. I took the lawyer at his gloomy word and was ready to sign whatever he put in front of me. It was Adam who stopped me, read all the papers, asked the right questions. It became obvious that the lawyer's advice would benefit himself much more than me. Adam recommended a new man of business, then steered me into the right investments to rebuild the family fortunes. It's taken four years to get the debts under control, but thanks to your cousin, the estate has been preserved and there will be something to pass on to the next generation of Launcestons."

As Antonia listened, she forgot to be ladylike, pulling her knees up and looping her arms around them as she gazed unseeing at the hills. "While my opinion of Adam has always been of the highest, it's strange to think of him as a merchant prince, a legend," she said reflectively. "On the other hand, it is easy to see him as a man who will go an extra mile to help a friend."

"It was far more than an extra mile," Simon said. "He even lent me the money to take advantage of his investment suggestions. I could never have come about without him." A husky note entered his soft tenor. "Yet his financial help is not the greatest service he has done me."

Antonia felt a premonitory shiver at his words. For the last week they had behaved with perfect propriety, saying nothing that could not be overheard by the world, but the awareness between them was acute. Praying that he was about to declare himself, she turned to him, knowing that her eyes were filled with longing.

"Best of all, Adam introduced me to you," Simon finished. His blue eyes were so close and intense that Antonia felt that she would melt right there, the force of her emotions causing her to dissolve like sugar in the rain.

He leaned forward, closing the inches between them to kiss her with exquisite slowness. At the feel of his warm lips on hers, Antonia gasped and pressed against him, raising her hand to bury her fingers in the dark curls at the back of his head. She had dreamed of this magic moment for a lifetime, and it was everything she had hoped for.

As his arms circled her waist and drew her nearer, the kiss extended and deepened, passion building until finally Simon broke away. He pulled her into a rib-crushing embrace against him while he fought to regain his breath and his self-control. "I'm sorry, Antonia," he said raggedly. "I had thought to behave with some decorum, but that was impossible."

"I'm not sorry, Simon." She lifted her head. "I don't want decorum. I feel like shouting from the rooftops."

The lean, beautifully sculpted planes of his face were classical statuary brought to warm life, and his dark lashes were ridiculously long, framing eyes the intense blue of cobalt. As their gazes locked, he began to smile, gently brushing a wisp of apricot hair from her cheek. "I have trouble believing that you might return my feelings."

"But I do, Simon, I do." She tilted her face, hoping he would kiss her again.

Instead, he said meditatively, "Being introduced to you in a parlor was so mundane and inappropriate. There you stood, looking like a goddess come to earth to give mankind a glimpse of higher things. I could scarcely believe you were real."

"It was like that for me, too. As soon as I saw you, I knew." She snuggled closer in his arms, knowing that if he didn't make an offer soon, she was going to commit the incredible *faux pas* of proposing to him instead. The moment seemed too wonderful to be real, yet his embrace was reassuringly solid.

"Antonia, I realize that we have known each other only a few days, but I want you to be my wife." Her heart tripped with excitement as he paused. "It may be too soon to speak, but tell me—is there any hope for me?"

It was the declaration she had waited to hear all her life. Her tone unsteady, Antonia replied, "It isn't too soon, Simon. Nothing could give me greater happiness than to wed you." Then the bubbling excitement rose in her and she laughed from pure joy. "And the sooner the better!"

It had been a pleasant excursion. Judith had needed silks for her embroidery, so Adam drove her into Buxton, the nearby spa town that an earlier Duke of Devonshire had tried to build into a resort as fashionable as Bath. The town had failed to reach such heights, but it was pleasant and prosperous, and the Crescent that Devonshire had built was every bit as fine as anything in Bath. Adam had accompanied her to the draper's, then they had taken a nuncheon at an inn.

They had been together almost constantly for the last week, and Judith had never been happier. After the scene in the garden when Adam had revealed so much of himself, a feeling of closeness developed between them very quickly. To Judith's perceptive eye, he seemed happier now that he had given up his hopes about Antonia; certainly he had become a charming and attentive companion to Judith. She liked his easy disposition and the gentleness that accompanied his great strength. More than that, there was a warmth in his eyes that kindled a glow of response within her. In her years with Antonia, there had occasionally been men who showed interest in the quiet companion, but none who made the effort to draw her out that Adam did.

When they arrived back at Thornleigh, Adam was recounting a hilarious tale of a trading voyage when an Indian boy had talked him into accepting a monkey for barter, and what had happened when the monkey had gotten into the liquor closet. She was laughing when they entered the foyer of the manor house to find Antonia and Simon. The other couple had obviously just come in, and they stood at the foot of the stairs, staring at each other as Antonia's hand lay on Lord Launceston's arm. Feeling an intruder, Judith stopped in embarrassment, her retreat blocked by Adam, who was close behind her.

Antonia turned at the sound of footsteps and smiled radiantly. Her bright hair flared like red-gold fire, and she had never looked more beautiful. "We have wonderful news. Will you wish us happy?"

It had been inevitable from the first moment Antonia and Simon had met; there was no reason for Judith to feel such a sense of loss. She shot a sidelong glance at Adam, who had come up beside her. She sensed him bracing himself as he absorbed the blow.

Then he stepped forward with an answering smile as his exhilarated cousin threw herself into his arms. "Of course I wish you happy, Tony." His powerful arms caught her up in a hug that lifted her from the floor.

As he set her back on her feet, Lord Launceston said to Adam, "As her ladyship's honorary brother, perhaps I should have asked your permission to pay my addresses."

Adam laughed and offered his hand. "Nonsense. For what it's worth, I approve, but Tony is her own mistress and always does exactly what she wants anyhow. It would take a stronger man than I to persuade her from a course she is set on."

Judith was proud of Adam's control. Surely there must be some distress under his good-natured congratulations, but he let no shadow of private grief mar the other couple's happiness.

Judith gave Antonia a hug, then offered her own hand to Lord Launceston. For just a moment her gaze met his deep-blue eyes and she mourned for all the romantic dreams that would never come true for her. Romance was for the bright and beautiful, the blessed of the gods. For women like Lady

Antonia Thornton. "Congratulations, my lord. I know you both will be very happy."

"Thank you." He sent a besotted glance toward Antonia. "I can't believe what a lucky fellow I am."

"I think the luck is mutual," Judith said softly.

Simon returned his gaze to her. They both realized at the same moment that he still held her hand, and he let go hastily.

"Have you made wedding plans yet?" Judith asked to fill the silence.

"Soon," Antonia answered for her betrothed. "Three weeks to cry the banns."

Lord Launceston appeared gratified but dubious. "Don't you want to go to London for bride clothes? And a settlement must be worked out."

Antonia gazed at him lovingly. "I have more than enough clothing to be married in, and who cares about tedious things like settlements?"

Adam's deep voice cut in. "Since marriage is an arrangement of property as well as affection, such things really cannot be ignored, Tony. However, it should be easy enough to reach an agreement. The wedding needn't be delayed."

"I'd like to talk with you on the subject, Adam." Lord Launceston gave a slow smile. "After all, you know more about my finances than I do myself."

"Of course." Adam waved his hand dismissively. "Whenever it is convenient."

Simon sighed. "It will never be convenient, but I suppose it should be dealt with as soon as possible. Why not right now?"

Adam chuckled, his gray-green eyes twinkling. "It never ceases to amaze me that a man who can do the most abstruse astronomical calculations has trouble understanding simple interest. Tony, it might be best if you join us. If we work out the general outlines of the settlement now, it will save the lawyers time."

"Very well. I'll meet you in the library when I have changed." Antonia noticed Simon's surprise when Adam invited her to join the men. Certainly it was most unusual for a prospective bride to participate in such a discussion; however, Antonia had been active in the management of her own estate and investments since she was eighteen and had no intention of stopping now. She slipped her arm into her companion's. "Judith, will you come and listen to me chatter?"

As promised, Antonia chattered like a magpie as she changed her dress and her maid restyled her windblown hair. Her principal topic was the utter splendor of her betrothed and what a lucky woman she was, opinions that Judith could endorse with all sincerity. After dismissing her abigail, Antonia turned to Judith. "You will stand up with me, won't you? I have assumed so, but I haven't properly asked you."

"Of course." Judith smiled at her affectionately. "The last and best office a companion can offer."

It took a moment for the meaning of the words to penetrate Antonia's excitement. Then she exclaimed, "The last? Surely you're not going to leave me?"

"As a married woman, you don't need a companion," Judith pointed out. "And I can't imagine that a newly married couple needs a third person constantly underfoot."

Antonia made a quick, impatient movement of her hand. "Don't be ridiculous. You did not join the household for reasons of propriety, but friendship. Acquiring a husband does not mean that one needs no other friends."

Judith wavered for a moment. It was true that if she stayed with Antonia there would still be friendship, and she would make herself useful in return for a lifetime of comfort and security. Then Judith thought of Simon bending adoringly over Antonia, and her resolve to leave firmed again. She wished them every joy in the world, but their felicity would underline her own solitary state; she would be a fool to subject herself to that. "It won't do, Antonia. I've loved every minute in your household, but I have always wanted to travel, and with the ridiculously high salary you have been paying me, I can now afford to do so. Perhaps I'll go to America. I've always wanted to see the New World, perhaps even live there permanently."

Antonia suppressed her protest, knowing she had no right to do so. "But . . . You will write?" she asked after a moment. "America is so far away."

"Of course I'll write. Even if I go, I don't know if I would stay there." Judith came and gave her a hug. "I may be too English to live in another land."

Antonia sighed and returned the hug. In a vague way she had thought of marriage as the life she already had, with the delicious addition of a handsome husband, but of course, it wouldn't be that simple. "I'd best go down and talk about settlements with Adam and Simon," she said ruefully. "It has just been brought home to me that there is a great deal more to marriage than falling in love."

Antonia, her cousin, and her betrothed settled in the library with a large pot of tea and a plate of cakes to fortify them for what was clearly going to be a lengthy discussion of jointures, inheritance rights of children yet unborn, reversion in the case of death without issue, and all the rest of the questions that must be decided. It came as no surprise that the business aspects of marriage were complex. However, two cups of tea later, as Antonia regarded her future husband's beautiful, startled face, it occurred to her that emotions could prove more complicated than financial issues.

"Your income is how much?" Simon asked incredulously.

"In the neighborhood of twenty thousand pounds a year," Antonia repeated obligingly. "More in a good year."

"I had assumed that your father left you comfortably well-off, but it never occurred to me that your fortune is so much greater than my own. Even when the mortgages are paid off, the difference will still be substantial." Lord Launceston shook his head in bemusement. "Had I know the extent of your inheritance, I would never have had the effrontery to offer for you."

"Then I'm very glad you didn't know." Antonia smiled mischievously. "Now your friends will think you vastly clever for capturing an heiress."

Simon was unamused. "I never fancied myself in the role of fortune hunter," he said stiffly.

Antonia looked at him uncertainly, not knowing what to say. A more venal man would have openly delighted in her wealth, but honorable sorts like Simon disliked the appearance of avarice. She wouldn't have loved him if he were not honorable—but at the moment, his scruples were a problem.

Adam looked up from the notes he had been taking. Because the newly betrothed couple trusted his honesty and his desire to see them both well-served by the settlement, he was acting as mediator in the negotiations. "No one who has ever seen you absently bestow a guinea on a potboy could think you overinterested in a fortune," he said soothingly. "Besides, Tony's father left her fortune tied up so thoroughly that you couldn't run mad with it even if you wished to."

"That's true," Antonia agreed, remembering some of the details of her father's will. She shot a guilty look at her betrothed. "One of the conditions is that my husband must take the Thornton name. My father didn't want to see his own line die out when the title went to my cousin."

Since men of fortune placed great value on continuation of their names, it was common for wills to require that an indirect heir or the husband of an heiress take on the name of their benefactor.

Lord Launceston was not an egotistical man, but as the possessor of a proud old name of his own, it was not to be expected that he received the news with enthusiasm. "Was the earl expecting you to marry a fortune hunter who would be eager to comply?" he asked with a trace of uncharacteristic sarcasm.

"Women are always expected to abandon their family names," Antonia pointed out with some asperity. "I believe England is the only country in Europe where a woman's family name is routinely lost on marriage. Is that fair?"

"It probably isn't fair," Simon admitted, "but it is the custom." He paused to consider, his brow wrinkled. "Though I never thought of myself as overconcerned with tradition, I find that I am reluctant to change my family name." He appealed to Adam as a fellow male. "Surely you can understand that."

"Not having an honorable old name myself limits my

ability to empathize," Adam said dryly. "However, if I recall correctly, the will permits the joining of both names, rather than requiring Tony's husband to abandon his own name completely."

"Thornton-Launceston will be a mouthful, but I daresay I'll become accustomed quickly." Simon's glance softened as it fell on his betrothed. "It is a small price to pay."

Relieved, Antonia smiled back, basking in the warmth of his vividly blue eyes. When two people loved each other, surely all problems could be solved as easily as the ones just surmounted.

4

One would have thought that a newly betrothed couple would find an evening of stargazing a highly romantic interlude. One would have been wrong. The night was just cool enough that a warm masculine arm would have been welcome, Antonia thought regretfully, but her beloved had been fiddling with his miniature telescope ever since they came outside. They had been betrothed for three whole days now. She suppressed a yawn; at this season the sky didn't darken until nearly ten, and it must be about midnight now. She wouldn't have minded if there had been enough light to admire Simon, but he was only one more shadow in a moonless night.

"There!" His voice was triumphant. "The telescope is now lined up correctly. Take a look through the tube, but be careful not to touch it or it will be knocked out of alignment."

Obediently Antonia stepped to the tripod that held the tube, which was less than a foot long and perhaps two inches in diameter. As her eye adjusted to the small eyepiece, she gasped in awe. "It's beautiful!" Hanging bright against the night was a white-gold sphere with sharp-edged rings above its equator, a vision as improbable as it was lovely. "I've heard of the rings of Saturn, but I never expected such majesty."

In her excitement, she straightened up too quickly, brushing one leg of the tripod and knocking the instrument away from its target. Guiltily she jumped back. "Oh, Lord, Simon, I'm sorry. After all your careful work."

"No matter." His slow voice was unperturbed. "Tonight

wasn't for serious observing. I've seen Saturn before. I just wanted you to see it too, because it's the loveliest sight in the heavens.'' He seated himself on a bench behind the telescope, taking the opportunity to put an arm around Antonia when she joined him.

She cuddled against him happily. "It's amazing that such a small instrument can provide such sights."

"It's a duplicate of one of Sir Isaac Newton's first reflecting telescopes. He presented the original to the Royal Society.'' Simon used his free hand to pat the small instrument affectionately. "I've carried this one all over the world. It only magnifies fifty times, but it has been invaluable when there was no observatory available." He chuckled. "Unfortunately, there is some kind of unwritten law that having a small telescope merely whets one's appetite for a larger one."

"Shall I get you a larger one for a wedding gift?" Antonia had been trying to think of a truly special present for her future husband.

"Definitely not. The really good ones are wildly expensive." He pulled her closer. "I'll get one someday. In the meantime, there are other telescopes available. The Greenwich Observatory for one. And Herschel himself said he would let me use his if I visited him at Slough, though that is not a privilege one would wish to abuse."

"Herschel?"

Antonia could feel Simon's quizzical glance even in the dark. "You've never heard of the Astronomer Royal? William Herschel is near seventy now, but still active and possibly the finest astronomer of our age. Why, he is the first man since the days of the ancients to discover a new planet. Some astronomers call it Herschel in his honor, though the classists who prefer the name 'Uranus' seem to be carrying the day."

"I'm afraid I'm not very knowledgeable about science and mathematics," Antonia apologized, making a mental note to inquire about getting him a telescope. She might not know much about the subjects that interested him, but she could use her fortune to help advance his work.

"And I am not very knowledgeable about politics, farming, or anything else practical." Simon's soft chuckle was intimate in the dark. He caressed her cheek with a lingering touch, then lifted her chin. "But, between us, we are very well-informed."

Before his lips met hers, he whispered the seductive promise, "When the moon is full, I'll show you the famous craters. That's another splendid sight."

Antonia preferred to leave contemplation of craters for a later moment; kissing was a much better way to use a dark night. But even as she slid her arms around her betrothed, she wondered doubtfully how often her husband would prefer to spend the night with a telescope rather than with her.

Antonia turned slowly in front of the mirror, studying the drape of the sari. It had taken time to fold, wind, and tuck the garment, but now the shimmering silk clung to her shapely figure in a convincing fashion. The gold-embroidered end was drawn upward over her left shoulder, then fell gracefully down her back. Her other shoulder was bare, and she felt daring and exotic, though the sari was actually no more revealing than an English ball gown. "Do you think this is correct, Judith?"

"I won't swear that you are wearing it properly, but you look magnificent," her friend said with a smile. "Derbyshire will be talking of nothing else for the rest of the summer."

"Good!" Like any woman in love, Antonia was eager for her man to admire her. Or, to be precise, she wanted him to be madly, passionately adoring. After a last touch to the curls of apricot hair that were permitted to escape her chignon, she accompanied Judith downstairs. She and her guests were invited to dinner and informal dancing at a neighboring estate. It was Antonia's first public appearance with her betrothed, and she was eager to show him off.

Both men were waiting in the drawing room, and Simon's intensely blue eyes showed a very satisfactory amount of adoring passion at the sight of her. "You look like a goddess," he said softly after he had kissed her hand.

For a moment she basked in his patent admiration, feeling warm and wanted. She had waited a lifetime for this. Antonia's gaze lingered on Simon's elegant height. He looked utterly, heart-stoppingly handsome in his black evening clothes; she felt quite a bit of passionate adoration herself.

Belatedly recalling that they were not alone, she released Simon's hand and turned to her cousin. Adam had been complimenting Judith, who was very fine in a white muslin gown embroidered with bands of silver thread.

"Do I look like an Indian lady?" Antonia asked. "Judith and I spent quite some time deciphering and practicing the sari instructions."

Regrettably, Adam was less impressionable than his friend. After his gray-green eyes had scanned her from head to gold-slippered feet, he delivered his judgment in a matter-of-fact voice. "You do not look in the least Indian, not with your coloring. I expect you are more interested in being told how beautiful you are than in how authentic the sari is."

Unable to suppress a smile, Antonia considered his words, then nodded. "Quite right. Given a choice, I prefer a compliment to almost anything else."

Adam laughed. "Very well. You look stunning, as well you know." A wicked glint showed in his eyes. "Are you worried about whether the sari will stay up if you do any dancing?"

"It has occurred to me that the potential for disaster exists," she admitted, "so I have a few discreet pins in places that don't show. I wasn't quite sure I trusted all the tucks to stay tucked." She gave Simon a mischievous glance. "As I recall, Sir Isaac Newton was quite specific on the unfortunate effects of gravitation on an improperly tucked sari."

They all laughed, and proceeded out to the carriage for the ride to Ansley Place, the seat of Sir Ralph Edgeton and his family. Antonia and Judith were frequent visitors to the house, but their escorts aroused a flurry of excited interest. Inevitably the other females present became wide-eyed and fluttery at the sight of Lord Launceston. In response, Simon withdrew into the cool, polite detachment that Antonia had not seen since his arrival at Thornleigh. By this time, she recognized his remoteness as a mask for his unexpected shyness.

Simon and Adam were an interesting study in contrasts, like classical statues of Contemplation and Action, or perhaps Thinker and Builder. Both were well-dressed and close to the same age, but the similarities ended there. Simon was taller, dark-haired, lighter in both build and voice, and wore an air of quiet containment.

While Adam didn't have Simon's breathtaking good looks —no one did—her cousin had a powerful, dynamic presence that drew the eye. Interestingly, Adam attracted almost as much attention as Lord Launceston, and he was a good deal more at ease with it as he moved around the room, greeting old acquaintances and making new ones.

No one had heard of Antonia and Simon's betrothal, and much time was spent in exclamations and congratulations to the future bride and groom. Later, after an excellent dinner and several sets of country dancing, Antonia mentioned the fact to her intended when they went outside for cooler air. "It seems odd that no one read about our engagement."

They had been strolling across the brick patio, but her words caused Simon to stop, a guilty expression on his face. "I daresay I forgot to post the notices to the London newspapers." Seeing Antonia's dismayed expression, he added apologetically, "I'm afraid I forget things with some regularity."

Antonia stared at him. How could he forget something so important? She made an effort to keep the sharpness from her tone. "It isn't really important. It's just that I want everyone in Britain to know how lucky I am."

"I'll post the letters tomorrow," he promised.

She thought a moment. "We might as well wait and send in a notice after the wedding, since it is only fortnight away."

"Very well." Simon gazed down at her, laying a hand over hers where it rested on his arm. "A fortnight seems an eternity."

"It does indeed," she murmured, her voice as husky as his. The light from the drawing room emphasized the clean planes of his face and shadowed the faint cleft in his chin. But even as they gazed raptly at each other, Antonia could not quite still her doubts. For the first time, she wondered if she was as important to Simon as he was to her.

Once planted, doubt grew with startling speed, and with it came tension. The next day when they were riding, Antonia presented a carefully reasoned plea for spending a substantial part of the year at Thornleigh. Of course, time must be spent in London and at the Launceston estate in Kent, but to her the Peak District would always be home. Though she could visit here alone, she would much prefer having the company of her husband; she had no desire to have a fashionable marriage where the partners scarcely ever saw each other.

Simon's noble brows were drawn together during her speech, and she believed he was well-inclined to her proposal. Then, when she finished speaking and asked his opinion, her betrothed remarked thoughtfully that the contours of the Peaks reminded him of an area in Switzerland where glaciers had gouged out the rock. Irritated that he had not been listening to something so important to her, Antonia snapped at her betrothed. His face had closed up immediately; she had seen before how he could withdraw behind an unbreachable barrier, but this was the first time he had done so with her. With a mental curse for her unruly tongue, she apologized immediately. Though he apologized in turn for his distraction and assured her that the spat was forgotten, they began to be wary with each other.

Ten days before the wedding, tension escalated to full-scale battle. They were having tea together in the morning room when Antonia asked about provisions for health care and education among the Launceston tenants.

Simon looked blank. "I have no idea what the situation is."

Raised by a Whig nobleman who constantly emphasized the responsibility that privilege carried, Antonia was deeply shocked by his answer. Not wanting to think badly of her beloved, she said, "I suppose you haven't been back in England long enough to become familiar with conditions on your estate."

With unfortunate truthfulness, Lord Launceston replied, "To be honest, when I was at Abbotsden it didn't occur to me to ask my steward about such things."

"Well, if you don't take an interest in your tenants' welfare, who will?" Antonia pointed out with what she considered perfect reasonableness.

"Isn't that what stewards are for?" Simon answered with equal logic.

"No matter how competent a steward is, one can't count on him to take an enlightened interest." Antonia struggled mightily to keep her exasperation from showing, but was not entirely successful. "For that matter, many of them will rob their masters blind if not closely monitored."

Simon sighed and studied his teacup. "I daresay you are right, but I find the idea of keeping my employees up to the mark quite tedious. I would far rather be at my studies."

"Natural philosophy is all very well," Antonia said tartly, "but one's responsibilities must come first. Are your tenants adequately housed and fed? Is medical care available? Did your father have an enclosure act passed, and if so, have the freeholders who are injured by such acts been properly compensated? Are promising children given the opportunity to advance themselves through education?"

With a flash of irritation, Simon said, "Since you are so concerned with the welfare of my dependents, I give you leave to arrange such matters after we are married. Certainly you enjoy managing far more than I do."

"An excellent idea," Antonia said tightly. "Someone must be concerned for their well-being, and obviously it won't be you."

Their ideas about what was important differed sharply, and with shocking suddenness they had gone from amiability to alienation.

Simon had withdrawn into the detachment that upset her so, his handsome face chilly and remote, but she could see the pain in his intense blue eyes. Impulsively she reached out one hand. "Simon, I'm so sorry. I don't mean to be a managing female. You were not raised to be the heir, and it is beastly of me to criticize you for not immediately becoming a model landlord."

He clasped her hand tightly, his expression softening with relief. "But you are right, Antonia. The Launceston estate supports many people. It is a disgrace that I don't even know how many dependents I have, much less what their condition is." He shook his head ruefully. "A tragedy that my brother died. He was much better at practical matters than I. That's why we never got on, actually. Will you help me learn what I should know? The well-being of my dependents is more important than my dabblings in natural philosophy."

In an instant she was in his arms, clinging as if an embrace could erase the unpleasantness, her face muffled against the smooth weave of his blue coat. "I should not have said what I did. Any country squire can oversee an estate. Your intelligence and talent for natural philosophy are far rarer and more valuable. In the long run, it is thinkers and scholars like you that will improve the lives of everyone."

He held her tightly and she raised her face to his. This time, when they kissed, an undercurrent of desperation ran between them.

A bespectacled gentleman was reading in the library when Judith entered, and for a moment she didn't recognize him. Then he glanced up and she realized it was Lord Launceston. Amazing what a difference a pair of gold-rimmed spectacles made; although he was still the handsomest man she'd ever seen, his scholarly air made him look more like a professor than a romantic hero.

Characteristically oblivious to the effect he produced, Simon rose politely and held up the volume he was reading. "I see from the inscription that this is your copy of *The Theory of the Earth*. I hope you don't mind my reading it. My own is in Kent, and there is something I wanted to check." He laid the book on the table. "Tell me, what do you think of Hutton's ideas?"

"I can see why he is considered sacrilegious by those who believe the earth only six thousand years old," Judith replied cautiously, "but his theories appear sound. It seems logical that the earth has been formed over eons of time, from many different processes of water, wind, and heat."

"I agree. Someday James Hutton will be considered the father of geology. His theories have the simplicity and logic of brilliance." After they had both settled in the comfortable library chairs, Simon asked, "Have you read much geology?"

She waved her hand deprecatingly. "Some. All nature is fascinating, but plants and flowers interest me more than rocks. When I was a child, nature was a great solace."

"Oh, yes, I recall that Antonia told me that you do wonderful drawings of wildflowers," Lord Launceston said with every evidence of interest. "I'd like to see them sometime, if you didn't mind showing them to me."

"Really?" Judith said doubtfully.

"Really." Simon's smile was reassuring. "Good art enables one to see the world in a new way, and I would expect you to draw very well indeed."

"My drawings aren't really art; they are just accurate records of local botanicals," Judith cautioned, but she was already going to the far end of the library, where a portfolio of her drawings was stored. It was impossible to resist the opportunity to show off work that she was secretly very proud of.

She had expected that he would flip through the portfolio quickly, but Simon took his time, examining every drawing carefully and reading the notes that she had written on the side. When he finally looked up, his blue eyes glowed behind the spectacles. "Your drawings are lovely in themselves, but far more important, you have the eye of a natural philosopher. Every detail is rendered with exquisite accuracy—at least, it seems that way to me. Have you considered having these published?"

"Publish my drawings?" Judith said, surprise even stronger than her pleasure at his good opinion. "Who could possibly be interested in common wildflowers?"

"Many people, when they are as well done as these." He grinned. "It won't be enough people to make you rich, but I imagine you would find it satisfying to reach a wider audience." He glanced down at the portfolio again. "I gather from your notes that many of these are flowers found only in the high country. That would make an interesting focus for a book."

"What you say is very flattering," Judith said, "but I haven't the faintest idea of how to find a publisher."

"I know a man in London who publishes serious works of natural science, including studies of wildlife. In fact, he is the one who has been alternately coaxing and threatening me to finish my paper on geology. With your permission, I'll send him a sample of your work."

"Of course you have my permission," Judith said with a delighted smile. She allowed herself to savor a warm glow of pleasure. Even if the publisher was uninterested, Simon's respect and approval gave her an insidious satisfaction. She might not be beautiful and charming like Antonia, but she had a few talents that the other woman lacked.

It was an unworthy thought, and Judith immediately chastised herself. Thinking of her employer, she asked, "Where is Antonia? I thought you were going riding together."

Lord Launceston glanced away, the enthusiasm he had shown for Judith's work fading from his face, leaving his expression cool and unreadable. "Antonia went alone. I find it unnerving to watch the suicidal way she hurls herself down the hills. I made the mistake of telling her that yesterday."

Judith rolled her eyes, trying to make a joke of it. "I'm sure you learned your error quickly."

"Indeed." His faint smile was humorless. "She said I could ride like a slowtop if I wished, but she had no intention of doing the same."

"Oh, dear." Judith's brow furrowed, knowing the words were inadequate. "You know she didn't mean it."

"Oh, she meant it, though she didn't intend insult," he said dryly. Then, with regret, "And Antonia's quite right.

I can stay on a horse well enough, but I'm no great rider. Nor a whip, for that matter. To me, horses and carriages are transportation, not a passion." He absently removed a red-gold hair from his sleeve. "She apologized."

Looking beyond his words, Judith asked quietly, "Is something wrong?"

Lord Launceston removed his glasses and stood, moving across the room with his natural grace to gaze out the window at the Peaks. His voice was halting. "I d-don't know. We keep quarreling. Then we are both aghast and make up immediately." He turned his palm up vaguely. "The issues are usually trivial, but we seem to be always on the verge of a row. I detest rows."

He turned to face Judith, appeal on the lean sculpted planes of his face. "You have been married. Is it possible for two people to be in love, yet to hurt each other constantly?"

Judith saw the same tension in Lord Launceston that had been visible in Antonia for the last few days. While she knew that her experience of marriage was hardly such as to make her an expert in love, she tried her best to offer guidance. "Perhaps you are suffering a reaction to the speed with which you fell in love with each other," she suggested. "All couples have disagreements; indeed, from what I have observed, much of a happy marriage is agreeing to disagree. You made a commitment to each other very quickly and are only now discovering your differences. That does not mean you will not suit."

He turned again to stare unseeing out the window. "Antonia and I seem to be doing that quite often—agreeing to disagree."

"That is the beginning of learning how to rub along comfortably," Judith said, trying to be encouraging. "It is just a matter of time, of learning each other's ways."

Simon sighed. "Perhaps that is what we need. More time."

Bending his head, he wearily massaged his temples. Lord Launceston was a very private man, and Judith felt honored that he treated her as a trustworthy friend. She ached for his unhappiness, wanting to say something that would take the shadow from his eyes. "When two people love each other, almost anything can be worked out. You will see."

He raised his head and gave her a long look, then smiled faintly. "Thank you, Judith. You're very wise . . . and very kind."

She felt absurdly warmed by his praise.

Even though there was strain between Lady Antonia and Lord Launceston, overall the four members of the house party blended well. Usually mornings were spent on personal activities; Antonia took care of her estate responsibilities, Judith conferred with the housekeeper or worked on her drawings, Simon read scholarly texts that he had purchased on his return to England, and Adam dealt with formidable quantities of papers sent to him by his London commercial agent. In the afternoons, they usually did things as couples, and evenings were spent with the four of them talking and laughing from dinner until bedtime.

The day after Simon and Judith had talked in the library was an exception. The weather was fine, and the four of them decided it was time to make an all-day excursion to the upland village of Castleton. The road wound upward through a wildly romantic gorge called Windgates because of the stream of air that constantly swept down it. Dramatic views of precipices or the Vale of Castleton met the eye at every turn of the road. At the top of the gorge, the village clustered at the foot of a peak topped by the looming ruins of a Norman castle. Peak Castle had been very nearly impregnable in its time; even now, without facing arrows and boiling oil, Antonia knew from experience that the climb up was a taxing one.

The special lure of Castleton was its caves. There were several in the area, but the best was Peak Cavern in the mountain beneath the castle. The cave was a well-known local landmark, and Simon had been interested in visiting as soon as he learned of it. Antonia had been less enthused; though she had lived in the district all her life, she had never been seized by a desire to go underground. But doubtless it would be interesting, and she was eager to participate in anything that would please Simon.

After a pleasant lunch at the village inn, they engaged a local guide to take them into the bowels of the earth. At the cavern, where a fast-flowing stream led into the dark gaping mouth, Simon surveyed the opening happily. "The action of water on limestone is what cuts the cavern from living rock," he informed his companions. "The stone slowly melts away."

"Fascinating," Judith said with a happy smile of anticipation. "I've always wanted to visit a cave, but have never had the opportunity. Have you been in many?"

Before Simon could answer, the wiry guide decided it was time to assert his authority. The cavern, he informed them portentously, went more than half a mile into the mountain. Many and wonderful were the galleries and chambers within, but the tour was not without danger. They must stay near the guide; the ladies in particular must be careful of their footing. After speaking, he lit three torches, giving two to Adam and Simon and keeping the last for himself.

Antonia eyed the entrance to the cave with distaste, reluctant to leave the sunshine. It could not be too dangerous, or there would not be so many visitors; nonetheless, she had to force herself to enter. The guide led, followed by Judith, Simon, and Antonia, with Adam bringing up the rear. After crossing a wide area that had once been used as a workshop by ropemakers, they squeezed through a tight passage that emerged in an enormous chamber. The ceiling arched high above their heads, blackened by the soot of centuries of torches, and the lights they carried were a feeble defense against the smothering dark.

"Welcome to the Devil's Cavern," the guide said, his voice pitched to echo hollowly from the stone walls.

Judith slowly turned in a complete circle, her dark head tilted back as she examined her surroundings with awe. "What a remarkable sight."

"In India, they would have put a temple here," Adam said, his deep voice behind Antonia.

"This is a splendid cave," Simon agreed as he lifted his
torch and explored the chamber, kneeling to peer into the
water, his long fingers testing the damp texture of the walls.
In the flickering light, he looked even more handsome and
romantic than usual as he spoke learnedly of stalactites and
stalagmites.

While Adam and Judith discussed their surroundings,
Antonia tried to focus on how handsome Simon looked and
what a lucky woman she was, but the farther they penetrated
into the depths, the more distressed she became. She felt the
dead weight of countless tons of stone hanging above her,
a nearly tangible pressure that constricted her lungs like a
band of iron.

They continued single-file along a narrow path by the
stream. The air was damp and very cold, and Antonia
shivered, chilled even through her heavy riding habit. The
wet rock beneath her feet was slippery, and she picked her
way carefully over the treacherous surface, the skirts of her
habit clenched in her rigid fingers. The pulse pounding in
her temples threatened to drown out the sounds of footsteps
and trickling water.

In the chamber called Roger's Rain House, water flowed
continuously down the walls in a glimmering sheet. Antonia
tried to join the other members of the party in appreciation,
but fear was mounting in her, choking her breath. This is
ridiculous, she told herself fiercely. People have been coming
down here for centuries. It's perfectly safe.

The guide warned in a sepulchral voice, "Mind your
heads. It's a low passage to the Orchestral Chamber." A
faintly accusing note was heard. "If your lordship had given
more notice, a choir could have been procured to sing in the
chamber. The sound is most remarkable."

Simon chuckled, then ducked down to follow the guide
to the next chamber. As he disappeared, Antonia stared at
the narrow opening and knew that not for love, nor money,
nor eternal life, could she make herself enter that passage.
Her heart pounded as if trying to escape her breast, and she
felt perspiration on her face and hands even as she shivered
with the cold.

Just before entering the aperture, Judith glanced back at her employer with an expression of concern. "Are you coming?"

Antonia tried to answer but could not make her voice work. On the verge of hysteria, she raised one hand to her mouth, knowing that if she were capable of speech she would begin screaming. Then a sharp question from Adam penetrated her rising panic.

"Tony, is something wrong?"

Instinctively she turned to her cousin. Recognizing the mute appeal on her face, Adam closed the distance between them and wrapped his free arm around her. Antonia clung to him, her breathing fast and shallow but knowing that she had found a secure haven in a precarious world.

"Don't worry, Tony, we'll go outside now." Adam's deep voice was infinitely soothing. "You'll be fine as soon as we leave the cave."

She swallowed and tried to speak evenly. "Don't let my foolishness spoil this for you." Her voice cracked on the last words and she slid her arms around Adam's muscular body, hoping his warmth would thaw some of her bone-deep chill.

He ignored her protest, his arm tightening protectively around her. "Judith, you go on. I'll take Antonia outdoors."

Her voice worried, Judith said, "I'll go with you."

Antonia was pressed so close to her cousin that she felt the vibration of his reply against her cheek.

"No, Simon and the guide need to know that we have left, not wandered into a side passage and broken our necks. Besides, like Tony said, there is no need for you to leave when you are enjoying the tour."

After a doubtful moment, Judith accepted the logic of his suggestion and ducked her head to enter the passage. In the distance the amplified voices of Simon and the guide could be heard, but Antonia ignored them. All that mattered was the reality of Adam's arm around her as they retraced their steps through the cavern, his comforting flow of words that anchored her to sanity. The torchlight caused grotesque shadows to swirl and dart around them, but with Adam she was safe.

His calm strength brought forth half-forgotten memories; there had been other occasions when Adam had held her close like this, protecting her from the demons of the dark. As a child, she had sometimes suffered night terrors, waking up screaming, and her nurse had soon learned that the little ladyship could be most quickly soothed by her baseborn cousin. The servants had found it a most affecting sight.

It seemed an endless journey, but finally they crossed the antechamber and emerged into the blessed, blessed sunlight. Antonia threw an arm across her eyes at the glare, gulping air deep into lungs that seemed to have expanded tenfold. It was incredible how quickly her panic dissipated. As it did, she began to feel embarrassment at her weakness.

Adam's arm was still supporting her, and as her breathing steadied, she looked up into his tanned face. She was so close that she could see the fine wrinkles at the corners of his eyes that came from squinting against a tropical sun. "You're all right now." His words were more statement than question.

When she nodded, he dropped his arm and stepped away from her, dowsing the torch in a pile of earth by the entrance of the cave.

She raised a still-shaky hand to brush a loose strand of bright hair from her forehead, saying with creditable calm, "I'm perfectly well. I can't imagine what came over me." She glanced back at the mouth of the cave, then quickly turned away, unable to suppress a shiver. "I feel a complete fool, having the vapors when there was nothing to be afraid of."

Adam's gray-green eyes studied her narrowly before he nodded, satisfied with her recovery. "Let's take a walk. The village is so small that our companions will have no trouble finding us when they are through."

Antonia took his arm and they began walking toward the village green.

As they neared the church, Adam said, "No need to castigate yourself for foolishness. If it will make you feel better, there's a name for what you experienced."

"Really?" Antonia glanced at her cousin in surprise. Already her fear had an unreal, dreamlike quality.

"It's called phobia, from the Greek word for fear, and it means blind, illogical panic. One can have a phobia about caves, heights, spiders, anything one likes. The fact that it is illogical doesn't make it any the less real."

Antonia mulled his words over. "Do you have a phobia?"

"Not a really first-rate one like yours," he said with mock wistfulness, "but I must admit I'm not overfond of caves myself. That was why I insisted on taking you out: it gave me a perfect excuse to leave."

She smiled, sure that Adam had made that up to make her feel better. Well, he had succeeded. "Is there a cure for a phobia?"

"Stay out of caves," he said cheerfully.

"I have every intention of doing so!"

They entered the churchyard and Adam glanced up at the square tower. "If I recall the guidebook correctly, there is a fine Norman chancel, an octagonal font, and doubtless other wonders. Shall we go inside and admire them?"

Antonia wrinkled her nose. "No, thank you. I've had enough cool, damp stone places for one day. Let's just sit in the sun."

There was a bench against the south wall and they sat down together. Antonia leaned against the wall with a sigh of release, letting the sun's warmth burn away the last of her deathly chill. There was no need for talk; they had known each other too long to fear silence. As a child, she had wished for brothers and sisters, but no natural sibling could have been a better brother than Adam. Perhaps it was because he had rescued her, as he had so often when they were children, that Antonia let herself admit, "I feel as if I let Simon down."

"Why? Because you don't like caves? He won't blame you for that." Adam's voice was reassuring. "In fact, he will be apologetic for taking you into one."

"I think he may be regretting our betrothal," she blurted out, fixing her gaze on her gold signet ring. It was engraved with the Thornton arms and had been a gift from her father on her eighteenth birthday. The motto said simply *Valor*. It wasn't always easy to live up to.

There was a long pause. She stole a quick glance at Adam. His tawny sun-streaked hair and aura of controlled power reminded her of a lion.

"Why do you say that?" he asked at length. He was staring straight ahead, his profile expressionless.

Antonia hesitated, not wanting to detail the host of minor difficulties that were symptoms, not the true problem. "He's getting more and more remote," she said finally. "Polite, not passionate. I'm doing something wrong, but I don't know how to change." She stopped, feeling fear again. Not the irrational panic of the cavern, but a piercing fear of loss that was all too genuine. "Perhaps I should give him his freedom back."

She took a deep breath, knowing herself on the verge of tears. "But I can't, Adam, I can't. I love him so." Her voice broke and she bent her head, wishing she was wearing a concealing bonnet rather than a tiny, saucy riding cap. Putting a hand across her eyes, she whispered, "What should I do?"

She wished that he would put his arms around her and offer the same uncomplicated comfort that he had in the cave, but he didn't. "I can't advise you on something like that, Tony. Only you can know what you must do." After a long pause, he continued, his words slow and careful. "Very few men are articulate in the language of the heart. The fact that Simon sometimes withdraws into himself doesn't mean that he doesn't care about you."

Feeling very confused and alone, Antonia reached a tentative hand to her cousin. For a moment she feared that he would not respond, but then his strong brown hand enfolded her slim fingers. The contact helped immensely; Adam had never let her down, except, perhaps, by leaving England. She said bleakly, "I thought that when I finally fell in love, everything would be magically right."

His fingers tightened on hers. "No one ever said that love was easy," he said, his voice rough. "That doesn't mean that loving isn't worth the effort."

Antonia closed her eyes, leaning her head against the sun-warmed stone. Odd that she, who considered herself a modern, independent woman, was so much a victim of romantic illusions. On some level, she had really believed that once she met the one right man whom she had been waiting for, she would recognize him instantly and there would be no problems more significant than choosing names for their beautiful healthy children.

She had recognized the man, all right, but she had certainly been wrong about the other part. Who had said that the course of true love never ran smooth? Shakespeare was a safe guess; the man must never have spoken an unquotable word. The thought made her smile faintly. Once again Adam had come to her rescue, as he had so many times before. He was quite right; no one had ever promised that loving would be easy, but the prize was worth the price. She would simply have to try harder.

She heard Simon speak her name and opened her eyes to see him swiftly crossing the churchyard, his face concerned. "Are you all right now? Judith said you were a trifle indisposed, but didn't tell me until we came out just how upsetting you found the cave."

At his approach, Adam stood and went to Judith, who was approaching more slowly than Simon.

Simon knelt on one knee in front of her, catching her hands in his, anxiety on his beautifully molded face. "I knew that caves have that effect on some people, but you are so utterly fearless that it never occurred to me that you would find it disturbing."

Antonia wryly supposed that that was a compliment. "I was fine as soon as I left the cave. I'm sorry to be such a poor creature."

Relief shone in his intensely blue eyes. "Forgive me for leading you down into the kingdom of Hades?" he asked softly.

He was so dear . . . "There is nothing to forgive." She stood and gave him her very best smile, the one that could melt the most obdurate of male hearts. "Shall we see if we can find a proper tea before we ride back to Thornleigh?''

As she tucked her hand in Simon's elbow, she made her resolution. However difficult love was, she would be equal to the task. After all, there was nothing she wanted more passionately than to love and be loved.

5

Early-afternoon sun touched the gilded harp to shining brightness, and the music room pulsed as Judith's supple fingers stroked forth a rippling cloud of melody. Sitting a few feet away, Adam was enjoying the sight of her as much as the music itself. In her simple white muslin dress, Judith looked exquisite and ethereal as she bent over the harp, her face rapt, her chestnut curls shining in the sunlight. The apparent fragility of her slight figure was belied by the strength and passion of her playing.

The sonata ended in a shower of notes of haunting purity. Immersed in the music, Judith kept her head bowed even after the last sound had died away and the air was still again.

When she finally looked up, Adam said, "You have a rare talent." His voice was low to avoid shattering the mood of closeness and tranquillity that lay between them.

Drawn back to the mundane, Judith smiled mischievously. "It used to irritate my Aunt Janet no end that her daughters had neither talent nor interest in music, while I had both. However, she insisted that my cousins continue with their lessons. Aunt Janet thought that a harp showed a young lady to best advantage."

"She was right," Adam agreed, his gaze warm.

"Only as long as her daughters didn't make the mistake of actually touching the strings." Judith chuckled. "That ruined the illusion immediately."

Adam laughed with her. "So you were the only one who took the lessons seriously?"

Judith looked down again, absently plucking a soft chord. "Oh, lessons were too expensive to waste on the likes of me. When the teacher came, I would sit in the corner and listen, then practice later.'' Glancing up, she saw his expression. "You mustn't feel sorry for me, you know. I was the lucky one. My poor cousins, who are incapable of understanding the joy of music, are the ones to be pitied.''

She had a gallant spirit, and the rush of tenderness Adam felt crystallized the resolve that had been growing in him over the last weeks. "Judith . . .'' He hesitated a moment, struck by the seriousness of what he was about to say. "You must know how much I care for you, and I think you are not indifferent to me.''

Judith raised her eyes to his, the strings of the harp motionless under her graceful hands. As he studied her small, finely cut face, Adam found that marriage was far harder to propose than any other contract. He drew a deep breath. "I would be proud, and honored, if you would consent to be my wife.''

She didn't answer, just regarded him somberly with her deep-set gray eyes.

"My money is from trade, but there is rather a lot of it,'' he continued hesitantly. "I would settle an income on you, so in the future you will never again have to be dependent on anyone. Not even on me.''

Judith shook her head slowly. "That is far less important than whether . . .'' She stopped, searching for words, before saying bluntly, "You have always loved Antonia. Are you marrying me because you can't have her, so any convenient female will do? I do not want to spend the rest of my life knowing that whenever you look at me, you will be wishing I were someone else.''

Adam stood and restlessly crossed the room, respecting the uncanny perception with which Judith had gone to the heart of the matter. That perception was one of the things he most admired in her. He took time to organize his thoughts, knowing how important it was to convince them both. At length, he turned to face her. "Yes, I love Antonia. We grew up together and she is the closest family I have. She will always have part of my heart.'' His voice roughened with sincerity. "But when I look at you, it is your wit and wisdom and gentle spirit that I see. You are yourself, and it is you that I am asking to marry.''

Her soft question was very steady. "You are sure?"

Adam crossed the music room to where she still sat at her harp. ''My youthful love for Antonia was only a romantic dream.'' He cupped her small chin with his hand, admiring the fearless directness of her fine gray eyes. ''This is reality.'' Then he bent over and kissed her, very gently.

Judith gasped, the harp strings making a sudden, discordant sound as her fingers clenched on them in unconscious reaction to the soft pressure of Adam's lips. Her husband had believed that sensual pleasure had no place in a godly marriage. There had been occasional intimacy before his illness weakened him too much, but it had been a furtive groping in the night, quickly ended, never alluded to in any way. Judith had patiently endured his fumblings, sure that the experience could be better, grateful that it wasn't worse.

Being kissed by Adam was quite unlike anything she had known before. She instinctively raised her hand to his shoulder, wanting to draw him closer, and he responded by clasping her slim waist and raising her to her feet. She felt very small in his circling arms, but safe and cherished. The gentleness Adam used told her that he had guessed a great deal about her marriage, and that he was taking exceptional care not to frighten her by going too quickly. Dimly she sensed the passion he was capable of, and as his hands expertly caressed sensitive areas of her back and neck, she knew he would be able to find matching passion in her.

Even so, Judith hesitated, wondering if what she felt was a strong-enough foundation for marriage. She had sworn that she would never marry again except for love. But what was love but comfort and caring? She and Adam had much in common, and they could cherish each other in a very special way.

And if she married him, she would never know want or helplessness again. Her decision made, she whispered, "Yes, Adam, I will be honored to marry you." As she spoke, Judith was surprised to realize that there were tears on her cheeks.

She felt Adam's tension ease, and he smiled in relief before producing a handkerchief and tenderly patting her cheeks dry. "Is marrying me such a fearsome prospect?" he asked, able to tease again.

"Not in the least." Judith found herself smiling through her tears. "I am merely having trouble believing my good fortune."

He pulled her close again and whispered a pledge. "I will do everything in my power to guarantee that you never regret accepting me."

"I won't," she said quietly, surer now that she had made the right choice. She and Adam would be very good for each other.

They settled close together on the sofa. "When and where do you wish to be married?" he asked. "You may have anything you like except a long engagement."

"I can see why you are a successful man of affairs, Adam. You waste no time." Judith melted within the circle of his arm, beginning to feel quite absurdly pleased. "I see no virtue in waiting, but I would rather not make any decision until Antonia and Simon are married. Even though their wedding will be very simple, it has kept me busy with planning." Her eyes narrowed in thought. "In fact, it might be better if we don't mention our betrothal until after the wedding. The household is in enough uproar already."

"I would rather announce it immediately, but I daresay I can keep the good tidings to myself for a few days," he said philosophically.

Judith was gratified that Adam showed no strain at discussing Antonia's marriage. It was not surprising that he had had a youthful infatuation for his beautiful cousin, but Judith believed that he truly had put that behind him. And if he had spoken no words of love—well, neither had she. Both of them were beyond the age of romantic delusion.

Lord Launceston realized that he had been staring at a blank sheet of paper for over an hour without making a mark. Allegedly he was working on his treatise refuting neptunism, the theory that rocks had been formed primarily from oceanic sediment and that volcanic activity was quite unimportant. He had been making observations and analyzing data on the topic for years, and the sentences should flow easily from his pen.

Instead, when he looked at the paper, he saw only Antonia, in all her brimming life and changeable moods. He had still not overcome his sense of wonder that such a glorious creature actually wanted him. While Simon realized that he was considered handsome, he knew himself for an absentminded and scholarly man without great charm or social skill. Certainly he was no special prize for a woman of Lady Antonia's birth, wealth, and incomparable loveliness.

Yet, in spite of his shortcomings, Antonia had been as dazzled by him as he had been by her, and he had won a woman he would never have dared dream of. For a few days —scarcely more than a handful of hours—he had known unadulterated happiness. Then, as subtle strains developed between him and his betrothed, he had come to fear that he could never be the kind of man she wanted and deserved.

Ever since confessing some of his doubts with Judith Winslow, he had been pondering her suggestion that he and Antonia needed more time. Indeed, he had thought of almost nothing else, and logic had led him to the decision that they should delay their marriage. Simon was sure that he was right; he was equally sure that his impetuous intended would not take such a suggestion well. In fact, to make it was to risk losing her.

He sighed and removed his spectacles to rub at his temples. Well, much as he disliked brangling, he could not delay speaking with her any longer. The wedding was less than a week away, and the longer he waited, the more difficult it would be.

Even as he was thinking the words, a knock sounded on the door of the study, followed almost immediately by Antonia's bright head. Her cinnamon eyes were sparkling, and at the sight of her he felt a tight knot of pain at what he must say. Surely he could convince her that a postponement would benefit them both.

"Are you interruptable?" she asked hopefully.

He rose to his feet. "Very much so. I have made no progress today. Besides"—he drew a deep breath—"I must talk to you."

For a moment wary alarm showed in her eyes. Then she said sunnily, "Very well, but first I have a surprise for you."

Since Antonia looked ready to burst with her surprise, Simon willingly followed her outside, knowing it was cowardly to be so relieved at a delay. She led him to the front door of an empty stone cottage some distance from the main house. Taking his hand, she said, "You must close your eyes now."

He obliged, unable to resist smiling at her childlike enthusiasm. One of the things he loved about Antonia was the zest she had for life, for making everything and everyone around her seem brighter and more alive. She steered him through the door, then to the right. "You can open your eyes now."

Simon obeyed her order, then gasped in shock. In front of him was all the complicated paraphernalia of a very large reflecting telescope.

As he stared at the pieces of equipment, Antonia said apologetically, "It's my wedding gift to you. I'm sorry it isn't assembled, but I knew you would prefer to supervise that yourself." When he didn't answer, she continued in a hesitant voice, "If you intend to erect the telescope here at Thornleigh, this building could be converted to an observatory, but of course you may prefer to move it to Kent."

Simon's emotions were chaotic. Such an instrument was fabulously expensive; even more than money, Antonia had expended great thought and effort to find something special. She had chosen well; if the opportunity had been offered, he would have given his left arm for such a telescope. It was a tribute to her efficiency that she had located and acquired such an unusual item in a fortnight, without even leaving her home. He was overwhelmed by her generosity. At the same time he felt intensely guilty that she had done such a thing while he was suffering doubts and when he himself had not even thought to buy her a wedding gift.

"I specifically told you not to buy a telescope." Guilt made his voice sharp. "You should not have done it."

"This is supposed to be a very fine instrument. Indeed, it was built by Herschel himself before he stopped manufacturing them." Her lovely face had changed from excitement to anxiety. "Would you prefer a refraction telescope? I was told that even the best of that type suffer from optical distortion."

Under other conditions Simon would have been impressed at how much she had learned about telescopes. Now the evidence of her desire to please him was a spur to his guilt. He stared at her helplessly. "It's too much, Antonia. Everything has been too much, too fast."

She froze, her slim body rigid, as if she sensed that he was talking about more than the telescope. "What do you mean?"

"We have known each other only a few weeks, and in another few days we intend to marry. It has all been too sudden."

"How can love be too sudden?" Her creamy skin had turned ash-pale. "Or do you mean that you have just realized that it was all a foolish mistake and that you don't really love me, after all?"

"That is not what I said." Simon took a step toward her, then stopped when she retreated an equal distance. "I do love you, but we have not taken the time to really know each other. Marriage is for a lifetime, and we are rushing in too quickly. I think we should postpone the wedding for several months."

"Why don't you just admit that you don't want to marry me?" she cried, an edge of hysteria in her voice.

Simon sought desperately for words that she would believe, cursing his maladroitness. "I do want to marry you, but you know how tense we have been with each other, how we have been making each other unhappy. I think that much of the problem is the speed of events. With the wedding so close, everything we do or say takes on added weight and we end up at odds with each other. We must take the time to learn to be comfortable."

Antonia just stared at him, her eyes wide and stark. Thinking that she was concerned with what people would say, he offered, "Very few people even know about the betrothal, so postponing the ceremony should occasion no embarrassment."

"I don't care what other people think!" she retorted. "What matters is how you feel. If you really loved me, you could not be saying such things. If, after several months there are still problems, would you wish to marry?"

Simon had known this discussion would be difficult, but he had not dreamed how painful it would be. The thought of losing Antonia, with her gifts of beauty and laughter, was intolerable. And yet . . . "Do you think that it would be wise to marry if we are making each other miserable?" he asked.

"What kind of love fears to take the pain along with the joy?" She was trembling with the force of her emotions. "The future is always a gamble, and waiting six months 'to get to know each other better' won't guarantee happiness."

There was some logic to her words, yet Simon knew that he was right too. "Of course there are no guarantees, but even if life is a gamble, we can improve the odds of happiness by being sensible—"

She interrupted him. "How can one be 'sensible' about love? I am not a theorem or a stone or a star. I am a woman, and I need to be loved." As tears welled up, she angrily dragged the back of her hand across her eyes. "Very well, I will be sensible. Clearly our notions of what constitutes marriage are incompatible and we will not suit. Therefore, I release you from the engagement you so foolishly entered into. Since you did not care enough to even notify the newspapers, you are spared the effort of writing a retraction."

Aching, he took several quick steps toward her. "Antonia, I don't want to end our betrothal. I love you."

She skittered back, her lovely face stark with misery. "Don't make it worse, Simon. You're right, it was all a mistake. I am a flighty, frivolous female, not at all a sensible choice for a serious man. God forbid that you should gamble on something as important as marriage."

He reached out a pleading hand, wishing that he had never spoken. Perhaps it really would be better to go ahead with the marriage and work out their differences after.

Before he could touch her or withdraw his words, she twisted away. "Just go, Simon. I don't ever want to see you again." Antonia slipped past him and darted out the door, tears pouring down her face. She looked very young and utterly desolate.

Lord Launceston knew a great deal about rocks, stars, and comets, but his knowledge of how to deal with distraught females was nonexistent. By the time he pulled himself together to follow Antonia outside, she was almost out of sight, racing toward the stables. He guessed that she was going to take one of her suicidal rides through the hills. If so, there was nothing he could do to stop her. He prayed that her usual skill and luck would prevent her from breaking her neck; if she injured herself, his guilt would be unbearable.

Paralysis held him in the doorway of the cottage, feeling that he had just made the worst mistake of his life. It was hard to assimilate that a few short minutes of argument had destroyed everything between him and Antonia.

The thought braced him. Surely the intensity of feeling that bound them could not just evaporate. Antonia was hurt and angry and had reacted emotionally. When she calmed down, perhaps she would miss him as much as he already missed her. He would wait two or three weeks, then contact her again. The worst she could do would be to dismiss him again, though God knew that would be bad enough.

It was a plan of sorts, and it gave Simon something to cling to through the mists of pain. In the meantime, he must leave Thornleigh immediately; he could not possibly stay under her roof after such a scene. He headed back to the house and ordered his valet to pack his belongings and arrange for them to leave before the afternoon was over. Then he went in search of Adam.

Adam was in the music room with Judith. If Simon had not been numb with unhappiness, he might have noticed the air of intimacy between them. Instead, he plunged into his own business. "I've come to say good-bye."

Catching sight of his friend's face, Adam immediately got to his feet and crossed the music room. "What's wrong?"

"Lady Antonia and I have decided we will not suit, so I am leaving Thornleigh." Simon tried to sound normal, but from the others' expressions, he was not successful. His voice lowered to reach Adam's ears only. "I think she has gone dashing off into the hills. P-perhaps . . . perhaps you can go after her. She might be too reckless."

"I will." Adam regarded him soberly, concern vivid on his face. "Is there anything I can do?"

Lord Launceston recalled his earlier thoughts. "When Antonia has had time to reconsider, she may regret that she has acted so hastily. I shall write you. Will you keep me informed of her feelings?" After speaking, Simon realized that he was asking his friend to act as a spy. Indeed, if Adam had to choose between supporting his cousin and Simon, he would certainly choose Antonia.

Fortunately Adam took Simon's words in good part. "In other words, Antonia has flown up into the boughs," he translated. "Don't worry, I shall do what I can."

Judith joined them, her gray eyes warm with sympathy as she offered her hand. "I'm so sorry."

Simon bowed over her hand, then tried to smile. "So am I." After a quick handshake with Adam, he escaped the room, fearful that too much sympathy would cause him to break down.

After Lord Launceston left, Adam swore a soft oath under his breath. Judith tried to interpret the meaning, then decided with bleak honesty to tackle her fears head-on. "Perhaps Antonia is no longer an unattainable dream, Adam. I will not hold you to our engagement if you regret making it."

Her words hung in the air for a painful eternity before Adam answered, his mouth twisted. "Do you think so little of my constancy? What happened between Simon and Tony has nothing to do with you and me."

Relieved, Judith forced herself to change the direction of

her thoughts; if she could not let herself trust Adam, she would poison the honesty of what was between them. "I'm sorry," she said quietly. "I just have trouble imagining that a man would prefer me when Antonia was available."

"The fact that she may not marry Simon does not make her available to me," he said rather dryly. "Besides, I think it likely that the breach between them can be repaired. When my cousin has calmed down, she will undoubtedly be sorry she sent Simon away, and he seems prepared to try again."

Judith remembered the sense of magic between Simon and Antonia at their first meeting. "I hope you are right."

"So do I, in spite of what you might think." He bent over to give Judith a light kiss. "Simon thinks that Tony has gone haring off into the hills, which sounds just like her. I'd best go after her."

"If anyone can find Antonia, it would be you." Judith wrinkled her nose. "I'll start canceling the arrangements for the wedding." As they went off on their separate tasks, Judith thought wryly that someone had to clean up the wreckage after the romantic leads had enacted their drama at center stage. Well, she had always been good at that sort of thing.

One of the grooms confirmed that her ladyship had stormed off on her favorite horse, and not even dressed for riding. The groom had been unsurprised; very little that the mistress did could surprise anyone at Thornleigh.

Adam took his time riding after his cousin. He had a fair idea of where she would end up, and it wouldn't do to get there too soon; his cousin would need some time alone. Later, she would need comfort, and he was experienced at giving that.

High in the rugged upland peaks was a protected ledge he and Tony had named the Aerie. An improbable patch of grass and flowers grew in front of a rocky overhang, making a comfortable spot to lie and watch the world. This had been their special retreat when they were children, and they had come often to talk, to dream, to watch the hawks soaring

over the valley. Adam had not come here for perhaps a dozen
years, but he could have found his way blindfolded.

Sure enough, his cousin's horse was tethered in the dale
below. Adam dismounted and tied his own mount, then made
the final scramble up the steep hillside. At the top he passed
through a narrow cleft in the rock and found himself in the
Aerie. Tony was huddled in the grass with her arms around
her knees, her yellow morning dress much the worse for wear
after her ride. She must have herd the sound of his approach,
but she didn't look up, just continued to gaze at a peregrine
falcon floating with effortless grace on an air current. Of
course she knew that only Adam would come here.

He dropped cross-legged beside her in the grass. "Can
you bear company?" he asked in a conversational tone.

"As long as it is you." Antonia still didn't look at him,
simply accepting his presence. She had been crying, and she
was so pale that he could see traces of the golden freckles
that had frosted her cheeks when she was a child.

There was also gooseflesh on her bare arms; the afternoon
was a cool one. Adam peeled off his coat and draped it around
his cousin's shoulders. It was large enough to go twice around
her, and she accepted it gratefully. "Thank you." There was
a long silence before she spoke again. "Simon told you what
happened?"

"Only in the most general way," Adam said carefully.
"He said the two of you had decided you would not suit.
He will have left Thornleigh by now."

His words rekindled her grief and she began crying again,
raw sobs wrenched from the depths of her heart. So Simon
had taken her at her word and was gone. She would never
see him again. Part of her had secretly hoped that he cared
enough to follow her, or at least to stay at Thornleigh; she
was willing to be convinced that he loved her. But she had
been right: Lord Launceston did not care as much for her
as she did for him. At this very moment he was probably
congratulating himself on his fortunate escape.

As Antonia doubled over in tears, Adam pulled her close,
cradling her securely against his broad chest. Once more she

accepted the refuge he offered, but this was not like her un-
accountable terror in Peak Cavern; this time sunlight would
not dissipate the black clouds. She cried for lost youth and
lost dreams, for all the bright illusions of love that she had
wanted so much to believe in. Adam wordlessly gave her
a handkerchief and eventually she subsided into hiccups, then
silence. The only other sounds were the perpetual soughing
of the wind and the occasional distant cry of a bird.

After a long time had passed, Antonia asked in a small
voice hoarse from crying, "Is love even possible, Adam?"

"Of course it is," he said, his certainty immensely comforting. "Unfortunately 'love' is an imprecise word, used
to describe a wide variety of feelings. The Greeks knew better
and had words for different sorts of loving. But even they
described only a handful of the complicated needs, desires,
and demands we call love."

Antonia considered his statement, her brain moving rather
slowly. "What do you mean?"

"There is the love of mother for child, of friend for friend,
of sibling for sibling, of a person for an object or nation or
ideal. Each of those is real, each different. And they are just
the beginning." He considered. "If I were a philosopher
trying to classify the kinds of love, I would divide them into
two categories: the first category is generous love, where
one wants the best for the beloved, even if it means personal
loss for the one who loves. It also includes the kind of love
that accepts the beloved as he or she is, knowing that differences are part of what makes love real."

Adam shifted his position, settling Antonia more comfortably under his arm. "My second category is selfish love,
where one is more concerned for oneself than for the other
person. It includes obsession, where one seeks to possess
and change the beloved. 'Because I love you, you must be
what I think you should be.' Generous and selfish love are
quite different, yet sometimes the two are intertwined so
closely that they cannot be separated.

"You asked if love is possible, but you were really asking
about romantic love. I know it is possible, but people have

different ideas of what it is. Often 'romantic love' means physical attraction. That is compelling, but without friendship and respect, it can be a volatile base for a marriage.'' He stopped to let that sink in, then finished slowly, ''Also, your personal ideal of romantic love might be one that is very hard to fulfill. If you know exactly what you mean by love, you should be able to answer your question of whether it is possible.''

Even in Antonia's present muddled state, she knew that he was offering her oblique advice as well as comfort. Was her love for Simon generous, or selfish, or some of both? Too often she had been critical, not accepting him as he was, yet she had genuinely wanted to please him as well.

It was easier to recognize that her idea of romantic love was a demanding one. Simon had been unable to meet it; perhaps no man could. Bleakly she accepted that the ending of the betrothal had been entirely her fault. Hurt and insecure, she had lost her temper and blamed him for the fact that he thought differently from her. She could not believe that Simon would be willing to forgive her when she had behaved so badly; he was a gentle and easygoing man, and she had made him wretched.

Adam made no attempt to draw her out. He simply held her, warm and undemanding. In all of Antonia's lifetime, he was the one person she had always been able to depend on. Ever since they were children, she had known that he cared for her even when she was at her naughtiest, even on the rare occasions when temper had made her lash out at him. Why could she not want to marry her cousin? There might not be romance between them, but there was certainly love, the generous sort that was based on kindness, friendship, and trust.

Well, why not marry Adam? He had offered for her, albeit casually. Antonia had never seen any sign that her cousin had a romantic bone in his body; perhaps his ideal of marriage was the kind of comfortable friendship that existed between them. If her own concept of romantic love was un-attainable, better to try for what was possible.

It was too soon to think of marrying anyone else; the image of Simon was too vivid, the pain too deep. But perhaps later . . .

It never occurred to Antonia that Adam's offer of marriage might no longer be open.

6

Antonia made no attempt to confide in her companion about the circumstances that had ended her betrothal. After she and Adam had returned from her escape to the hills, she had been relentlessly cheerful with everyone, only her deep shadowed eyes revealing her unhappiness. It hurt Judith to watch her.

By mutual agreement, Judith and Adam did not announce their engagement; it would seem like a cruel flaunting of their happiness when Antonia was so miserable. The only comfort Antonia seemed to find was in her cousin's presence, and every day she went for a long ride with him. Judith watched Adam very carefully, but saw no signs that he was regretting his betrothal and yearning after his cousin. Judith was immensely grateful for that; she could not have blamed Adam if he was still in love with Antonia, but she would much rather keep him for herself.

Several days after Lord Launceston left, Adam received a short note from him, giving a hotel in London where he could be reached. Adam showed the note to Judith, who saw that his lordship intended to return to Derbyshire soon to plead his case. If he did, Judith suspected that Antonia would probably welcome her erstwhile lover with open arms.

A very long week after Simon left, Adam announced that he was going to visit an engineer working on the outskirts of Macclesfield and would either of the ladies like to visit the shops while he was examining Mr. Malcolm's steam engine? Thinking that it would be good for Antonia to get away from Thornleigh for a day, Judith accepted for both of them.

As they drove west to Macclesfield, Judith asked, "What is special about Mr. Malcolm's engines?"

"They work at very high pressures, so a compact engine can produce a great deal of power," Adam explained. "There are many possible applications in industry, transportation, and mining."

Judith thought about that a bit. "If the pressure is very high, isn't there danger of explosion?"

"Potentially, but not if the device is well-built and well-maintained," Adam answered. "Malcolm has had good success with his engines throughout the Midlands, and is looking for investment to build a larger manufactory."

Judith nodded thoughtfully. Based on what she had observed of Adam's business acumen, if he decided that a project was worthwhile, success was virtually assured.

Apprentice engineer Dickie Stokes used the massive spanner to tighten a bolt on the steam engine, then temporarily hung it on the convenient arm of the safety valve while he rummaged through his wooden tool chest for a screwdriver. As he straightened up, he was unable to repress a yawn. Bit of a pity that the barmaid at the Stars and Garters had chosen last night to succumb to Dickie's charm; he'd not gotten a wink of sleep. Usually it wouldn't matter, but today some nabob was visiting Mr. Malcolm and the gaffer was all aflutter to impress him. He'd had his apprentice rushing about all morning, first cleaning the sheds, then testing every cylinder, rod, and bolt in the engine. The old man should have brought more than one apprentice on this project; but of course, money was short.

Dickie checked the water level and the furnace, then nodded, satisfied that everything was right and tight. Lastly he began gathering his tools; 'twouldn't do to leave them lying about with an important visitor coming.

The engine made such a racket that at first he didn't hear Mr. Malcolm calling, but finally the yells of "Dickie, get in here!" penetrated the clamor. The apprentice stifled another yawn. The gaffer must have found something else to worry about. Well, the engine itself was singing as sweet as you could please.

"Dickie, get over here, you worthless Geordie!"

Dickie started moving more smartly; the gaffer never called him a Geordie unless he was right peevish. Not that there was anything wrong with having been born in New-castle, and Dickie Stokes would draw the claret of anyone who claimed otherwise.

As the apprentice closed his tool chest and left the pumping shed, he completely forgot the heavy spanner weighing down the arm of the safety valve.

After the carriage dropped him off at the mine site, Adam crossed the field to the flimsy shed that James Malcolm used as an office. An equally flimsy shed fifty yards away housed the steam engine, chugging away as it pumped water from a badly flooded old mine. Malcolm had been challenged to get the water out; if he was successful, the mine could be profitably worked again and Malcolm's prestige would be enhanced enormously.

The engineer saw his approach and came bustling out. He was a short muscular man with the powerful hands of some-one who had started life as a laborer. "Mr. Yorke, a pleasure to meet you, sir. I can't offer you any refreshment just now, but my apprentice has gone off to purchase some tea."

"No matter." Adam shook hands agreeably, wanting to reduce the engineer's anxiety. His research had indicated that Malcolm was a talented inventor, and Adam was already pre-disposed in his favor. "It's your engine I'm interested in, not tea."

The two men entered the office, and within a few minutes every available surface was covered with detailed drawings of Malcolm's designs. It became clear that the two men were kindred spirits, and before long, they were deep in a lively discussion about flues, crankshafts, and plunger poles. Examining the actual engine was deferred until later.

In the adjacent hut, the pumper roared on. With the safety valve jammed shut, the internal pressure slowly began to rise, driving the engine faster and faster.

* * *

At the George inn, Ian Kinlock shifted restlessly as he waited for the carriage to come. He'd already finished his newspaper, and lack of activity was in a fair way to driving him mad. As a physician and surgeon, leisure was not something he had ever had a chance to become accustomed to. It didn't help that his visit to a distant cousin in Macclesfield had been tedious in the extreme; he should be old enough to know that his mother's social suggestions should be ignored. Unfortunately Lady Kinlock had known that her son would be passing through the area, and he hadn't been able to think of a good reason not to call on Cousin Euan. He had, however, been more inventive about finding reasons for cutting his visit short after a mere two days.

Kinlock pulled his watch out and checked the time; still a quarter of an hour. He gave a sudden chuckle at his own impatience, then crossed his legs and settled back in the coffee-room chair. Any man who had heard as many dull medical lectures as he had should be able to sit still for fifteen minutes.

Macclesfield was a center for silk manufacturing, and the shops had a fine selection of the local products. Antonia eyed the bolts in the draper's shop, wishing she could summon more enthusiasm.

Judith glanced across at her. "Not in the mood for shopping?" she asked sympathetically.

"Not really," Antonia admitted. Her companion had been a model of tact and sympathy lately, never prying, but always willing to offer the silent comfort of her presence. Antonia knew that she was most enormously lucky to have friends like Judith and Adam, and she should make more of an effort to be agreeable. She smiled brightly. "Actually, I'm rather curious about Adam's steam engine. Silk one can see anytime. Do you have any interest in walking back to where we dropped Adam off so we can see the engine? Anything that noisy must be interesting."

Judith gave the quick smile that made her quiet face

sparkle. "Actually, it sounded interesting to me, too, but I thought you preferred shopping."

Antonia made a wry face. "Clear proof that we shouldn't make assumptions about other people's preferences. Shall we go see Mr. Malcolm's marvelous machine?"

Abandoning the shops, they set off through the hilly streets for the edge of town. A brisk twenty-minute walk brought them to the top of the last hill, where they paused. Below they could see the mine buildings and, a bit beyond, a coaching inn called the George. "I believe I can hear the sound of the engine all the way up here," Judith remarked. "When we set Adam down, I didn't realize just how noisy it was."

Antonia listened, then nodded. "You're right. I see why Adam said that steam carriages on the roads would probably never be feasible because the noise terrifies horses."

Judith gave a soft chuckle. "I'm not ashamed to admit that it would frighten me!"

They started down the hill.

Adam studied Malcolm's drawing with interest. "You really think that you can run an engine at 150 pounds of pressure?"

Malcolm nodded. "Aye. We'll go even higher when we find a way of sealing the joints of the boiler plates better." He unrolled another drawing. "You may find this interesting, too."

Adam cast an experienced eye over the drawing. "I see that you attached the connecting rod directly to the piston. It certainly makes the engine more compact, and it should be cheap to build. Hasn't Trevithick done something like this?"

"Aye." The engineer shook his head regretfully. "The man's a genius, but he never stays with a project long enough to make a success of it. All over Britain, there are men like me building on Trevithick's ideas."

Adam smiled inwardly, admiring the dexterity with which Malcolm implied that he himself was competent and reliable. Adam preferred men who were reliable. He neatly rolled the latest drawing up, then cocked his head, realizing that the background noise had changed. He frowned. "Your engine is running much harder than when I arrived. It's really designed to work at such a pace?"

All of Malcolm's attention had been absorbed by his discussion with this knowledgeable potential investor, but now he stopped to listen. "Bloody hell!" he swore. Without another word, he dived toward the door of the shed.

It was already too late. Even as the engineer's hand touched the door knob, the pressure of the steam engine, denied the relief of the safety valve, reached explosion point.

Antonia and Judith were about three hundred yards from the engine house when it exploded with a deafening roar that could be heard on the far side of Macclesfield. The concussion hit the two women with a blast that staggered Antonia and almost knocked the smaller Judith from her feet.

Right in front of their eyes, the engine house disintegrated into clouds of steam and fragments of wood. Huge chunks of iron hurtled through the air in all directions to bury themselves in the earth up to a hundred yards away. One such chunk just missed a young man who had been approaching the office and who now lay motionless on the ground in the wake of the blast. Other iron missiles tore into the office itself, combining with the shock wave to knock the little building into an untidy jumble of beams and boards.

Deafened by the noise, Antonia stared in horror at the devastation. Then she screamed, "Adam!" and began running full-speed toward the wreckage, Judith hard on her heels.

The coach was ten minutes late, which did nothing to improve Ian Kinlock's mood. Eager to make up for lost time, the coachman was stopping just long enough to change his team and pick up passengers. The doctor was passing his bag up to the coachman when the engine exploded. Even several hundred yards away, the blast was stunning in its intensity, and the horses began plunging in their traces and trumpeting with fright.

"Damnation," Kinlock swore, grabbing at the side of the carriage to steady himself.

As thunderous echoes of the detonation rolled between the bare hills, the coachman gasped, "Gawdamighty, what was that?"

"I don't know," Kinlock said grimly, "but throw my bag down again. The odds are that someone is going to need a doctor."

Antonia never recalled the aftermath of the explosion except in a jumble of disconnected images. She remembered men pouring out of the inn down the road, remembered clawing at the steaming wreckage of the shattered engine house, tears pouring down her face. When a man caught her in his arms and tried to drag her away, she pummeled him with her fists, crying out that her cousin was there and she must save him.

The burly workman looked down at her with pity. "If he was in there, miss, he's past saving."

Judith was also tugging her away, her white face showing the same terror that Antonia felt, but her voice almost steady when she said that perhaps Adam had been in the office and would be pulled out unharmed at any moment. The young man who had been walking up to the shed lay unconscious on the ground, a white-haired man expertly checking him for injuries.

The rescuers drawn by the explosion cleared the wreckage away with slow care. Antonia wanted to shriek at them to hurry, but even in her present state she knew that haste could unbalance the debris, causing further injury to anyone trapped inside. At some point Judith passed on the news that apparently no one had been in the engine house, so there was a good chance that Adam was in the office.

The first victim uncovered was a stocky middle-aged man, unconscious but with no obvious injury. Antonia ignored him, her eyes riveted to the ongoing work. Finally, after an endless, aching interval, they brought Adam's bloody form out of the ruined building. Antonia fought her way through the ring of men to kneel at his side. He was so still . . .

"Get a physician," she begged. Adam's light-brown hair was saturated with blood, his face partially obscured, his powerful body completely limp. She clenched his unresponsive hand, refusing to believe that he might be dead.

"I'm a physician." The clipped words had a Scottish burr, and Antonia looked up to see the man who had already examined the other two victims. Later, she would be surprised at how youthful the face under the white hair was, but now only one thing concerned her.

"Is he . . . ?" she stopped, unable to complete the sentence.

The physician knelt beside Adam and felt for a pulse in his throat. "He's alive. For the moment."

Judith pulled Antonia to her feet and together they watched while the doctor made a quick examination. The blood came from a long gash across the right side of Adam's skull; it was hard to believe that a man could lose so much blood and still survive. So much blood . . .

Antonia gripped Judith's hand fiercely, fighting her feeling of nausea.

The physician improvised a head bandage, then stood and signaled for the makeshift litter. As two husky fellows carried Adam to the inn, Antonia intercepted the doctor. "Will he be all right?"

He shrugged. "Sorry, lass, but I cannot say. It's hard to tell about head wounds. Even minor ones bleed something fierce, so it may not be quite so bad as it looks. There isn't much a surgeon can do except sew the wound up and hope for the best." He considered telling her that at least the skull hadn't been broken away to expose the brain, but decided that that might be more descriptive than this terrified young beauty could bear. "The gentleman is your husband?"

"No, my cousin." Antonia shook her head numbly. "More than that, really."

"Well, he seems a strong fellow. He may be awake in an hour, wanting to know what happened."

In spite of the reassuring words, Antonia didn't think that the doctor believed that any more than she did.

* * *

Judith had known that Antonia and Adam were close, but never had she seen the bond so clearly demonstrated as after the explosion, when Adam hovered near death in a coma. Her employer's attention was totally focused on her cousin, as if only her watchful concentration would hold him to life. She did not even know that her hands were bleeding from when she had torn at the wreckage of the engine house.

It was left to Judith to perform the mundane tasks, and the responsibility helped her own precarious equanimity. She had the doctor attend to Antonia's hands after the major victims were cared for; she sent to Thornleigh for clothing and for Antonia's maid; she arranged for rooms and food, welcoming all the distractions. She also sent a note to Lord Launceston in London, feeling that he should know about his friend's injury.

It was Judith who dealt with James Malcolm and his anxious questions, wondering cynically if the engineer's concern was rooted in worry over losing a potential investor. Malcolm had escaped the collapsed office with only a broken arm, while his apprentice, who apparently caused the explosion by accidentally jamming the safety valve, had no injury beyond a temporary loss of consciousness. It seemed bitterly unfair that they were hale and hearty while Adam's life lay in the balance.

Antonia spent all her time at Adam's side, paying attention to what was happening around her only twice. The first time was when she told Judith to arrange a reward for all the men who had participated in the rescue, leaving the details of how much to her companion. The second time was when she bent all her formidable powers of persuasion to convincing the doctor, Ian Kinlock, to stay and attend Adam.

It was the sheerest chance that had put Kinlock on the scene, but his obvious competence had quickly won the respect of everyone present as he tended first the blast victims, then the minor injuries of the rescuers. He spent a long time with Adam, cleaning and sewing his head wound, then checking thoroughly for possible other injuries. The following morning he had intended to resume his journey to Scotland, but under Antonia's urging, Kinlock agreed to stay on for at least a couple of days more.

While the physician didn't strike Judith as being oversusceptible to the female sex, it would have taken a heart of granite to deny Lady Antonia. Most women would have looked haggard under the fear and sleeplessness that her ladyship was undergoing, but Antonia had the fine-drawn beauty and burning eyes of a saint in a Renaissance painting.

It was difficult to persuade Antonia to lie down; only the knowledge that Judith would be with her cousin allowed her to rest. Most of the time both women sat with Adam as he lay quiet and pale as a marble effigy, his immense vitality diminished to an erratic flicker, the only sign of life the slow rise and fall of his chest. Judith briefly considered telling Antonia that she and Adam were betrothed, but dismissed the idea as grotesque when his life might be measured in minutes or hours. Besides, she preferred to keep her grief as private as possible.

Only when she rested, leaving Antonia in the sickroom, would Judith allow herself the luxury of tears. She wept for Adam, whose kindness and intelligence ebbed so close to extinction, and she wept for herself, that the greatest happiness she had ever known seemed likely to end before it had truly begun.

It was the third night since the explosion, and Antonia sat alone with Adam in the dark reaches after midnight. In the last twelve hours Adam had started to move restlessly, which Kinlock thought encouraging, but he had not yet regained consciousness. One terrifying possibility the doctor had mentioned was that Adam might survive, but with his mind so damaged that he would never be himself again. And the longer Adam was in a coma, the greater the likelihood of that kind of damage even if he did survive. Antonia would not think of that. *She would not think of it.* She guessed that the doctor and Judith both expected the worst, but Antonia refused to believe that full recovery wasn't possible.

She, who had always assiduously avoided sickrooms, spent

hours trickling broth in her cousin's mouth, a few drops at a time. It maddened her to know that the one time in her life when Adam needed help, there was so little she could do for him. It seemed monstrously unfair when he had so often assisted her, usually out of muddles of her own making.

Though she had known Adam since she was four years old, only now did Antonia fully realize what an enormous emptiness his death would leave in her life. Even when he was in Asia, she had known that he was alive and that someday she would see him again. But now he was perilously close to the voyage from which there was no returning.

In the bleak honesty of the last two days Antonia had faced the knowledge that Adam's proposal to her had been in dead earnest. He had spoken lightly, testing the waters, and she had treated his offer as a joke because she hadn't wanted to accept and a serious refusal might have created awkwardness between her and her cousin. She had been a coward. More than that, Antonia had felt a lingering anger over the fact that he had left so casually years before; perhaps she had wanted to punish her cousin by treating him as casually as he had treated her.

Adam, unwilling to show vulnerability, had calmly accepted her teasing refusal. He might not love her in the way that she considered romantic, but she did not doubt the depth of his feelings. In her selfishness, in her desire to avoid unpleasantness, she must have hurt him badly, but he had carefully spared her any hint of reproach. No wonder he had been able to speak of generous love.

Now her prayer was not just that Adam survive, but that she have the opportunity to make up for her past insensitivity. There was ironic significance in the fact that Antonia had scarcely thought of Lord Launceston since her cousin's injury; though she had fancied herself in love with Simon, her feelings for Adam ran much deeper.

Lightly Antonia laid one hand on his cheek. His valet had shaved him the day before, but now there were bristles under her palm. Aching with tenderness and guilt, she made a solemn promise to herself: if Adam survived, and if he still wanted her, she would marry him. Not that she was any great bargain, but if she had the opportunity, she would spend the rest of her life making up for the way she had taken Adam's love for granted in the past.

His tanned skin was warm under her hand, and by the dim candlelight she studied his face, trying to see him through fresh eyes. His square jaw showed a stubbornness that he never used with her, and the faint lines were a product of laughter, not ill-temper. No one would ever stop and stare as they did with Lord Launceston, but it was a pleasant face, more familiar to her than her own. She leaned forward and pressed a light kiss on his well-formed lips.

Then, as she lifted her head away, she gasped in shock. Adam's eyes slowly opened and fixed on her. She was so close that she could see the brown flecks in the gray-green irises, could see the confusion in the depths.

"Adam?" she whispered tensely, scarcely daring to breathe.

"A-dam?" he repeated in a scarcely heard whisper. The word was drawn out experimentally, as if unfamiliar to him.

At the sound of his rasping voice, she straightened and picked up a glass of water from the bedside table, then helped him drink some.

When Adam spoke again his voice was stronger, but there was still a quality of tentativeness, as if English was foreign to him. "Where—am—I?"

"In an inn in Macclesfield, near where the explosion was."

His brow furrowed under the bandage. "Ex-plo-sion?"

Dr. Kinlock had said he might not remember what had happened just prior to the accident. "Yes, you were visiting an engineer, Mr. Malcolm, to talk to him about his steam engine. It exploded and you were injured." Antonia considered whether she should wake either Judith or the doctor, but it was three o'clock and both were asleep. Time enough to tell them in the morning.

Adam raised an exploratory hand to his head, feeling the bandage, so she explained, "You received quite a crack on the head and a good few bruises, but there are no bones broken."

His eyes shifted away from her and she could almost see

the slow process of his thoughts as he tried to make sense
of her words. Finally he glanced back. "Who are you?"

His question hit Antonia like a blow. It was hard to believe
that Adam wouldn't recognize her unless his brain was
irrevocably damaged. Pray God this was just temporary
confusion. She forced herself to answer calmly. "I am
Antonia."

Surely there was intelligence in the eyes that regarded her
so seriously. Adam slowly raised one hand and touched the
thick braid of red-gold hair that fell over her shoulder. "Pretty."

She smiled at him. "You have always admired my hair."

"Who am I?" Adam's next question was even more
frightening, but now Antonia was better prepared.

"Your name is Adam Yorke and I am your cousin. You
are twenty-nine years old. We grew up together, mostly at
a place near here called Thornleigh."

"Like brother and sister?"

"Not exactly." In an impulse borne of tenderness and her
earlier vow, Antonia found herself saying, "Actually, we
were going to get married."

7

That statement had certainly gotten Adam's attention. His eyes widened and he stared at her for a long moment. "How did I talk you into that?"

For the first time, Adam's voice had his familiar wry humor, and Antonia felt a rush of relief. He could not possibly sound like that if there was anything permanently wrong with him; he was just disoriented now. "You didn't talk me into a betrothal." She smiled teasingly. "It was as much my idea as yours."

Then a less-welcome thought struck her: when he was back to normal, he would remember that they were not precisely betrothed. He had asked her to marry him, and she had accepted—but those two events had been widely separated in time, and she hadn't informed him of her acceptance. How could she, when it had only just occurred? Antonia realized uneasily that a purist might feel that she was not telling the truth.

The thought was an embarrassing one; she didn't want to be caught in a fib. Well, Dr. Kinlock had said that patients with serious head injuries didn't remember things that happened around the time of the accident. "Though we've known each other forever, the decision had only just been made," she explained. "No one knew." Not even Adam. Antonia's conscience was clear; it wasn't as if she was really lying.

Her cousin was watching her with unwavering intensity, so she continued rather shyly, "Of course it was just an understanding, not a formal betrothal. You can change your

mind if you like.'' It was certainly not her intention to coerce
him into a marriage he didn't want.

His eyebrows lifted in a characteristic Adam gesture.
''Crying off already, Antonia?'' His hand moved across the
counterpane to rest on hers. Even if he didn't consciously
remember her, he obviously felt comfortable in her presence.

''No, most assuredly I am not crying off.'' She squeezed
his fingers affectionately, still savoring the miracle of his
recovery. Now that Adam was awake and in possession of
his wits, she was sure that he must be out of danger. ''It's
just that the most important thing is for you to get well.
Whether or not we marry can wait until later.''

With that same disconcerting intensity, he murmured, ''I
can't imagine that anything is more important than whether
or not we are getting married.''

Suddenly suspicious, Antonia fixed him with a sisterly eye.
''Adam, do you really remember everything and you've just
been teasing me?''

She saw bleakness in his eyes before he closed them and
sighed. ''I only wish . . . that I were teasing.''

Good Lord, here she was bantering with him when he had
just emerged from a coma. Waking up without memories
must be unnerving, to say the least. Antonia pressed his hand
gently. ''Don't worry, love. Dr. Kinlock said that when you
first woke up, you'd be confused. In a few days you'll be
as good as new.'' The endearment slipped out with remarkable ease.

The next time he awoke, he knew it was daylight, even
though his eyes were still closed. Some animal instinct that
feared the unknown kept him still as he searched his mind
for memories. All that he found were a few brief minutes
of conversation with a woman so beautiful that it was
impossible to believe that he could have forgotten her. Odd;
while there were no memories, there was language. Words
floated through his mind and he understood them. Horse.
He knew what a horse was. Was the image in his mind a
particular horse, perhaps one he owned, or was it just an
essence of horseness?

He put the problem aside as unanswerable from available data. He appeared to have a logical mind that could handle concepts and could even question that fact. How was it possible that he had a sense of himself even though he had no idea who he was? Another question to put aside. His body had tensed at the direction of his thoughts and he forced himself to relax; physically he was in no danger. And mentally? The glorious Antonia had assured him that in a few days he would be as good as new, however good that was. He would like to believe her, but guessed that she was speaking from hope, not certainty.

Enough time had been spent in the dark. He opened his eyes, hoping she would be there, and experienced a wash of disappointment that she was not. A different woman sat sewing by the bed, her head bent over an embroidery hoop. She was small and sweetly pretty, but she was not Antonia. Sensing his movement, she looked up and smiled, the gesture warming her fine gray eyes. "Thank heaven you are awake. How do you feel today, Adam?"

"Since both of you called me Adam, I suppose that must be my name," he murmured, half to himself. "I have no better suggestion."

His words disquieted her and she set her embroidery aside. "You still don't remember who you are?"

"No." Seeing her disappointment, he said apologetically, "I'm sorry, I don't remember you, either. Are you another cousin whom I should know?"

She regarded him gravely. "No, my name is Judith Winslow, and I am Antonia's companion. You and I," she paused as if wondering how much to say, "first met several weeks ago, when you returned from India."

"India?" The word triggered several simultaneous images: a map, a ship, a bazaar that teemed with humanity in a rich potpourri of scents and sounds and colors. "I seem to have a great deal to catch up on." He wanted to sound unconcerned, but for the first time he felt fear. He was awake, feeling reasonably well, words came easily to his tongue, yet his life was a blank. With iron discipline he suppressed the fear. "I didn't even remember Antonia, which is something of an insult when she and I are to be married.''

Judith Winslow was so still that only the beating pulse in her slender throat showed that she was alive. ''You and Lady Antonia are betrothed? I thought you could remember nothing.''

''I see the news is a surprise to you. Antonia said no one had been told.'' Adam thought back to the night before, his brow wrinkling as he tried to recall his reaction to the information. ''I didn't remember the betrothal any more than I remember anything else, but when she told me, it sounded right. Just as I didn't really recognize Antonia, but she seemed familiar.''

Judith opened her mouth to speak, then stopped, her eyes stark and unreadable. ''I see. Yes, the news is a surprise.'' Her voice shook and she stood before he could speak again. ''I'll call Dr. Kinlock. He wanted to be informed when you woke up.''

Adam wondered at her strong reaction; there had been more than just surprise on her face. Then he sighed and set the thought aside as one more thing he could not understand. After the door closed behind her slight figure, he cautiously pushed himself up in the bed. His head swam for a minute and he had a variety of aches and pains, but everything seemed to work.

While he was in the process of propping pillows behind himself, the door opened to admit a compact man with startlingly white hair over a young, dark-browed face. From his brisk air, doubtless this was physician Kinlock.

''Should I know you?'' Adam inquired with a touch of dryness.

''No, you are in the clear this time,'' the doctor said cheerfully. ''I'm Ian Kinlock, and I happened to be in the vicinity when Mr. Malcolm's engine chose to explode. I would have been in Scotland by now, but your charming cousin persuaded me to stay on for a few days.'' Without further comment, Kinlock began the poking and prodding universal to physicians.

After the physical exam, the doctor asked questions. Some were about his patient's past, and for those Adam had no answer. Others were about things and places and ideas, and most of those Adam did know, though sometimes considerable thought was required to dredge up the information.

After the interrogation, the physician presented him with a pencil and a blank sheet of paper and asked him to write his name. The pencil felt natural in Adam's hand, but he had no idea how to write and felt a frustration that bordered on fury. Kinlock was watching narrowly, and he retrieved the writing implements and printed the words "Adam Yorke" on the paper, then handed it back. "Does that help?"

Seeing the words was like setting a spark to tinder. Adam duplicated the printing easily, then, without thought, wrote his name in a bold script. He stared at his signature, knowing that he must have written it thousands of times before, yet feeling no kinship. "My hand remembers, but my mind doesn't."

"I won't tell you not to worry, because advice like that is both smug and useless." Kinlock sat back in the bedside chair, ready to share his evaluation. "Not remembering one's personal past must be disquieting in the extreme. On the other hand, in most ways you qualify as a singularly well-informed man. Even things that seem strange at first, like the writing, will probably come back to you quickly."

"Are you preparing me for the fact that I am unlikely to recall whatever I was?"

"No." The physician's mouth quirked up wryly. "I can't really say what will happen. You are suffering something called amnesia, which means loss of memory. The medical profession doesn't really know a damned thing about it, but being able to name a condition makes us feel wiser. The likelihood is that your memory will return very suddenly, and within the next few weeks. If and when it does, you will probably never remember events close to the accident, and you may forget all or most of the period from now until your memories return."

"But I might not remember?"

"Perhaps not." Kinlock sighed. "We know very little about the human body, and even less about the mind. Cases like yours are too unusual to have been much studied. You are fortunate that there appears to be no damage to your mental abilities. You can write, speak clearly, and reason well. My personal belief is that you will soon remember your past.''

"But if I don't . . . ?"

"If you don't, your new life begins today," the physician said bluntly. "Even if you never remember your earlier life, you have a strong foundation of knowledge and intelligence and friends willing to help however they can."

"You're saying that matters could be worse."

"They could indeed. Try to remember that if your situation seems too infuriating." Kinlock rose. "I'll be leaving on the noon stage. It has been five years since I have seen my family, so I trust you will forgive my unseemly haste. I don't think you have any further need of medical care. The rest of your recovery is not in human hands."

"Thank you for your help, Dr. Kinlock." Adam knew that the doctor's uncompromising advice was wise, though it might not be easy to follow. He offered his hand, but could not stop himself from asking with a trace of bitterness, "We are the sum of our experiences, choices, and memories. What is a man with no past?"

The physician's grip was firm, his keen blue eyes compassionate. "He is still a man, Mr. Yorke." With a brusque nod of his head, he turned on his heel and left the room.

Judith managed to leave Adam's room and send the doctor to him with an appearance of normality, but her real attention was on the words ricocheting around inside her mind: "She and I are to be married." During the past fearful days, Judith had accepted the fact that she might lose Adam to death, or that he might survive mentally crippled, but she had never imagined losing him to Antonia. Even after the rupture with Lord Launceston, Adam had treated Antonia like a fond brother, with nothing the least loverlike in his attitude. It was Judith he had confided in, Judith whom he had kissed.

At the memory of his tenderness, her teeth sank into her lower lip, nearly drawing blood. She entered the coffee room, which their party was using as a private parlor, and it was blessedly empty at the moment. Moving carefully, as if she were made of porcelain and might shatter, she sat in a Windsor chair in the corner. Could Adam have offered for Antonia and been accepted, and not yet ended his betrothal to Judith? The Adam she knew—whom she thought she knew —was too honest to behave in such an unpardonable way. But love had made fools of men before Adam, and he had always loved his cousin. Perhaps Antonia, heartbroken by the loss of Simon, had indicated that she was available and Adam had been unable to resist the woman he had wanted for so long.

Judith forced herself to analyze objectively her feelings about losing Adam. How much of her distress was simple possessiveness, how much was anger at losing the security he represented, and how much was regret about losing the man himself? Reluctantly she conceded that she was affected by all three considerations. She cared deeply for Adam, she had also looked forward to being protected and supported by him, and it seemed bitterly unfair that Antonia should have Adam's love as well as Simon's.

As her thoughts reached that point, the door opened and Antonia walked in, followed by a maid carrying a tray of food and coffee. She must have just risen, and she looked years younger this morning, her apricot hair tumbling around her shoulders, her face shining. The two women had talked briefly in the early morning, when Antonia was going to bed and Judith rising to take her place. At that time Antonia had revealed the happy news that her cousin had been awake and coherent, and the less-happy information that he did not remember his past. There had been no mention of marriage.

In contrast to Judith, Antonia was exuberant. "I assume that Adam woke up this morning and you sent Dr. Kinlock to him." She perched on a chair and prepared to eat, telling the maid to pour coffee for both Judith and herself. After the servant left, she began buttering a warm muffin. "Did Adam remember more this morning?"

"I'm afraid not." The hot coffee scalded Judith's mouth,

but she needed its warmth. "He didn't recognize me or remember anything of his past. He did, however, mention that you and he are betrothed."

Antonia choked on her muffin. When she stopped coughing, she said guiltily, "I daresay you think it too soon after Lord Launceston and that I am some kind of monster of fickleness."

Judith wanted to scream, "You don't know what I think!" But, of course, she didn't. She merely made the astringent comment, "It does seem rather sudden."

Antonia concentrated hard on spreading strawberry preserves on the other half of her muffin. "It's not like that, you know," she said in a low voice. "I've always cared for Adam, and he for me. After Simon and I ended our betrothal, I realized what an infatuated fool I had been, fancying myself in love with a handsome stranger whom I really didn't know. It made me realize that it was Adam I wanted."

Her words had a sickening ring of truth. "How fortunate for you," Judith said, unable to keep the caustic edge out of her voice. "Adam didn't mind being second best?"

"Adam is not 'second best.'" Antonia looked up, her cinnamon eyes wide and stark. "You see why it seemed better not to speak of the betrothal for a while. I knew other people would not understand. Even you don't."

Judith's coffee was bitter on her tongue. "When did you reach an agreement? I must be very dense not to have seen another romance budding under my nose."

A tinge of color showed high on Antonia's cheekbones. "It was . . . only a few days ago, just before the accident," she said vaguely.

Judith knew instantly that Antonia was not telling the whole truth; her ladyship was a terrible liar.

Antonia continued earnestly, as if needing her companion's approval, "Truly, I intend to do everything I can to make Adam happy. He deserves the best."

It was impossible to doubt Antonia's sincerity; whatever her motives, she genuinely cared about Adam and wanted to marry him. If it had been any other woman facing her, Judith would have fought for Adam, claimed him as her own.

But this was Antonia, who had been more than generous to a hopeless young widow, who had given trust and love and respect, asking only friendship in return. What kind of friend would attack Antonia when she was so vulnerable? Moreover, how could Judith lay claim to a man who didn't even recognize her and who had accepted Antonia's claim?

Her only chance was that Adam would recover and remember his engagement to Judith. But she was unable to avoid thinking of another bleak possibility. Even if he recovered, would he choose Judith over Antonia if his cousin truly wanted him?

Dr. Kinlock entered the coffee room at that moment, saving Judith the necessity of answering her employer's last remark. The physician had baggage in hand and was dressed for traveling. "I wanted to have a word with you before I left." Briefly he explained his patient's condition and the uncertainty about whether he would regain his memory.

"Is it safe to move him?"

"Aye." The doctor's mouth quirked in a half-smile. "In fact, from what I've seen of Mr. Yorke, it would be well-nigh impossible to keep him in bed any longer. Just try to prevent him from doing anything too dangerous for a while."

Antonia flashed a quick answering smile. Then her expression turned serious. "What can we do to help him?"

"You can reacquaint him with things he has known in the past—that might trigger his recovery. But don't treat him as a freak and don't pressure him," Kinlock cautioned. "The harder he tries to remember, the more difficult it will be. Be patient if he is angry and frustrated." He thought a moment more, then said slowly, "And don't be too surprised if he seems different than the man you are used to."

"What do you mean?" Antonia asked, not liking the doctor's implication. "Can a head injury result in madness?"

"Possibly, but I see no signs of that in your cousin." Kinlock frowned, trying to define his idea more clearly. "We all choose what facets of ourselves we will show to the world. Since Mr. Yorke doesn't remember how he presented himself in the past, you may see aspects of him that are unfamiliar to you."

"But I know Adam!"

"How well does any person ever know another?" Kinlock asked philosophically. "The people we have known the longest are sometimes the ones we see the least clearly. And in this case, you hadn't seen your cousin for years."

"Perhaps." Antonia shrugged in disbelief, then rose to her feet. "Thank you for everything you've done, Dr. Kinlock. Words cannot begin to express how much I appreciate your staying here."

Kinlock grinned. "I spent several sessions at the local hospital doing surgery on charity patients, so the time wasn't wasted." He reached inside his coat and brought out a piece of paper. "Here is the address of my family home in Scotland. I'll be there for several weeks before going to London to take up an appointment at St. Bartholomew's Hospital. I would appreciate your keeping me informed about Mr. Yorke's progress. A most interesting case."

"Of course." Antonia folded the piece of paper carefully, thinking that physicians had a morbid idea of what was interesting. "If you will be heading south again in a few weeks, perhaps you could stop and see Adam?"

"Surely Derbyshire has other physicians," he said with amusement.

"I like you," Antonia said as she offered her hand and honored him with one of her devastating smiles. "You're the least pompous medical man I've ever met."

"I'll take that as a compliment." Kinlock chuckled, bowing over her hand. "Very well, if you wish I will call on my journey back to London." Outside, the sound of an arriving coach was heard. "Lady Antonia, Mrs. Winslow."

After the physician had left, Judith asked, "Do you wish to go back to Thornleigh today?"

Antonia shook off the concerned expression induced by the doctor's words. "Yes. I should think that Adam would recover more quickly in familiar surroundings."

Judith nodded agreement. She had her own personal reasons for wanting Adam to recover as soon as possible.

* * *

At his hotel in London, Lord Launceston returned from a visit to the Royal Greenwich Observatory to find Judith Winslow's letter waiting. Simon had been closer to Adam than to his own brother, and the thought that his friend might be dead already was unbearable.

He had been intending to go to Derbyshire soon to see if the estrangement with Antonia might be repaired. Now, his face a tight mask of anxiety, Simon sent his servant to book coach seats to the north.

8

Dr. Kinlock was correct, Antonia decided: Adam was behaving differently, though perhaps no more so than anyone else suffering from a complete loss of memory. When they arrived back at Thornleigh she had suggested he rest, but he had politely refused, asking her permission to reacquaint himself with the house. A little uncertainly, she accompanied him, knowing how easy it would be for a stranger to get lost in the long corridors. But it was impossible to think of Adam as a stranger.

He looked quite normal except for the discreet bandage that ran through his light-brown hair, but he reminded her of a cat exploring new territory as he prowled through the house, his eyes sharp and assessing. For all the solidity of his muscular frame, he moved lightly, again like a cat; if he had had whiskers, they would have been quivering with wariness.

Antonia supposed that he sought something that would trigger memories, but he had no success. After moving through the west wing, including the ballroom and the portrait gallery, she suggested going to the schoolroom. It was part of the nursery suite at the top of the house, with low ceilings and a splendid view of the Peaks. "We spent a great deal of time here as children," she remarked as they entered the room.

He stopped by a battered desk and brushed his fingers across the top, where generations of bored children had carved their initials. "Here is an 'A.Y.'," Adam commented. "I suppose that must have been me."

She nodded. "Yes. I've always thought those the most

elegant initials in the schoolroom. You were always good at carving. Later I'll show you some of the wooden figures you made when you were older.''

He considered her words for a moment, then gave a faint shake of his head as they failed to stimulate any associations. Restlessly he went to scan the shelves of well-worn books and toys, pausing at the shelf where a dissected map of the world had been left in the assembled position. ''Is this how we learned geography?''

''It was the beginning.'' She gestured across the room. ''You were always interested in faraway places. That globe in the corner was my present to you on your eleventh birthday.''

Adam lifted the map piece that represented France and said reflectively, ''The Emperor Napoleon, the Continental System, the blockade. The capital is Paris, important products include silk and philosophers.'' Neatly setting France back into Europe, he crossed to the globe and studied it. ''St. Helena, the Cape of Good Hope, Madagascar, the Indian Ocean. I could set out today and navigate a ship to Bombay, yet my own name means less to me than the name of a foreign country.''

He gave the globe a spin of frustration and watched it twirl in its frame. ''You say this globe was mine, yet I haven't the faintest shred of recollection. Bizarre, isn't it? It's like a glass wall in my head separates personal and impersonal knowledge.'' He raised a hand to brush at his hair, then dropped it abruptly when his fingers encountered the bandage. ''How did I come to live with you?''

''You were orphaned at the age of seven.''

While Antonia debated how much to tell him about his childhood, Adam glanced up. ''Who were my parents?''

''Your father was a cousin of my father. His name was James Thornton.'' She stopped, seeing by the sharpening of his eyes that he understood what that meant.

''I see. I assume that my mother's name was Yorke.'' His voice was flat. ''What was she, a chambermaid or an actress?''

''Neither.'' Antonia swallowed, wishing that she did not

have to discuss something that could be so hurtful. But lies would not help him rediscover himself. "She was respectably born, the daughter of a very strict Noncomformist minister. As I understand it, your father was a political radical, a poet who did not believe in anything as conventional as marriage. Your mother ran away with him, and both families cast them off. They lived together until your father's death. Then your mother supported you both as a seamstress until her own death. For a few months, before my father could locate you, you were apprenticed to a chimney sweep."

From the tightness of his expression, Antonia realized that Adam also understood what that meant, but his question came from an unexpected direction. "Was my father a good poet?"

"I don't know." Antonia blinked a bit. "I expect we could find out."

"Not really necessary. It's a fair assumption that he wasn't very good." Adam wandered over to the nearest window and stared out at the hills, his face hard and expressionless. "How did I feel about my background?"

"I'm not sure. You never talked about it much." She chose her words with great care. "You seemed to think that being illegitimate was something of a stigma."

"Well, isn't it?" he asked dryly.

Unable to think of a good answer to that, Antonia kept silent.

Next Adam asked, "What was my relationship to the Earl of Spenston?"

"He approved of you, considered you a good influence on me." Antonia smiled, more at ease. "He was quite right about that. You usually kept me from getting into worse trouble than I might have. Father also thought it was a good thing for me to have a companion in the schoolroom, since I was alone here so much of the time."

Adam turned and leaned against the windowsill, folding his arms across his chest. "You were alone here?"

"Oh, not really alone," she assured him. "I had my own household, rather like a Tudor princess. Since the principal family seat, Spensford, was entailed, I couldn't inherit it.

So my father decided when I was born that I should receive Thornleigh, which had been in the family almost as long.'' She found herself adding, ''As a female, I was a sad disappointment to my parents. They tried so long for an heir, and I was all they could manage.''

''One would have thought they would be proud of their efforts,'' he said quietly.

Antonia gave Adam a suspicious glance, unsure whether she was getting a compliment or a tease, but could not read his expression as he stood against the light from the window. ''As a leader of the Whig reformers, my father believed that landlords should be intimate with their tenants and obligations,'' she explained. ''That's why he arranged for me to spend as much of my time here as possible, and to be trained in land management by the steward. He had very advanced ideas about female abilities.''

''Did your parents ever come to visit you?'' Adam asked with a suggestion of dryness.

''Of course they did,'' Antonia said defensively. ''And you and I always spent Christmases at Spensford.''

''How very good of the earl and countess,'' Adam murmured. This time the dryness was unmistakable.

''They weren't neglecting me, or at least, not by choice.'' Antonia flushed at the implied criticism. ''What they were doing in London was important. My mother was a great hostess, as involved with politics as my father. Their efforts improved the condition of people all over Britain. And my father had his own responsibilities at Spensford.''

''How did you feel about that?''

''I understood, of course. My father was a great man.'' Antonia found that she had pulled a lock of hair over her shoulder and that she was twisting it nervously. With a scowl, she tossed the hair back and lifted her chin. ''He believed in education and made sure that I had the best available servants and teachers.''

''What persuaded him to admit the bastard son of a mad radical and a female with no common sense into the household?''

In spite of the casualness of the way Adam leaned against the windowsill, Antonia could see tension in him. What must it be like to hear all this as if for the first time? "When you were found in London, you were sent up to the nursery in Spenston House to have the soot cleaned off. Father was planning on finding you some respectable foster home or apprenticeship, but I liked you and started crying when they came to take you away. So he let you stay and be educated with me."

"So I was rather like a toy to keep you quiet?"

"It wasn't like that!" For some reason, tears were stinging her eyes, and Antonia felt an ache so deep that she had been able to deny its existence. "My parents cared about me, they really did. About you, too. It's just that they had other responsibilities, important things that needed to be done."

Adam made a move as if to go to her, then subsided back on the windowsill with an oath. "I'm sorry, Antonia. I didn't mean to upset you. It just seems like such a bizarre arrangement. If I was raised with you, one would think I would be less surprised by it."

Antonia randomly picked up the nearest toy, a painted wooden top, and examined it with a great show of interest, not wanting to meet her cousin's eyes. Even among the aristocracy, setting up a five-year-old girl in a separate household was unusual, to say the least. But it didn't mean that her parents didn't care, she told herself fiercely; they were different, special. It was wrong to judge them by the standards of common people. "Perhaps you always thought the arrangement bizarre, but never mentioned it aloud because it would seem ungrateful," she said stiffly.

He turned to stare out the window again, his face brooding. "Am I unnerving you?"

Another surprising question. "A little," she admitted. "I don't know what to expect. You are so utterly familiar to me that it is hard to remember that, in your eyes, I am the veriest stranger."

"I unnerve myself," he said bleakly.

She saw the tension in his shoulders and swiftly crossed

the room to lay a comforting hand on his arm. "I know you must find this terribly difficult," she said softly. "To be surrounded by people telling you what kind of person you are and what you should remember."

His gaze fell to her fingers where they rested on his forearm, and his mouth tightened. Antonia had touched Adam with the casual intimacy of a family member, but the expression in his gray-green eyes was not casual. Memory was a bond that stretched two ways; in a sense, since her cousin did not remember their mutual past, her concept of her cousin could no more exist for her than Adam existed for himself. When she touched him, he must see her as a virtual stranger behaving with provocative familarity.

As taut silence twanged between them, for the first time in her life Antonia was sharply aware of Adam as a man, an intensely and disturbingly masculine one. Over the years she had remembered him in terms of friendship, kindness, and trust, but now he was an unpredictable stranger, not simply an adult version of the cousin she had grown up with. The disquieting moment convinced her that they were truly strangers to each other as nothing else could have.

With studied casualness, as if there had not been that flash of insight to change her perceptions, Antonia withdrew her hand. "I want to help you in any way I can, Adam, but I'm not quite sure how to go about it. Tell me how you want me to behave. If you want company, or a guide, or questions answered, I will oblige the best I can. If I am too much in your pockets, feel free to chase me away. I promise I shall not take it amiss."

"Thank you. I will need that, I think," he said. "This must be as difficult for you as for me."

"Nowhere near as difficult as it would have been if you had died." Antonia paused, then said unsteadily, "I never felt as alone in my life as when I thought you must have been killed in the explosion."

He watched her gravely. "Perhaps the Adam you knew is dead. I certainly don't know who or where the fellow is."

Her eyes met his, searching. "I can't believe that the basic material of your personality will change that much,'' she said slowly, willing him to believe. ''You still have humor and intelligence and kindness. If you never regain your memories, we will just have to create new ones.''

Adam tried to smile. ''Whatever the rest of my family is like, certainly I have been fortunate in having you. Thank you, Antonia.'' He thought of Adam Yorke as a stranger whose life he himself had inherited, or perhaps purloined. What had a baseborn man of unremarkable appearance, and surely unremarkable fortune, done to win a woman like this? Her inflammatory beauty drew him, but even more than that, he craved the warmth and honesty in her cinnamon eyes.

The only personal memory he had experienced since waking up after the explosion was a single flash of Antonia laughing up at him, delight in her eyes, her lithe body vibrant in his embrace. That image had come to him when she first told him that they were betrothed, and it had haunted him since. It had made it possible to believe that they were in love with each other, yet his lack of memory hobbled him in his dealings with his cousin. The last thing he wanted was to alienate her by behaving inappropriately.

He wished that he knew Antonia well enough to take her in his arms, but he daren't touch her for fear of undoing whatever miracle of charm the original Adam Yorke had performed to convince Lady Antonia Thornton to marry him. Even at the most optimistic estimate, it would take time to rebuild whatever relationship had been between them; he felt like a blind man fumbling around a china shop, risking the destruction of the unfamiliar objects around him. Wearily he raised his hand and rubbed his temples. ''Perhaps now I should take your advice and rest. I have enough to think about for the time being.''

Adam was more than tired; he was emotionally and physically drained. It had been foolish of him to insist on exploring the house when they returned from Macclesfield, but he had had an intense need to develop a sense of place to fill some of the voids in his mind. He had also hoped that some sight or sound would have meaning for him, but there had been no such event. The closest he had come was experiencing a vague sense of familiarity at the sight of the Peaks.

As he followed his cousin to the bedchamber said to be his, Adam tried to formulate a strategy for learning about himself. He had a servant, a valet cum groom named Bradley, whom he would have to become reacquainted with; so far they had only exchanged the simplest of sentences. Perhaps Bradley would have more alarming information about his alleged past.

Antonia had also told him that he was involved in various commercial enterprises and that there were papers to examine, and that the engineer whose invention had put him in this state wanted to talk to him when he felt capable. At the moment, the only thing he felt capable of was prolonged sleep. Maybe he would wake up and this whole mad affair would turn out to have been a nightmare.

Adam slept from late afternoon straight through to the next morning. When he awoke, his memory, alas, was as blank as it had been the day before. As he began stirring about the room, Bradley magically appeared with a pitcher of hot water. The valet had grizzled hair, an eye patch, and a villainous scar across his cheek—not the usual discreet gentleman's gentleman. After washing up had revived him, Adam eyed his servant warily. "You know that I have no more memory than a newborn?"

"Aye. Mrs. Winslow explained the situation to me," Bradley said, unperturbed.

"How long have you been with me?"

"Five years. I went out east with the Indian army, and after I was discharged, I had a run of bad luck in Singapore." A pained expression crossed his battered face. "In fact, you bailed me out of the local jail."

"What were you doing there?" Adam stopped. "Forget that I asked that. I'm probably better off not knowing."

"That's what you said then, too," Bradley said, a glint of amusement in his one visible eye.

Adam smiled back, feeling more relaxed. "What else should I know about myself?"

Bradley considered. "You always preferred shaving and dressing yourself."

"That is still true." Adam felt obscurely glad that some traits hadn't changed. Next question. "Were you privy to all my disgraceful secrets?"

Bradley looked distinctly uncomfortable at being asked to draw conclusions about his master. "You didn't have any disgraceful secrets."

"I sound like a dull dog," Adam murmured.

"Never that, sir. But you kept yourself to yourself." The servant thought some more. "You were always gentlemanly with everyone, high and low. Too much so, in my opinion," he added with a burst of candor.

Adam grinned, understanding why he had kept the old reprobate around for five years. "I think that is about as much information about myself as I can absorb at the moment. Where are my clothes?"

Examining his possessions was another way of establishing what kind of man he was; the afternoon before he had been too tired. Apparently he liked good quality in material and tailoring, but there was a total lack of ostentation, which Adam approved of. He supposed that being comfortable in his own clothing was a reasonable place to start defining himself.

After dressing in what Bradley assured him was correct country attire, Adam went downstairs. He paused at the bottom of the main staircase, trying to remember if he knew the way to the breakfast room. Instead, in the morning stillness he heard the lilting sound of a harp. Curious, he followed the melody to the music room, where he found Judith Winslow bent over a golden harp, her face absorbed in the melancholy tune she played.

He cleared his throat and she looked up in surprise, then greeted him with an uncertain smile. He smiled back; while she lacked Antonia's splendor, Mrs. Winslow was a most attractive female. "Good morning. I didn't mean to interrupt you."

"That's all right. It is rather early to be playing, but I find it soothing."

"Do you need soothing, Mrs. Winslow?"

Judith watched as Adam circled the music room, his quick glance registering everything. He had not been prone to probing questions before, but then, he had not been in such a situation. "Well, the last few days have been rather . . . tiring."

He grimaced. "It must have been very difficult, even with two of you to share the nursing."

"We did it because we wanted to," Judith said. "Antonia could have hired someone, had she wished."

His inspection done, he came to stand in front of Judith where she sat by the harp. "I appreciate your efforts on my behalf, Mrs. Winslow, particularly since I am not even related to you. Many thanks."

He was standing in the same spot as when he had asked her to marry him, but the moment that was so vivid to Judith no longer existed for Adam. She could have wept from frustration. Instead, she said, "You used to call me Judith."

"We were friends?"

His gray-green eyes were so intent that she wanted to pour out the whole story: that they had been more than friends, that he had made her feel special as no one ever had before—most of all, that he had wanted her, not Antonia. But Adam had enough complication and confusion in his life; if she truly cared for him, she could not add more. She swallowed hard. "Yes, we had not known each other long, but we had become friends."

"Then I may call you Judith?"

"Please."

He smiled at her, and he was so like her Adam that she could scarcely bear it. Fortunately he turned away and resumed his restless pacing before she could lose her control. "How long have you been with Lady Antonia?"

"Something over two years. Her father and my husband died about the same time. I needed employment, Antonia needed a companion, so a ferocious aunt of hers, Lady Forrester, brought us together." Judith managed a smile at the memory. "Antonia and I are as unlike as chalk and cheese, so it really shouldn't have worked, but it has."

Adam glanced at her. "Is there anything I should know about you, so I won't give offense in some way?"

She tensed. It was a perfect opportunity to speak, but once again, she could not. The truth could be destructive to both Adam and Antonia, and might do Judith herself little good. After an appearance of deep thought, she said, "Well, I prefer not to be referred to as small. I like to think of myself as average-sized. It is just that almost everyone else is taller."

He laughed aloud. "Duly noted, Judith. I guess the next question is, are there things that I should know about myself?"

This was without a doubt the strangest conversation Judith had ever had in her life. "I would rather not answer that," she said soberly.

Suddenly serious, Adam murmured, "As bad as that?"

"Not bad. Complicated."

He looked at her quizzically. "In that case, for the time being I will accept your judgment that it is better not to know." His tone lightened. "Can you direct me to the breakfast room? I can't deal with too much drama on an empty stomach."

"Neither can I," Judith admitted. "If you don't object, I'll go with you."

As she led the way to the other wing, Adam asked, "Are we likely to find Lady Antonia there?"

"No, she is probably riding about the estate now. Often you would accompany her." Glancing askance, Judith saw that her words seemed to please him. She had the sinking feeling that Adam-as-he-was-now was ripe to fall in love with his cousin all over again. But for the life of her, Judith did not know what she could in conscience do about it.

That afternoon Adam decided to investigate his intimidating pile of business documents. After warning that she knew nothing useful about his enterprises, Antonia had volunteered to keep him company, even if she was no help.

Adam had been glad to accept; he felt better when she was around.

They sat on opposite sides of a double desk in the library, a mound of papers between them. Adam lifted a document and stared at it, his expression tightening. "I don't think I am able to read anymore," he said in a flat, suffocated voice. "This is so much gibberish to me."

Quick concern on her face, Antonia rose and came to stand behind him and look over his shoulder. She inhaled sharply, then reached down to take it out of her cousin's grasp. "Don't worry. This is gibberish to me, too." She frowned. "I don't even recognize the alphabet. If I had to guess, I would say it is some Asian tongue, but I really have no idea." She laid a light hand on his shoulder. "Try something else."

Adam opened a thick folder and perused the top sheet, then gave a sigh of relief. "This I can understand." He glanced at Antonia ruefully. "I was so worried that for a moment I forgot that I had already done a little reading."

"I don't blame you for being upset. I can imagine few worse fates than being unable to read." She gave him an encouraging pat, then returned to her seat and began leafing through a stack of documents.

There was silence for some time, broken only by the shuffle of papers. Antonia found records of a startling variety of transactions, but she did not gasp out loud until she came to the bank statements.

When Adam looked up inquiringly, she explained in a choked voice, "According to this, you have accounts of almost fifty thousand pounds in three different banks. Hoare's, Eaton and Hammond, and Mortlock and Sons, to be precise."

Adam gave her a startled glance. "I have almost fifty thousand pounds sterling on deposit?"

"No, fifty thousand in each," Antonia said weakly. "The total is just under a hundred fifty thousand pounds."

He stared blankly ahead before venturing, "That's rather a lot of money, isn't it?"

"To say the least," she said, still stunned. "I suppose you

used three banks as a precaution against possible failures.''
She started to mention that Simon had said that her cousin
was something of a legend in India, then stopped. She would
rather not have to explain who Simon was. "I supposed that
you had done well, but I had no idea that you had done this
well.''

He smiled wryly. "It gets worse. Apparently I own a
trading company and a merchant fleet of a dozen ships.''
He held up another paper. "And if I am interpreting
correctly, partial ownerships in plantations in Ceylon,
Indonesia, and India.''

Antonia shook her head. "You said you were 'something
of a nabob,' but I thought you were funning.'' She waved
her hand at the mass of documents. "I never expected
anything like this.''

His gaze intent on her face, Adam asked, "Does this alter
your opinion of me?''

"No. Yes.'' She stopped. "Yes and no. I would always
expect you to be successful at whatever you did, but this goes
beyond mere success. You have built a royal fortune in only
eight years. I can't imagine how you did it.''

"Legitimately, one might hope,'' Adam said, his voice
flat.

"That goes without saying,'' Antonia retorted. "You were
always quite maddeningly honest. I could never get you to
tell even the smallest fib to keep us out of trouble.'' Setting
her elbow on the desk, she propped her chin on her palm
and stared at her cousin. "I am beginning to think, Adam,
that I knew you much less well than I thought.''

His bleak gaze caught and held hers. "Then neither of us
knows who I am.'' He pushed his chair from the desk with
suppressed violence and stalked across the room, his
muscular figure taut with a sense of energy barely contained.
"Am I really like I was before, Antonia, or have I changed
out of all recognition?'' His deep voice was despairing.
"Perhaps that blow on the head is making me mad.''

"Nonsense, Adam, there is nothing mad about you.'' She
made her voice cool to counteract her cousin's explosive

tension. It was the first time a crack had appeared in his controlled facade, and she sensed and understood his fear. To be a stranger to oneself was difficult enough; to wonder if one's mind and emotions were dangerously warped would be infinitely worse.

"Remember that I had not seen you in eight years. It is too easy to see people we know in terms of what we already know about them, rather than as they are now," she said with a sudden insight that was as valid for her as for her cousin. "The fact that you have grown and changed more than I realized means that I lack perception, not that there is anything wrong with you."

Adam had halted by the fireplace and was staring at himself in the mirror that hung above the mantel. The afternoon sunlight touched his hair, making it glow like polished oak, and Antonia was struck with the feeling that he was both stranger and intimate friend at one and the same time.

He himself saw only a stranger reflected in the mirror. "Wouldn't one think that one's own face would be familiar?" he asked. "Perhaps I am not really your cousin at all, but a changeling dropped into his body."

"Dr. Kinlock said that you might seem different," Antonia chose her words carefully, "because we show different sides of ourselves to different people. With amnesia, a person cannot remember what faces he has shown the world. For me, this is a golden opportunity to see more of you, to learn to know you better, because you have obviously been far too modest about your achievements."

Adam's tension diminished, and when he turned from the mirror, his wry smile was back in place. "That does sound better than being mad," he admitted. In a return to pragmatism, he continued, "I appear to have a man of business in London who oversees the day-to-day details of my investments. Fortunately he seems very capable, because at the moment I certainly am not."

"Once your agent in London is informed of what happened, he should be able to handle routine business for a few days or weeks without your personal supervision. I'm sure that you wouldn't have hired him if he wasn't honest as well as competent.''

"I suppose." Adam ran his hand through his sun-streaked hair, leaving it boyishly tousled. "But I still can't imagine why I ever wanted to work hard enough to earn all this.''

In spite of her comforting words, Antonia herself was perplexed. The Adam she had grown up with had not been particularly interested in money and had planned on a military career that might have won him glory but would have yielded precious little gold. Yet it was obvious to even the meanest intelligence that he must have worked with incredible intensity the whole time he was away to amass a fortune like this. When had her cousin decided that he wanted to be rich? And why?

Over the next few days Judith saw little of Adam except at meals. Most of the time he spent with Antonia, and they were obviously on very easy terms with each other. While Judith observed no public expressions of affection, when Antonia was present the majority of Adam's attention was always on her, though he was never less than polite to Judith.

Interestingly, Antonia was equally attentive to Adam. Judith tortured herself trying to decide if her mistress was showing the protectiveness of a woman with an ailing favorite relation, or the romantic affection of a woman with her intended husband. In either case, hour by hour Judith felt Adam slipping away from her, and her desperation grew proportionately.

Then help appeared in the guise of a note from Lord Launceston. He had just arrived in Buxton, and since he was unsure of his welcome at Thornleigh, he requested that she call on him as soon as possible. As Judith reread his words, she felt a wave of gratitude so intense that it weakened her. She needed an ally most desperately, and there could be none more welcome than Simon Launceston.

9

As soon as he received word that Judith Winslow waited in the private parlor, Lord Launceston hastened downstairs to see her. She had just removed her rain-soaked cloak when he entered; he thought irrelevantly that she had the true English mist-born complexion. "Thank heaven you came so quickly. Is Adam . . . ?"

"Alive and reasonably well," she said quickly.

"Thank God," he said, the relief like a breath of fresh air. "All that the innkeeper could tell me was that Mr. Yorke had been injured and that his life was despaired of." Then Simon gave his visitor a melting smile. "That was incredibly rude of me. How are you, Judith? It's good to see you again."

"Well enough." The fine-drawn tension of her delicate features belied her statement, but she refrained from saying more while a maid bustled in and set down a tea tray. After the maid had left, Judith said, "While Adam's life is no longer in danger, he is still suffering the effects of his injuries. He has lost his memory of everything before the explosion."

"Good Lord," Simon said blankly as he sat opposite where Judith perched on an oak settle. "He remembers nothing?"

"Not a thing. Not his name, not Antonia, not me. Nothing." Judith's voice wavered, and she glanced down, lifting the teapot and pouring as if it were the most important task in the world.

It took time for Simon to assimilate the import of her words. At length he said softly, "Total amnesia. So he would not remember me, either." At Judith's nod, he asked, "I assume that a physician has been consulted about the prognosis?''

"Yes, there happened to be an excellent man within earshot of the explosion, and he tended Adam through the critical period. Antonia also summoned the best physician in Buxton after we returned from Macclesfield.'' Judith spread her hands helplessly. "They both agreed that when a head injury causes amnesia, memory usually returns within a few days or weeks, but there is no way of knowing for sure until it happens. He may never remember his previous life.''

"Is Adam suffering any mental effects from the injury?'' Simon asked sharply. The thought of his friend's quick, questing intelligence being destroyed was almost as hurtful as the prospect of his death had been.

"No, he can read and speak and write normally, and he seems to recall all his abstract knowledge. Some things he forgot, but he relearns them almost instantly. It's his personal life that is a blank.''

Now that his worst fears for Adam had been allayed, Simon was able to proceed to a topic of nearly equal urgency. "Does Antonia ever mention me?'' he asked haltingly. "Do you think she would see me if I called?''

"If you had returned to Thornleigh before the accident,'' Judith said slowly, "I think Antonia would have fallen in your arms. She was desperately unhappy after you left.''

So they had both been desperately unhappy. Why had he decided to give her several weeks to recover her temper? Why had he gone as far as London just because he wanted some new books? "I should never have left Derbyshire,'' Simon burst out. "I should have been here to help Antonia. Even with you to support her, it must have been the very devil of a time.''

"Oh, it has been, and for more reasons than you can imagine,'' Judith agreed, her voice laced with pain. "Adam's injury has changed everything.'' She paused, as if groping for words, then said baldly, "After the accident, Antonia informed me that she and Adam have an understanding.''

Simon stared at her, unable to accept the usual meaning of that simple phrase.

Judith watched him with compassion. "She told me that they had decided to marry," she elaborated.

The teacup in Simon's hand jerked so badly that scalding liquid splashed on his hand. "How could Antonia turn around and fall in love with Adam so quickly?" White-faced, he set the cup on a table. "It has only been a fortnight since I left. Good God, she always thought of him as a brother. How could she?" Then, with bitterness, "How could he?"

"Something havey-cavey is going on," Judith said bluntly. "I heard nothing about their betrothal until after the accident. I think that Antonia invented it."

"She couldn't possibly lie about something so important." Simon's usually precise mind seemed numb as he tried to make sense of Judith's words. "I understand that Adam offered for her in the past. Perhaps he renewed his offer and in a moment of loneliness she accepted him."

"No. I would wager anything I own that he did not renew his offer to her." Simon looked up, wondering at her vehemence, and saw that Judith's gray eyes were drowned with tears. Her voice breaking, she cried out, "I know because, before the accident, Adam was betrothed to me."

In her face was an agonized reflection of his own pain. "Oh, my dear," he said softly. Rising, he went to Judith and enfolded her in his arms as her slim body shook with sobs. So she had suffered through the misery of Adam's accident not just as a friend, but as a woman who loved him. And in the aftermath, not only did Adam not remember her, for some unknown reason he had been claimed by Antonia.

Eventually Judith's weeping diminished and she pushed away from Simon with a wavery smile. "I'm sorry to behave like such a watering pot, but the last week has been dreadful, and there has been no one I could confide in."

She stopped to dig a handkerchief from her reticule and repair the ravages of her tears before continuing in a more controlled voice. "Adam and I had reached an understanding just before you and Antonia ended your engagement. She was so miserable that we decided to keep silent for a while." Judith shook her head in disbelief. "Even though our betrothal had not been announced, I can't believe Adam would have offered for Antonia when he had just asked me to marry him.''

''You are right, he would never behave so despicably.'' Simon leaned against the settle, his brows knit. ''I had noticed that you and Adam always seemed to be together, and I even remember thinking that the two of you would suit very well. I was so happy that I wanted all my friends to be as well.'' He swallowed. ''But why would Antonia pretend that there was an understanding between her and Adam? And why didn't you tell her the truth right away?''

''I think I know the answer to your first question.'' Judith poured more tea and took a revivifying sip. ''You know how fond Antonia and Adam have always been of each other. She may have decided that if she couldn't have you, she might as well take Adam, who said just after he returned to England that she could always marry him.''

''I assume that that was before he had a chance to know you,'' Simon interposed.

Judith gave him a grateful glance; it soothed her lacerated spirit to have someone take her seriously. ''Exactly. He was half-teasing when he said that, but he was also half-serious. Perhaps right after the accident, when she was feeling so distraught, she decided to marry him if he survived.''

''And if that happened, she wouldn't let a little thing like amnesia stop her,'' Simon said dryly. ''Lord, why did I have to fall in love with such a headstrong female?'' The question was rhetorical; her heart-stopping beauty and charm were sufficient answers. ''But why didn't you tell her the truth?''

Judith spread her hands despairingly. ''How could I? Adam doesn't remember me and seems willing enough to believe Antonia. And however confused her motives for wanting to marry Adam, she certainly seemed sincere.'' She sighed and absently pleated the fabric of her cambric round gown. ''Besides, Antonia is the best friend I have ever had. I couldn't bear to call her a liar to her face, not with all she has had to endure.''

Simon briefly laid his hand on hers. ''Your sentiments do you credit.'' Then he rose and restlessly crossed the parlor, thinking hard. "It's a damnable situation, but when Adam regains his memory and recollects his feelings for you, the problem will solve itself. Certainly he would never break his word to you, nor do I think that Antonia would try to persuade him to do so."

"What if he doesn't regain his memory?" Judith had had longer to imagine the pitfalls than Simon. "Or what if they become so involved that they must marry?"

Simon flinched, not wanting to think about what she was implying. His jaw tightened. "Then we must do what we can to end their engagement as soon as possible."

"But how?" Judith asked. "I've already said that I can't bring myself to confront Antonia and call her a liar, and I can't think of a better strategy."

She watched as Simon paced around the parlor, avoiding furniture with his usual grace. It seemed unfair that worry made him look more handsome, the beautiful bones of his face more prominent under the drawn flesh; Judith knew that she herself merely looked haggard.

Half to himself, Lord Launceston muttered, "Ideally, Antonia would call it off by telling Adam that she had taken her fences too fast and they had not really been betrothed. The question is, what could persuade her to do that?"

As Judith watched Simon, she knew the answer to his question. "That's simple," she said. "The one thing that will surely undermine Antonia's resolve to marry Adam is you. Antonia fell in love with you the moment she met you, and if she had not believed that you were gone for good, she would never have considered another man."

Simon turned to her uncertainly. "Do you really think so? I've wondered if what she felt was temporary infatuation, not real love."

He was too modest to believe that no woman could possibly resist him, so Judith said merely, "I'm sure. Unfortunately, Adam stands between you and a reconciliation. If you went to Thornleigh and said that you still love her and want to renew your betrothal, Antonia would feel honor-bound to stay with Adam because of his injury. After all, he believes that they were already betrothed.'' Judith frowned, her thoughts uncomfortable. ''I wish I knew how Adam felt about Antonia. He is very easy with her, but that may be partly because on some level he senses that they grew up together.'' It was also possible that he was falling in love with his cousin, and that if she withdrew from their engagement, he would be deeply hurt, but Judith dared not think of that.

Simon considered, then shrugged. ''All we can do is work on one problem at a time. First of all, will Antonia let me call at Thornleigh to see Adam, or am I still persona non grata?''

''She will certainly let you call on Adam, but we need some reason for you to run tame at Thornleigh again. The more she sees of you, the sooner she will set her nobility aside.'' Judith smiled wryly. ''But I have no idea how that can be accomplished; if you try to court her openly, she will show you the door from loyalty to Adam.''

Simon was staring abstractedly into space. ''What if I called on her to ask about Adam, told her that she was quite right that she and I wouldn't suit, and wished her happy with him? If she thought that I could not press my attentions on her, she would have no reason to feel threatened by my presence.''

''That's well enough as far as it goes, but we still need a reason for you to call often. Adam is good for several visits a week, but that might not be enough.''

An expression of uncharacteristic deviltry touched Simon's chiseled features. ''That is simple enough. I'll call on you.''

''What!'' Judith positively squeaked. ''Simon, have you run mad? Why would you be calling on me?''

''Why, for the obvious reason,'' he said teasingly. ''You are an attractive woman. Why should I not seek out your company? What objection could Antonia make without sounding gothic?''

''This is not a good idea,'' Judith said emphatically.

His amusement fading, Lord Launceston came and knelt on one knee before Judith, his face pleading. ''I know that we are grasping at straws, attempting to predict how other people will react. There is nothing very wise or honorable about trying to play God. But the alternative is to stand by and watch while Antonia and Adam's betrothal develops so much inertia that it can't be stopped.''

Distracted, Judith asked, "What is inertia?"

"The propensity of matter in motion to stay in motion or matter at rest to stay at rest, unless influenced by an outside force." Not sure that his explanation had helped, he translated, "In other words, if we don't try to stop them, the betrothal will take on a life of its own, and they will end up marrying even if it is a mistake for both of them. Is that what you want to happen?"

"Of course not," Judith said helplessly, "but we are playing with emotional fire here. We might all of us be burned."

"There is a risk of that," Simon agreed soberly. He said nothing more, just looked at her with his intensely blue eyes.

As sure as the sun rose in the east, Judith knew that the consequences of such a charade could be disastrous. She had agreed to marry Adam, to bear his children and share his days and nights for as long as they lived. But in a small corner of her heart, the image of Simon was enshrined as her beau ideal, the quintessence of her romantic dreams. A fantasy was harmless as long as it stayed a secret, but what would happen if Simon went through the motions of courtship with her? If she was the recipient of his devastating smiles, that fantasy might come alive and interfere with the solid reality of her feelings for Adam. She closed her eyes in anguish. It was not fair that any man should be so attractive; he made it impossible for her to think. She stood and slipped by Simon, putting a safe distance between them so she could evaluate his suggestion on its merits.

The damnable thing was that his idea might work, though Judith doubted that he understood the female mind well enough to realize just what a potent plan he was proposing. If his lordship appeared to be courting Judith, not only would Antonia see him constantly, but jealous pride would help undermine Antonia's determination to marry Adam. Would

Antonia really be able to stand by and watch her man go to another female, especially one so inferior in looks, charm, and fortune? Judith doubted it; Antonia had her full share of pride. Very soon she would feel the need to reassert her claim to Simon, leaving Adam to Judith. How fortunate that polyandry was not permitted in England, or Antonia would end up with both men.

She turned to Simon and said gloomily, "You realize that we may all end up hating each other? Antonia may throw me out of her house and never speak to me or you again; Adam may call you out; heaven only knows what other catastrophe might befall."

At her tacit agreement, Lord Launceston gave a relieved smile. "Perhaps, but I doubt it. The most likely outcome is that Adam will regain his memory before our plotting has gone too far. It may have even happened while you are here in Buxton."

"We will not be that lucky," Judith said with conviction.

"Probably not," Simon agreed. Then his face brightened. "I have some good news for you. My publisher friend is eager to do a book of your wildflower studies. He thought they were exquisite, both as art and as natural history, and hopes that *The Flowers of the High Country* will be the first of a series on flowers of different parts of Britain."

"Really?" Judith was startled, having almost forgotten that Simon had sent the drawings to London. Then her lips curved involuntarily into a smile of delight. "How wonderful! I didn't really believe he would be interested, in spite of what you said. Thank you, Simon, for sending them off in spite of me."

His faith in her work was deeply gratifying. Beyond that, perhaps the acceptance of her drawings was a sign that Judith's luck was changing and this dreadful tangle would soon be sorted out. She most fervently hoped so.

The ladies of Thornleigh were sitting in the morning room after a light nuncheon when the butler brought in a calling card on a gilt salver. Antonia was surprised; while a number of neighbors had left cards as a sign of concern for her cousin, it was generally understood that she was not receiving for the time being. Who would have insisted that the card be brought in?

When she saw the card, Antonia understood.

At her small inhalation of shock, Judith glanced up from her embroidery. "Is something wrong?"

"Simon is here."

Judith's eyebrows arched speculatively. "No doubt he heard about Adam's injury."

Antonia made an effort to collect herself. "Of course. I should have thought to write him, but I was too distracted." She turned to the butler. "Send Lord Launceston in."

Judith stood and packed her embroidery into her work-basket. "I assume that you would prefer to see him alone."

Antonia was by no means as sure of that as Judith was, but she did not attempt to stop her companion from leaving. Nervously she touched her hair, wondering how she looked, before telling herself forcefully not to be a goosecap. She was betrothed to Adam, and all her starry-eyed foolishness about Simon was behind her.

That being the case, why did her heart twist in her breast when Simon entered the room? He halted just inside the door, dark-haired and elegant, more handsome than any man had a right to be. His expression was contained, giving little away, but she saw no signs of anger or the withdrawal that she found so alarming.

"I realize that this is an imposition, Lady Antonia, but I heard about Adam and have been very concerned. I hope you will forgive my intruding on your property."

She found that she could still breathe, if she thought about it. "Of course. You are Adam's friend and have every right to be concerned. If I had been thinking more clearly, I would have written myself." Antonia waved him to a seat, asking hesitantly, "How much do you know about the situation?"

"Quite a bit, I think," he said as he sat down. "I arrived in Buxton last night. Since you are the great lady of the district, events at Thornleigh are much discussed."

Antonia nodded, unsurprised. Most of her servants were local, so the great house held few secrets. "Then you heard about Adam's amnesia?"

Simon nodded, his dark-blue eyes grave. "Yes. And also about your betrothal." Antonia tensed for condemnation, but her former intended made no attempt to rail at her. "I won't deny that the news was a considerable shock, but when I thought about it, I understood. You and Adam have always been close, you share many of the same interests." He gave her a sad smile. "You were right, you know. Much as it hurts for me to admit it, you and I would not suit." After a deep breath, he added, "May I wish you and Adam happy?"

Antonia felt a sharp sting of tears. Simon was such an incredibly nice man that it hurt. In a choked voice she said, "Of course you can. You are very generous." She shook her head, refusing to give way. In a more normal tone she said, "It would be more appropriate to say that Adam and I have an understanding rather than a formal betrothal. Nothing more specific can be decided until Adam is better."

"How is Adam feeling?"

"Physically he is quite well, though he has headaches and sleeps more than usual. In fact, he is resting now. However, the doctor said that was to be expected and should pass soon."

Her qualification did not escape Simon. "How is he mentally and emotionally?"

Antonia paused to choose the best answer. "Although he doesn't complain, it is obvious that he finds the situation rather distressing. Or perhaps maddening would be more precise."

"One can certainly understand why," Simon said feelingly. "Since I heard the news, I have tried to imagine what it would be to wake up a stranger to oneself, surrounded by other strangers." He gave her a questioning look. "I'd like to see him, unless you think it would be a bad idea."

"No, I think you should. Adam is coping amazingly well, actually. He asks a lot of questions, trying to establish what his life was like. Since you knew him in India, which was such a large part of his life, you can tell him things that I know nothing about.'' She glanced down at her well-groomed fingernails. ''I have discovered that I knew him less well than I thought.''

''That must be very disconcerting,'' Simon sympathized.

''I prefer to think of it as educational.'' Antonia smiled suddenly, feeling very much in charity with Lord Launceston. ''It is too easy to take our nearest and dearest for granted. Adam and I are having a unique opportunity to rediscover each other.'' She stopped when she saw a slight tightening of Simon's face; really, it was not at all the thing to be discussing the man she intended to marry with the gentleman who had previously occupied that position.

Simon rose. ''When would be the best time to call on Adam?''

Antonia glanced at the mantel clock. ''He should be awake soon,'' then absently bit her lip as she thought. ''Where are you staying?''

''At the White Hart in Buxton.''

''It seems silly for you to be staying there,'' she said tentatively, not quite sure how she wanted him to respond.

''Well, I could hardly expect you to welcome me here,'' Simon said reasonably.

He was being such a perfect gentleman . . . ''Oh, bother with propriety,'' Antonia said with exasperation. ''This is the most absurd situation. Surely we can be friends, since we are in agreement that our betrothal was a mistake. As my friend and as Adam's, you will always be welcome at Thornleigh. It would make much more sense for you to stay here while you are in the area. And I think it would be good for Adam to have a male friend near. There is some danger that Judith and I will smother the poor man in solicitude.''

Simon laughed, his blue eyes lightening. ''There is no one like you, Antonia. If you can bear to have me underfoot, I should be happy to stay here.'' Then, with a subtle shift in tone that did not escape his hostess, he asked, ''Speaking of Judith, how is she?''

"Very well. She was a tower of strength after Adam's accident. I would have gone mad without her." Antonia sighed, then shook off the recollection. "When you were announced, she tactfully disappeared." Antonia made a rueful face. "Unlike me, Judith is always tactful."

Simon chuckled. "If you are sure that my presence will not distress you, I will go into Buxton to fetch my belongings."

Antonia offered her hand, and after an infinitesimal pause he bowed over it. The gesture was a tense one for both of them, and the feel of his fingers lingered on hers, but the moment passed without incident.

After Lord Launceston left, Antonia sank into the sofa and congratulated herself. They had both carried that off very well. Of course, she had felt a few daft girlish flutters at the sight of him—Simon could make a stone Madonna turn her head in admiration—but she hadn't made a fool of herself. Proof positive that her infatuation was a thing of the past. She was so sure of that that it would have seemed foolish not to invite Simon to stay. One must be hospitable. Of course, the fact that his presence would be beneficial to Adam was the most important aspect. Of course.

As he went outside to his carriage, Lord Launceston breathed a sigh of relief that the first hurdle had been surmounted so easily. Antonia was really the most splendid woman; she might be impetuous, but she was also fair and uninterested in holding grudges. Which made his own duplicity all the more contemptible; only the belief that his actions would be ultimately beneficial to all four of the people involved could justify his behavior.

Simon was startled and not best pleased to discover after thirty-one years that he had an alarming talent for duplicity; it had been remarkably easy to act the role of the sorrowing but noble suitor. He hoped Judith was right that Antonia was still in love with him; he himself was not convinced. There had been nothing tentative about the way she talked about Adam. When he analyzed her manner, he decided that she spoke as if she was one-half of a couple, and that did not bode well for his hopes.

He shrugged and snapped the whip over his horses. Only time would tell. Meanwhile, he was doing everything he could to promote a desirable outcome for all concerned.

10

Adam was sifting through his business papers in the library when Lord Launceston was announced. Antonia had prepared Adam for the visit of an old friend, but he still tensed; it was hard not to feel wary around people who knew more about his past than he did himself. But in the event, Lord Launceston made it easy. He entered quietly and offered his hand. "Hello. You always called me Simon. Do you mind if I call you Adam again?"

"Not at all." As Adam shook his visitor's hand and indicated a seat, he was impressed at Launceston's grasp of what it was like to be a stranger in one's own mind. "Antonia said that we met in India?"

"Yes. You came into the Bombay observatory one night and wanted to use the telescope."

Adam's gaze drifted for a moment, then he nodded. "I remember seeing the surface of the moon through a telescope and trying to identify the seas. Mare Imbrium, Mare Crisium."

"You actually remember that?" Simon said eagerly.

Adam shook his head. "It's like everything else: I remember the results and what I learned about astronomy, but not you or the occasion. It seems that everything personal has been excised from my mind."

"Well, it has only been a week or so since a roof landed on your head," his visitor said philosophically. "One can hardly blame your memory for wanting to go on holiday."

Adam grinned and settled back in his chair behind the desk, thinking that his old self had had good taste in friends. "Perhaps you can tell me some things about my life in India.

I never wrote Antonia much detail about my business activities, so there is little she can tell me.''

''I don't promise to be an expert—we seldom discussed business—but I'll do my best,'' Simon promised. ''What do you want to know?''

Adam waved his hand at the documents spread across the wide desk. ''I seem to be the possessor of an indecently large fortune. What did I do to earn it? I can't imagine how I did— at least, not if I was honest.'' His mouth twisted. ''I'm not sure I want to hear your answer.''

''You can rest easy on that head,'' his visitor assured him. ''I never heard a hint that you behaved dishonorably, and considering how ingrown and gossipy the European community in India is, it would have been hard to keep secret. Though, mind you,'' he added reflectively, ''you would have attracted as much admiration as censure.''

Adam smiled. ''Then how did I do it?''

''By sheer, unremitting hard work and a willingness to take risks. You told me once that you made your original stake playing hazard on your voyage out from England.''

''Really?'' Adam was startled. ''I wouldn't have thought that I was a gamester.''

''You weren't. How did you explain it?'' Simon lounged back in his wing chair and crossed his long legs, thinking that it was interesting how they could still converse easily even without knowledge of a common past. ''You said that a real gamester was addicted to the thrill and that he needs the likelihood of defeat to give the game savor. You played in cold blood, and for one reason only: to win. You never gambled unless the odds were good, and a man who is clever at calculating probabilities will always do well at hazard.

''By the time I met you, you did no gaming at all, though you took some fearsome risks in your business. From what I could see, they almost always turned out profitably.''

''What kind of risks?''

Simon considered for a moment. ''As I said, I wasn't well-informed about your business, but I have personal knowledge of one such transaction. There was a mixed-blood sea captain who had lost a ship under mysterious circumstances and was drinking himself to death in a shack near the Bombay water-front. You staked him to a new ship, with him to receive half the profits if he would risk sailing through an area of the East Indies that was notorious for piracy. Everyone thought you were mad to let him have a ship, but your risk paid off. The reason I know is because you suggested that I invest in some of his cargoes when I was on the verge of financial disaster, and I benefited enormously from your advice.''

"So I let other men risk their lives while I waxed rich on the profits?" Adam raised his brows. "Certainly not illegal, but somewhat parasitic."

"It's not parasitic to give a man a new lease on life. Eventually, the captain earned enough to buy the ship from you. Besides"—Simon grinned—"if you are thinking yourself cowardly, I should mention that you went with him on his first voyage. I believe that you have a saber scar on your left forearm?"

"Is that what that is?" Adam asked, automatically glancing at his coated arm.

"You had to fight your way through the Strait of Malacca."

Adam sighed and ran his fingers through his brown hair. "I suppose that is better than letting others always run the risks for me. But sometimes I wonder who Adam Yorke is. The man seems like a complete stranger to me."

"You were—are—a complicated man, Adam. I was probably closer to you than any of your other acquaintance in India, yet I could not have said that I knew you really well."

"How did you see me, then?" Adam's gaze was steady.

Simon hesitated before answering. "As a man who had genuine intellectual curiosity about many things. You strove for wealth, yet did not have an acquisitive nature. Much of your success came from being a good judge of people, as with the mixed-blood sea captain. You gave opportunities to people who deserved them, and in return, you earned loyalty and your employees' best efforts." Then, slowly, he tried to define a more subtle impression, "I always thought that some secret passion drove you, but I never knew what it was."

Adam sighed and rubbed absently at his head bandage, now much reduced in size. The more he learned, the less he understood. Was there really a dark secret at the heart of Adam Yorke? One would think that he would be aware of it, even now, if that was the case. The thought suggested another question. "Did I have a personal life in India, or was it all work?"

"You avoided most of the usual social events," Simon said. "You said once that you misliked the fact that a fortune made you acceptable to families that would have sneered at your birth a few years earlier." He thought of another relevant fact. "You did have a mistress. A young Chinese girl that you bought from a slaver, I believe. You bought her to set her free, but she didn't want to leave you."

"Good Lord," Adam said, startled. "What became of her when I left India?" Then, with alarm, "I didn't bring her back, did I?"

"Never fear, she isn't stashed somewhere in London," his friend assured him. "You gave her a substantial dowry and she was planning on going to Singapore to find a husband after you left. A practical race, the Chinese."

Adam smiled wryly. "As rakish pasts go, it could be worse." But as they drifted to more neutral topics, he couldn't help wondering what other surprises his past held.

Lord Launceston was a pleasant addition to the household, and the next few days passed smoothly. Adam was grateful that the other three people treated him casually, as if his amnesia was no more than a mild summer cold that would soon pass. They were all willing to talk when he felt the need for information, but the atmosphere was always unstressed. It would have been harder if they had made him feel the weight of their anxieties or expectations.

Most of his time was spent with his cousin, and their tastes and thinking meshed so exactly that it was obvious why they had decided to marry. Nonetheless, he sensed a slight withdrawal on Antonia's part whenever they were in circumstances conducive to physical intimacy. It was baffling; Antonia was in most ways spontaneous and affectionate, but there was a line of reserve that warned him not to behave as a man usually would with his future wife.

Adam admired her exquisite figure and wondered if her exuberant red-gold hair was as silken as it looked, but he controlled his desires. There was too much he didn't know about their mutual history; perhaps Antonia was reserved now because he had been too importunate in the past. It was not a subject that he felt he could discuss with her, so he bided his time.

In the week after Lord Launceston moved to Thornleigh, he and Judith spent considerable time together. They hunted for fossils and flowers, admired the seas and craters of the moon, discussed books they had read, and generally lived in each other's pockets. Judith found Simon's companionship enormously, and dangerously, enjoyable. Unfortunately, their closeness seemed to have no effect whatsoever on Antonia. Not only was the lady of the house singularly unjealous; she scarcely seemed to notice her companion and guest because all of her attention was on Adam. Unable to bear watching the other couple, more and more Judith turned to Simon.

The summer weather turned unusually hot, and after a late dinner everyone decided to take a turn in the garden in hopes of cooler air. After Antonia took Adam's arm, Simon offered his to Judith and they followed the other couple into the lingering dusk. The roses were luxuriantly fragrant at this time of the evening, and Judith inhaled deeply. Her nerves had been strung as tightly as her harp strings for the last week, and it was pleasant to simply enjoy the moment and the presence of the man at her side.

Ahead of them they saw Adam pluck a yellow rose, then present it to Antonia with a flourish and a comment that made her laugh out loud. Still laughing, she tucked the blossom behind her ear before taking her cousin's arm again.

Watching from their distance, Simon said ruefully, "We have not made much progress in our attempts to separate Adam from Antonia, have we?"

"It would be easier to do that if we were malicious." At Simon's questioning glance, Judith explained, "My years in other people's houses have taught me that the most effective troublemakers are those who enjoy causing other people pain."

"Then that must be our problem: neither of us intends harm. We just want everyone to live happily ever after with the right partner." There seemed nothing more to add to that, so for the next half-hour they followed the winding paths, saying little. Judith had always loved Thornleigh's gardens, and never more than tonight. Though the sky was not yet dark, already one star shone bright not far above the horizon. Judith pointed to it. "Is Venus the evening star now?"

"Yes," Simon said, pleased with her knowledge. "Venus is the brightest object in the heavens after the sun and the moon, and she makes the best of evening stars. Did you know that the word planet means wanderer? That's what the ancients called planets, because they wandered through the heavens."

"If it isn't a real star, does that mean that one can't make a wish on it?"

Her companion glanced at her, an odd expression on his face. "Of course you can. Wishes and dreams come from a higher place than astronomy, and what better star to wish on than Venus, the planet of love?"

Judith stared at the bright point of light, then shook her head. What she wished for was impossible, beyond even dreams. Better not to think the words or admit that hopeless longing.

Eventually their peregrinations brought them to the stream, and they stopped to listen to the softly splashing water. In the quiet, they could hear the sounds of the other couple approaching along the same path. Just before Adam and Antonia would appear around the bend in the trail, Simon turned to his companion. "It's time that we gave Antonia something more to think about." Judith saw a quick flash of mischievous smile before he pulled her into his arms and bent over for a kiss.

Judith gasped, knowing that this was the greatest mistake

possible, but she could not prevent her arms from sliding around Simon's neck, nor stop herself from straining up against him, responding to his kiss with every iota of desire that she had ever suppressed. Dimly she heard the other couple's steps and words stop abruptly, then the sounds of quiet withdrawal, but that was infinitely far away.

Reality was the feel of Simon's arms around her, his flare of passion at her response, the warmth of his mouth against hers. She had been wise to fear the consequences of letting Simon pretend to court her; what was subterfuge to him had come achingly alive for her. Judith, who had never allowed herself to dream, found that she was drowning in a lifetime of longing. She had no idea how long they stood wrapped in each other—an endless time that was far too quickly done.

Knowing that the longer they continued, the harder it would be to deal with the consequences, she broke away. In the near dark, she could see just enough of Simon's expression to see that he was as shaken as she was. Of course he was unnerved; he had undertaken a make-believe embrace to stimulate a reaction from Antonia. It must have been a shock to have the quiet companion turn into a wanton in his arms, kissing him as if he was her last hope of heaven . . . or of hell.

After a struggle with her pulse and breathing, Judith was able to speak lightly, as if she had been only acting. "That should have stirred the broth a bit. Let us hope that the results benefit our little conspiracy."

There was a long, long pause. Simon's face tightened, then smoothed out to look like cool marble sculpture, the deepening night emphasizing the faint cleft in his chin. "Let us hope."

As they returned to the house, they did not touch in even the slightest and most casual of ways.

Antonia had been telling Adam an amusing story of how as children they waded in the stream, to the intense irritation of their keepers. Then they rounded the bend in the trail and came on Simon and Judith embracing, oblivious to the world around them. Antonia's breath wooshed out like a collapsing bellows at the sight, and she would have stood gaping had not Adam grasped her upper arm, turned her around, and led her away.

She clung to him numbly as he led them away from the brook. Why shouldn't Simon be kissing another woman? Antonia had given him his *congé*. Did she really want him pining for her? Yes! She was behaving despicably, like a jealous female, a breed she had always despised. She should be happy at the thought that two people she cherished were interested in each other. Now that she thought of it, Judith's gentle bluestocking ways and quiet understanding were just what Simon needed.

Since that was the case, why did she feel like sitting down in the middle of the path and howling?

Adam's deep voice said with amusement, "Why are you so surprised? It has been obvious that there is something between them. Do you object to your companion having a suitor?"

Antonia realized that her fingers were digging into her cousin's arm, and she forced herself to relax. Who was she to object to Simon seeking consolation elsewhere? She herself had decided to marry Adam within a matter of days. But that was different! She called herself a rude name. "As I have said before, I am not always very perceptive. Most of my attention has been on you."

"I think I should be flattered," he murmured, stopping in the middle of the path and turning to face her. In the gathering dark his gaze was very intense, his eyes more green than gray as they probed too deeply for comfort. Adam raised a hand and, with butterfly delicacy, traced the lines of her face, skimming from brow to cheek, then along the edge of her jaw to the sensitive curve of her throat. His touch was deeply erotic, and Antonia shivered in a mixture of desire and fear. She craved his touch, yet it felt wrong to want her cousin in such a way.

"And why has most of your attention been on me, little cousin?" he asked softly. "Because I am an injured unfortunate who must be cared for, or because I am your future husband?''

His hand had circled to the back of her neck with soft strokes that warmed and soothed her. Antonia's emotions were hopelessly tangled between wanting and doubting. ''Some of both, I think,'' she said, her voice unsteady.

''What a pity,'' he said. His hand dropped away and Antonia felt bereft. She was sharply aware that she did not know what she wanted of Adam. What was worse was that Adam knew it.

When Adam returned to his bedchamber, Bradley materialized to see if his master required anything. Underneath his piratical visage, Bradley had the soul of a solicitous mother hen.

Untying his cravat, Adam asked, ''Did I speak often of my cousin?''

''Lady Antonia? Hardly ever, sir.'' Bradley pondered. ''When her letters arrived, you would look pleased, like a cat in the cream pot, but you never spoke of her.'' More thought. ''Did you know that you have a miniature of her in the back of your watch case?''

''No, I didn't know that.'' Adam dug his gold watch out. It had simply been one of his possessions, and he had paid no particular attention to it, but now investigation disclosed a catch that caused the back panel to snap open. Inside was a portrait of Antonia, her apricot hair and eager smile caught with vivid life. She must have been sixteen or seventeen when it was painted.

Adam studied the portrait, as he must have done often over those long years at the opposite end of the earth. He could venture a good guess about the ''secret passion'' that had driven him in India. Regrettably, he had no better idea what to do about it now than he must have had then.

Antonia slept badly and decided to skip her usual early-morning ride; Thornleigh could get on without her personal supervision for a few hours. Instead, she lay abed later than usual, then went down to the breakfast parlor, where she found Judith drinking tea and restlessly crumbling toast into a pile of crumbs. At Antonia's entrance, her companion looked up, then flinched. It was most unusual for the mistress of Thornleigh to be here at this hour.

Gathering her courage, Judith said, "About yesterday evening—"

Antonia halted her with a quick gesture. "There is really nothing that needs to be said." She knew that she sounded stiff, but could not bring herself to be gracious.

"If you are distressed, there is much to be said," Judith said gravely.

This time Antonia managed to sound more natural. "I was . . . surprised," she admitted. "I had not realized waht terms you and Lord Launceston are on. I fear that I have been sadly unobservant."

Judith still looked anxious. "I do not want you to think that we have been sneaking behind your back . . ." She stopped and bit her lip, looking unhappier than ever.

"It is hardly a question of sneaking." Antonia gave a brittle laugh. "You and Lord Launceston are both of age, and unencumbered with spouses. I don't think that he is the sort to trifle with a female's affections, and even if he was, it would be presumptuous of me to be dropping hints in your ear. You are supposed to be my chaperon, not vice versa."

Vexed, Judith said sharply, "Antonia, you are babbling. I think I would prefer that you were angry. It has to be upsetting to see someone you were so recently involved with embracing another woman. What happened was something of an accident. Please believe that I would rather not see Simon again than to have my friendship with you damaged."

Judith's directness dissolved Antonia's brittle manner. She flopped down in a chair. "Lord, Judith, I'm acting like a widgeon, and I know it," she said ruefully. "It was a shock to see you together when Simon and I were betrothed just a few weeks ago, but who am I to talk? I accepted Adam in half the time."

She leaned forward earnestly. "When I thought about it,

I realized that you and Simon are really much better suited than he and I ever were. You are more intellectual, far more accepting, and would never plague the poor man like I did. If you and he are truly attached, I will be the first to wish you happy.''

Judith feared that she was going to melt into a little puddle of pure guilt. So much for theories of jealousy and pride; Antonia was being so understanding that it was almost unbearable. If that wasn't bad enough, it was obvious that Judith and Simon's strategy was failing; it was looking more and more impossible to separate Antonia and Adam. And worst of all, their conspiracy was having disastrous and unexpected consequences for Judith. She took a deep breath. "I don't know what is going to happen, but good wishes are definitely premature. What you saw was a—a momentary aberration of no significance.''

Antonia looked skeptical but didn't press the point, for which Judith was intensely grateful. More and more, she had the feeling that the four of them were caught in the toils of a Restoration comedy, the kind with revolving doors and ever-changing partners. A bad Restoration comedy.

Adam and Antonia tethered their horses in the narrow dale, then climbed the steep hillside, Adam carrying a hamper of food while Antonia coped with the voluminous skirts of her riding habit. For some reason their rides through the hills had not brought them to the Aerie, perhaps because on the last occasion she had been mourning the loss of Simon. But the spot was a significant part of their mutual past; it was time she reintroduced Adam to the place, so she had invited him for a picnic.

They passed through the narrow cleft in the rocks and emerged on the ledge to see the peaks rolling out to the hazy horizon. Setting the hamper on the soft grass, Adam inhaled sharply, his eyes fixed on the breathtaking prospect. Antonia watched him from the corner of her eye, hoping that he might recognize the place but not wanting to ask. Sensing her unspoken question, he said, "I don't actually remember being here, but I am sure that I must have been, many times.''

"Yes. We called it the Aerie, and it was our favorite retreat when we were children."

Adam's gaze scanned the flower-strewn patch in front of the rocky overhang, then went out to the vastness of space before them. "I can see why. Up here, we can almost pretend that we are birds ourselves."

"You spent hours watching the hawks, wondering what it would be like to fly."

He turned to her with a smile. "What did you do while I watched the hawks?"

"I was always too restless to watch for long, so I would bring along a book and read." She grinned. "If I finished it and hadn't brought another, I would tease you until you decided that it was easier to leave than to put up with me."

He chuckled. "Brat."

"Undoubtedly," Antonia admitted, "but you were always most tolerant." She gestured at the hamper. "Traditionally, the first thing we did was sample Cook's wares."

"Heaven forfend that we should break with tradition," Adam said with amusement, taking a blanket from the basket and spreading it so they could sit without acquiring grass stains.

Cook's crumbly crusted meat pies were always delicious, and outdoors they were even better. They were accompanied by pickled onions and tangy ale, and one could not ask for a better meal. The day was warm, and both of them removed their jackets and used them as pillows as they lay back on the blanket and absorbed the sunshine. It was the sort of intimate, mindless contentment that they had often shared as children, and Antonia was drowsing when Adam said with deceptive casualness, "Of all the things that I can't remember, the most frustrating is that I know so little about past relations between you and me. You say that we have known each other all our lives and that we are to marry, yet there is a reserve between us that seems wrong, at least for a betrothed couple."

Abruptly Antonia was wide awake, wondered if her too-perceptive cousin had somehow deduced that their engagement was somewhat irregular. Propping herself up on one elbow, she looked across the two feet of space that separated them and found herself mesmerized by the intensity of Adam's gaze. His wide, powerful shoulders were emphasized by his white shirt, and even half-reclining on the grass, he radiated controlled strength. "Have I forgotten something important that I should know about you, Antonia?" he asked. "Did I hurt you, frighten you so badly that you fear me?"

She was acutely aware of his virile intensity, and she realized that she did fear him, a little. The cousin Antonia had grown up with represented safety, and all her life she had depended on his protective strength. But Adam was not her brother, nor a eunuch content to admire her and no more. She had chosen him to be her lover and her husband, and if they were to have a true marriage, she would have to yield herself to that frightening masculinity, trusting him not to harm her.

If she could not trust Adam, there was no trust or hope anywhere. "You have never hurt me, ever. I know that I have held myself back, and your amnesia has much to do with that," she replied, speaking some of the truth. "Since I was a stranger to you, I did not want to make demands or overwhelm you when you were adrift in a strange new world."

Her breath quickening with a blend of anticipation and anxiety, Antonia leaned forward, closing the distance between them. "I want no barriers between us."

Her lips met his and Adam made a sound deep in his throat, his arm going around her waist to pull her against him. Her kiss had been tentative, but his response was not, and the length of his body burned against hers. He untied the ribbon that held back her hair and buried his fingers in the glitter-bright mass, whispering, "I have wanted to do this since the moment I first woke and saw you."

Antonia clung to him, shaken by the passion that lanced through her. There was nothing brotherly in Adam's embrace, and nothing sisterly in the hungry way she kissed him back. In an instant the entire nature of their relationship had changed, and it could never be the same again. She had always loved Adam, and now, that love expanded into a new dimension she had never entered before. She lay back on the blanket, wrapping her arms fiercely around him, surrounded by his strength, glorying in the feel of his weight and hard muscles. Her earlier anxiety burned away like morning mist in the sun, already almost forgotten.

When Antonia had kissed Simon, there had been the sweetness and magic of romantic dreams come true, but what she felt with Adam was fire and earth, passion and reality. When his hand found her breast, she gasped with pleasure and arched against his expert caress, hating the fabric that separated them, wanting to possess and be possessed.

For a few intoxicating minutes they shared madness, all Adam's questions about Antonia's feelings swept away by desire and his judgment very nearly gone as well. He wanted her with an urgency that was pain, and he knew that she would welcome whatever he chose to do. But the blanks in his memory made him wary, and with his last shreds of control he lifted himself away from her. "I don't suppose that we have ever actually . . . ?"

Antonia's eyes opened, the cinnamon depths dazed, her breasts rising and falling as she gulped for breath. Understanding his incomplete question, she shook her head. "No. No, we had not become lovers."

If they were already lovers, nothing could have stopped him, but they had not been and it made a difference. Adam rolled onto his back, gripping her hand in his with numbing force. "I did not think I could have forgotten that," he said raggedly. "Was I behaving as a gentleman of honor or a slowtop?"

She made a choked noise that was part laughter, part frustration. "You have always been the soul of honor."

"What a pity." Adam lifted her hand and kissed it, then held it against his cheek. "It is also a pity that I've forgotten much that is useful, but still remember that society would censure us for doing what is so utterly natural."

"I have never cared greatly what society thinks," Antonia said. In her eyes he saw the same mixture of desire and doubt that he himself felt.

"I'm not sure that I do either, not for myself." Under

control again, he rolled onto his side so they lay face to face, a foot of space between them. "But for you, I want everything to be right." Antonia's lips were parted, soft and inviting, and her shining apricot hair lay in a cloud around her face and shoulders. He ran his hand along her slim body from shoulder to hip in a lazy caress, then cupped her breast.

She gave a gasp of pleasure, then smiled mischievously up at him. "That feels very right to me."

"To me also." Exercising all of his considerable willpower, Adam pulled away from her and sat up. "If I don't stop now, my good intentions are going to be lying in the grass in broken flinders, along with all of the pieces of that very complicated riding habit."

Antonia sat up as well and began raking her fingers through her hair to remove the tangles. "Doubtless prudence is the wiser course," she said wistfully, then laughed a little. "You are always right. When we were growing up, I used to think that was the worst thing about you."

He was immensely grateful that they could laugh together about what had happened or, more accurately, what hadn't happened; he had never felt closer to Antonia. Even so Adam felt a need to explain himself more fully. "I feel incomplete. There is too much of myself missing, and I think that I should be careful about doing anything that would have serious consequences for anyone else." He reached out and caught Antonia's hand, needing to touch her. "You say that I have never hurt you in the past. I don't want to begin now."

Antonia tensed. "Is this a roundabout way of saying that we should not be betrothed?"

"No!" His grip on her hand tightened. "Just that it is better not to set a date quite yet. In a few weeks or months, I will either have remembered my past or come to terms with my life as it is now. When that happens, I hope you will marry me with all possible speed."

Antonia sighed with relief, then closed the distance between them, sliding her arm around his waist and laying her head against his shoulder. "Good. I was worried for a moment." She raised her face for a kiss. "We have waited a long time. We can wait a little longer."

This kiss was gentler, deliberately restrained, though fire still burned beneath the sweetness. There would be time enough for passion later; for the moment, sweetness was more than enough.

11

Something had changed between Adam and Antonia; Judith could see it in the way that they looked at each other, the way they found reasons to touch. Nothing vulgar, but unmistakable to a watchful eye. She didn't know if they were technically lovers, but the emotional bond between them was so strong that it was almost tangible. Even if it could be broken, she no longer believed that she or Simon had any right to do so.

Judith accepted that Adam was lost to her and that perhaps that was for the best. She herself, in the bitter nights, had admitted that she loved Simon Launceston. At the beginning she had pretended that she was attracted to him only superficially, that she felt no more than a normal woman's admiration for his striking good looks. But when they had kissed, she had lost her ability to delude herself. She loved Simon's dreamy brilliance, his innate kindness, and his occasional flashes of unexpected mischief. In her heart Judith believed that she would make him a better wife than Antonia could; if Simon won Antonia back, there would be less room in his life for the matters of the mind that absorbed and challenged him. But it was Antonia that Simon wanted, and who could blame him?

Since the evening in the garden, the easiness between him and Judith had disappeared, and he had withdrawn behind his mask of impeccable politeness. She knew that she had upset and confused him, and sometimes she felt his quizzical gaze on her. He also watched Antonia, and Judith suspected that he was beginning to realize that the situation was hopeless. When Simon finally accepted that fact, he would leave Thornleigh, and Judith knew that she would never see him again. She took advantage of the present to store up secret images. When she was old and gray, in some distant place, she would still remember the turn of Simon's head, the abstracted beauty of his face in thought, his unconsciously graceful movements, his long deft fingers.

In spite of the pain of unrequited love, Judith was grateful for all that had happened. Without even knowing it, in a few moments of one-sided passion Simon had restored her ability to dream.

Adam had written his man of business, Whittlesey, about his amnesia, and Whittlesey now sent documents with a brief description of the history behind a transaction, probable results, and his own recommendation. Assuming that Whittlesey wasn't seizing the opportunity to rob his employer blind, it was an excellent system, and if Adam was half as good a judge of character as people said, his agent should be honest.

A new sheaf of papers had just arrived from London, and Adam was perusing them in the library. There was also a letter from Manchester, and Adam opened it, then chuckled over the contents.

Antonia was curled reading in a wing chair, and she glanced up when she heard. "Something amusing?"

"Rather. James Malcolm, engineer of the infernal steam engine, has written to say that the explosion made him aware of a serious design flaw that he has now rectified. From now on, all Malcolm engines will hae not less than three forms of safety device." Adam glanced down at the letter. "There will be two safety valves, one of them tamper-proof, a mercurial steam gauge that will blow out if the safety valves don't work, and a lead plug that will melt and release the pressure if the water level becomes dangerously low. Mr. Malcolm commends the new design to my attention, and is willing to call it 'the Yorke safety engine as a commemoration of the most regrettable incident.' "

Antonia slammed her book shut and jerked upright in her chair. " 'The most regrettable incident'! That man's engine almost killed you, and now he's trying to turn you up sweet so you'll invest in his company anyhow.''

Adam laughed. ''That's true in one sense, but he's just being a good businessman. The fact is, most progress is a result of changes made after something goes wrong. At least, no one was killed in the process of learning that the engine needed some improvements.''

Antonia gave him a mock scowl. ''You may be casual about your *pas de deux* with St. Peter, but I am not.''

''Good.'' The sunlight gilded her hair to a halo of fire, and Adam feasted his eyes on the sight. ''Have I mentioned recently that you are incredibly beautiful?''

Antonia laughed. ''Now you are trying to turn me up sweet.''

''Precisely.'' He rose from his desk and circled around to her chair, then lifted her chin for a kiss. ''And no one tastes sweeter than you.''

She reached up to link her arms around his neck so he couldn't escape, then returned his kiss with enthusiasm. There were many stolen kisses like this, embraces that left them both in a state of simmering desire. There was an aching pleasure in the denial, and Antonia knew that in the future, when they were married and could make love whenever they wished, she would still remember this interval with a special kind of nostalgia. Now was the season for anticipation, and the richness of it would make fulfillment all the better.

When the need for air ended the embrace, Adam pulled back and kissed the end of her nose. ''I've finished with business for the day. Shall we go out to the summerhouse to read?''

''Sounds delightful.'' Antonia retrieved her novel, which had slipped unnoticed to the floor. ''Do you have an interesting book?''

''Simon recommended this volume on the natural history of the Midlands. He said there were some intriguing theories in it.''

The weather was continuing warm, and the summerhouse was a delightful retreat from the heat. The upper part of the structure was vine-covered lattice that admitted air and light, and the wide padded bench that ran around the inside walls was a comfortable spot to lounge and read. Antonia was just settling down when Adam remarked, an odd note in his voice, "Lord Launceston has interesting taste in bookmarks."

She glanced up curiously and saw that he was reading an unfolded sheet of paper. "According to this, the world is notified that Antonia Thornton, Lady Fairbourne of Thornleigh, has done Simon Launceston, Lord Launceston of Abbotsden, the honor of consenting to become his wife."

He looked up, his eyes filled with cool question. "Was this wishful thinking on his part, or is it one of those things I should know about?"

Blast Simon and his absentmindedness! It must be one of the announcements he had forgotten to send to the London journals. Still, while it wasn't information that Antonia was eager to explain, there was no avoiding it. "We considered marrying," she admitted, "but very quickly decided that we would make each other miserable, so we ended it and he left Thornleigh."

"Everything must have been very quick indeed," he said dryly. "I seem to recall being told that Lord Launceston and I returned from India on the same ship, about two months ago. My present memory goes back three weeks to Macclesfield, so you must have met Simon, fallen in love, separated, then accepted an offer from me in five weeks or less."

"It sounds rather awful, put like that," Antonia said, her cheeks coloring, "but that is substantially what happened."

"What was I doing when all of this high drama was taking place?" Adam asked with dangerous mildness.

"You were right here," Antonia's answer was less than steady, "soothing me and giving me good advice when I was having the vapors."

"What a boringly virtuous person I seem to have been." Adam's voice was lightly reflective, but underneath Antonia heard a note that frightened her. "Do you know, I had become so accepting of the amnesia that I had forgotten how woefully uninformed I am about the most important things in my life.

"Did you accept me because I was the most convenient

choice to make Lord Launceston jealous? Or was it to prove that you were not wearing the willow for him? Either way, I find that I dislike being in the dark about what must be common knowledge for everyone else at Thornleigh.''

Setting his book aside, he stood and strolled across the summerhouse, not looking at Antonia. "No wonder there was a lack of physical intimacy between you and me. There had hardly been time to develop any." He turned to face her, and the angry ice of his eyes was a vivid reminder that weak men do not make fortunes in a handful of years. "Was it difficult to pretend to enjoy the touch of one man when you were longing for another?''

Antonia gasped in shock, but he continued inexorably. "And I have to wonder how much I don't know about what is going on under the surface of our little gathering. Ignorance is such a dangerous thing. You and I are together all day, but I really don't know how you spend your nights. Did Lord Launceston return to Thornleigh to persuade you to a reconciliation? If so, what kind of arguments does he make and how much do you enjoy them?''

Aghast, Antonia stared at her cousin before she jumped up and crossed the summerhouse to stand in front of him, her heart pounding with fear. "Adam, it wasn't like that," she said intensely. "Ever since I was four years old, you were the one person in my life whom I could rely on. It took my brief infatuation for Simon to make me realize just how much I cared for you. Wanting to marry you was not some form of retaliation against Simon; he was already gone from my life. Only your accident and his genuine concern for your welfare brought him back to Thornleigh. Simon has not said one single word to indicate that he still wants me. You saw him with Judith. Did he look like a man mourning the loss of another woman?''

In her fierce desire to convince him, Antonia laid her palms on Adam's chest, feeling the hard strength of bone and muscle. "I should have explained the whole history to you, but it was not very flattering to me, and the more time that passed and the closer you and I became, the less important it seemed.''

The ice in Adam's eyes was thawing as he weighed her words, and she knew that he wanted to believe her. She bent her neck, resting her forehead on his solid shoulder as her fingers curled around his lapels, feeling that she could not bear it if he hated her for withholding information from him. She finished, "I wanted to marry you because I need you in my life."

Adam was quite still under her touch, and she could feel the steady beat of his heart. Then she felt him sigh and his arms came around her. "Poor little cousin," he said, his baritone voice soft. "So much needing, so much hurting."

To her horror, she began to cry and did not even know why. "You have always been much too good for me," she whispered.

"That has been the problem, hasn't it?" he said bleakly. "You speak of needing me, but you have never said a word about love."

Suddenly she knew what was really upsetting him. Raising her head, she locked her gaze with his, ready to reveal the whole truth that she only now understood. "I told Simon that I loved him too quickly, and to say the same to you so soon seemed a cheapening of the words. More than that, I had always loved you as a brother, and it seemed almost incestuous to desire you. That all changed the day that we went to the Aerie. There I discovered that I loved you in quite a different way, as a woman loves her man."

Standing on tiptoe, she lightly pressed her lips to his before saying, "I love you, with no qualifications or limits, and I want—most desperately—to marry you. And that, I swear, is the whole truth."

His arms crushed around her, pulling her tight against him. "Lord, Antonia, I have wanted so much to hear you say that. The worst part of not remembering is not knowing how you felt about me and being afraid to ask." Adam's kiss was demanding and possessive, and she rejoiced in it. "I thought that there was something very warm and real between us, and finding that marriage announcement was a ghastly shock. It made me wonder if I had been wrong about everything."

"I understand. I should have explained sooner, but it was

easier not to speak.'' Antonia leaned back in his embrace, relaxing into a smile. ''You know, I am not the only one who has avoided talking about love.''

Adam smiled ruefully, then pulled her closer and rested his cheek against her head. ''Even with amnesia, I know that I've always loved you. It's like knowing how to breathe—something that can't be forgotten while one is still alive.''

Antonia gave a sigh of pure delight, relaxing within the safe circle of his arms, and they stood locked together for a long time. Finally she chuckled. ''It's like the steam engine.''

Adam loosened his grip and looked inquiring. ''What is?''

Smiling, she sat on the padded bench, tugging her cousin to sit next to her. ''It wasn't until it exploded that Malcolm knew it needed improvement. It's the same with you and me: I thought we were happy before, but something went wrong, we made improvements, and now I'm happier than ever.''

His laughter was rich and deep. ''You have a talent for analogy.'' Absently he rubbed at the healing wound on his head. There was no longer a bandage, and the stitched gash and the shaved area around it were almost covered by longer hair.

''Is your head hurting?'' Antonia asked.

''Some,'' he admitted. ''I wonder if I'll spend the rest of my life getting headaches whenever I become overset.''

''I've never known you to anger easily, and I will certainly do my best to avoid provoking you in the future.'' Antonia tilted her head reflectively. ''You can't imagine how glad I am that you challenged me when you were angry rather than becoming all cool and maddening. Simon could withdraw like an oyster, and that more than anything convinced me that we would never suit.''

''I can see how little that would appeal to someone like you, who prefers open battle,'' he agreed with amusement. ''I think that you and I have more compatible styles of fighting, though I shan't repine if we don't do it very often.''

Though his tension was gone, Adam had a drawn look that implied fatigue as well as headache. Antonia knew that he was still having occasional attacks of drowsiness, so she suggested, "Why not lie out on the bench and relax? I make a tolerably good pillow."

"An irresistible offer," Adam murmured, swinging his legs up on the bench and laying his head on her lap, dozing off almost immediately.

Antonia felt vastly content. The altercation between them had been painful, but in the aftermath she felt closer to Adam than ever. They loved each other, and she sensed that in the future there would be still deeper levels of closeness. When they married and became lovers, when they had a child . . .

Leaning back against the wall, Antonia herself dozed, and when she woke up, the sunlight had shifted noticeably. Adam was still sound asleep, and she enjoyed the sight of his still face, which had a boyish quality in repose. While he did not have Simon's stunning handsomeness, she thought him quite irresistible, and she leaned over to kiss his forehead.

At her touch, Adam's eyes opened. As his gaze slowly focused on her face, she saw confusion, then shock, in the gray-green depths. "Tony?" he asked uncertainly.

It took her a moment to appreciate the significance of the fact that Adam had used her nickname, but when she did, a wave of excitement coursed through her. After the accident, she had introduced herself to Adam as Antonia, and he had called her that ever since. But for most of her life, she had been Tony to her cousin. Scarcely daring to breath, she asked, "Adam, do you remember what happened?"

His expression puzzled, he sat up, pulling well away from her while he raised one hand to his head. Encountering the healing scar, he murmured, "What the devil . . . ?" Adam scanned his surroundings, then glanced at his cousin. "What do you mean by asking what happened?"

"I mean the explosion, and the head injury you suffered." At his blank expression, Antonia asked, "Adam, what is the last thing you remember?"

He stood and walked across the summerhouse, a frown creasing his brow. "I was going to Macclesfield to see an engineer named Malcolm." He unconsciously rubbed the scar on his head. "I—I seem to recall asking you and Judith if you wanted to go at breakfast, and Judith accepting for both of you.'' He shook his head, disoriented. "Did that happen this morning? It's very vague. I can't remember if we went to Macclesfield. Nor do I remember coming out to the summerhouse with you"—he smiled faintly—"much less how I ended up on your lap, pleasant surprise though that was.''

"In Macclesfield, Malcolm's steam engine blew up, and you were unconscious for two and a half days. When you woke up, your personal memory was entirely gone, though you recalled abstract facts well enough," she said succinctly. "That was three weeks ago. You remember nothing of that time?"

"The devil you say! I've really lost three whole weeks?" His expression was astonished. "How bizarre."

"The physician who attended you, Dr. Kinlock, said that your memory would almost certainly return, and do so quite abruptly and thoroughly," Antonia explained. "In fact, I think he said it might happen while you were sleeping. Kinlock also said that you might not remember the interval between the accident and your recovery of full memory."

While Adam digested the information, Antonia bit her lip suddenly. Her first reaction to the apparent return of her cousin's memory had been delight, but now she saw that the whole time of their falling in love was gone from Adam's mind; the kisses and promises so recently exchanged no longer existed for him. Even worse, his behavior to her was subtly different, without the nuances of intimacy that had grown between them.

She shrugged philosophically. They would have to start over again, and he might never be able to share the sweeter moments of the past three weeks with her, but certainly it was better if he was now restored to his full self, no longer incomplete. And coaxing him back to their recent state of closeness would have a certain delicious appeal of its own.

"While it's difficult to believe that a whole piece of my life has disappeared, the evidence seems to be written on my skull," Adam said, fingering the scar on his head again. "Have I missed any important events?" His eyes scanned Antonia with approval. "You look much happier than you did. Has Simon returned and persuaded you to renew your engagement? I shouldn't think that anything else could have restored you so quickly."

"Oh, dear, this is going to be much more complicated than I anticipated," she said ruefully, then patted the bench next to her. "If my looks are improved, it is because you and I have been betrothed for the last three weeks, and it has agreed with me famously."

Adam had started walking toward her, but at her words he froze. "That's impossible," he said, his eyes narrowing. "What about Judith?"

Antonia stared at him. "What has Judith to do with anything?" she asked in bewilderment.

"I can't have asked you to marry me"—Adam's face was utterly rigid—"because Judith and I are betrothed."

Antonia's heart congealed within her even as she tried to deny Adam's words. "How can you be? Neither of you ever mentioned such a thing."

"She and I reached an understanding just before you and Simon ended your betrothal. Because you were so unhappy, we did not speak of it." Adam's words were clipped and precise, but his eyes showed something of the same confused pain that his cousin was experiencing.

Bemused, Antonia shook her head. "But if you two had an understanding, why did she never speak of it?" Her mind flashed back to the time of the accident. She herself had been half-mad with grief. How had Judith behaved? Of course she had been distressed, but she was less demonstrative by nature. Could she have been as worried over Adam as Antonia? Certainly she had nursed him as devotedly.

Then Antonia recalled Judith's face when her employer had announced that she herself was engaged to Adam. Judith had been more than surprised or disapproving of the rapid betrothal; she had looked very nearly ill, and if she was in love with Adam, no wonder! It was not hard to deduce why Judith had not spoken up then; it must have seemed as if it was already too late. Antonia buried her face in her hands, her whole body chilled with shock. "God help us all," she said dully.

She felt Adam's weight settle next to her, and he put his arm around her shoulders. His restrained touch was no longer that of a lover, but a brother; she felt the difference instantly. "Tony, you must tell me what has happened," he commanded.

Only the whole humiliating truth would do. "I was distraught when you were injured," Antonia said unsteadily. "I couldn't bear the thought of losing you. Simon was gone for good, and you had said once that I could always marry you, and you seemed to mean it. So I decided to accept." She swallowed hard. "When you came out of the coma, I said that we were betrothed and you accepted the statement without question, perhaps because I seemed somewhat familiar to you. I wouldn't have held you to it against your will, but you seemed satisfied with the arrangement."

She straightened up, but continued to stare at her hands, which lay knotted in her lap. "So, for the last three weeks, you and I have been betrothed." Antonia finally dared look in her cousin's face, and she recoiled at what she saw there. "Adam, don't look at me like that!" she cried.

He stood and walked away, explosive tension in his steps. "What a damnable tangle," he swore softly. "Poor Judith."

Poor Judith, indeed. It did not escape Antonia's notice that her cousin's first thought was for Judith, whom he wanted to marry. Had Adam not been in love with Judith, Antonia was sure that he could have been persuaded to fall in love with herself, but now Judith held his first allegiance. Judith, her best friend, whom Antonia had unintentionally put through hell. Briefly she wondered about the overseen embrace with Simon, but in the light of what she knew now, Antonia guessed that it was not what it seemed; in fact, Judith had implied as much.

"Adam, please don't be angry with me," she begged. "I would never have knowingly done anything to hurt you or Judith."

His face eased, though his body was still tense. "I'm not angry with you. There is more than enough blame to go around. Had Judith and I not kept our understanding a secret, had she spoken up after I was injured, none of this would

have happened.'' Adam's mouth twisted in a smile tinged
with bitterness. ''This would be amusing if it weren't so
painful for all concerned. Do you know where Judith is? I
must speak with her at once.''

''Of course,'' Antonia agreed bleakly, still stunned by his
news. There would always be a bond between her and Adam,
but in the future it would be Judith who must come first with
him. Judith whom he would cherish and protect and love.
''She is in the house, I believe.'' There was something else
he should know. ''Simon is at Thornleigh, too. When he
heard about your accident, he returned from London immediately.''

Adam looked at her, his eyes hooded. At length he said,
''I see.'' Then he turned and headed toward the house.

Antonia watched his broad figure vanish among the
shrubbery, feeling as if a knife were being twisted slowly
in her heart. Surely God must be punishing her for every
act of willfulness and selfishness that she had ever committed.
Did love exist if it was not part of a person's memory? Yes,
surely for a handful of days, Adam had loved her. Had she
had the wisdom to love him sooner, he could have been hers;
she knew it as surely as she knew the peaks and dales of
Thornleigh. But the Adam who had loved her was gone; in
a sense, he had never even existed.

Unfortunately, the love that she felt for him was piercingly
alive. As the soft summer breeze caressed her, Antonia
closed her eyes in a futile attempt to stop the tears that coursed
down her face.

Lord Launceston was a methodical man and he had spent
several hours making a list; it seemed the best way to order
his confused emotions. Then he struck a light and burned
the list, which was not the sort of thing that one should leave
lying around. Staring at the ashes in the grate, he knew that
the precise weighing of pros and cons had merely confirmed
what he had already known: that he was in love with Judith
Winslow.

Simon had never thought of himself as an unsteady man,
but he must be. Or perhaps Antonia's brilliant beauty had

temporarily blinded him to the gentler qualities of Judith, just as the sun outshone the moon when they shared a sky.

He had liked Judith from the beginning, had admired her intelligent, thoughtful mind, but it had taken that moment of passion by the stream for him to realize how much more he felt than liking. Strange how the lower animal nature had such an influence on the emotions. He stood, smiling at his attempt to be the natural philosopher even now. Love was a mystery, and only a poet would dare attempt to explain it.

Judith may not have been as moved by that kiss as he was, but she had always seemed to enjoy his company, and their minds and emotions matched well. Perhaps, now that Adam and Antonia seemed bound for the altar, Judith might consider marrying elsewhere. Simon's fortune was nothing like so large as Adam's, and he was all too aware of his defects of character, but he could offer a comfortable existence and the status of a married woman as well as love. In time she might come to love him as much as he loved her. Or if not that much, at least to love him a little.

His decision made, he set off purposefully to find her.

12

Judith was studying a newspaper in the morning room, looking at the shipping news. Very soon now it would be time to leave Thornleigh, and she was making plans.

At the sound of quick masculine footsteps she looked up, and when she saw Adam's face, she knew instantly what had happened. He had always been polite and friendly in the weeks since the explosion, but he had never once looked at her like this, with the remembrance of past intimacy in his eyes. "Your memory has come back," she exclaimed, not really needing confirmation.

"Yes, I was dozing in the summerhouse, and when I woke, I remembered everything until shortly before the explosion, though nothing since then." He took a seat near Judith. "Antonia was with me and she explained what has happened. All of it." His grave eyes intent on her face, he asked, "It must have been dreadful for you watching Antonia and me together. Why didn't you tell her about us?"

"How could I, when you didn't remember me?" Her hand turned up in a gesture of impotence. "There was no proof of a betrothal, apart from my word."

"And you didn't want to set your word against Antonia's." Adam smiled wryly. "It was all quite absurd. My impetuous cousin told me that she had decided to accept my standing offer, not knowing that it was no longer open." He regarded her questioningly. "Has anything happened in the last three weeks to make you wish to cry off from our betrothal?"

No, nothing at all, except that Judith had fallen in love with a man she could not have. She searched Adam's face, seeing the kindness that had attracted her to him from the

first time they met in London, when he had brought a present
for a woman he didn't even know. He would be a considerate
husband; she still wanted children, the security and companionship of marriage, everything that he had once offered and
she had accepted. "No, nothing has changed," she answered
in a soft voice, reaching out for his hand as if it were a
lifeline. It was very frightening to contemplate leaving
Thornleigh and being alone in the world once more. "Not
if you still want me."

He lifted her hand and kissed it. "Then we shall continue
as we were before?"

"So be it." Judith's phrase was a solemn ratification of
their renewed agreement. The warmth of Adam's gesture
was deeply appreciated; she needed that warmth. She would
never let him know of her foolish passion for another man.

"How is Antonia?" Judith asked hesitantly.

"Badly upset." Adam glanced down at their joined hands,
his fingers tightening. "When she learned that I was already
pledged to you, she was horrified at what she had done."

Her raw emotions very near the surface, Judith ached with
sympathy for her friend and employer. Where Antonia gave
love, she gave wholeheartedly, and whatever her initial
reasons, she had done that with Adam. The thought pushed
Judith toward a difficult decision; just as Adam had asked
her if she wanted to continue their engagement, she should
ask him the same thing. She had seen Antonia and Adam
together; there had been an intensely real bond between them.
But with his memory of the last three weeks gone, perhaps
that bond had vanished.

As she mentally debated, Lord Launceston entered the door
of the morning room. At the sight of Judith and Adam holding
hands, he stopped, his startled expression showing that he
had drawn a quick and accurate conclusion. Then his face
took on the cool chiseled hardness of granite. "Your memory
has returned, Adam?"

"Yes, just a few minutes ago. I have forgotten everything
since the explosion, but Antonia explained what has been
going on, in all its improbability." Adam released Judith's
hand and stood, his steady gaze meeting his friend's. "I hope

that you have not been too distressed by the unlooked-for engagement between Antonia and me. That was a temporary aberration, now ended. I did not intend to come between you and my cousin.''

''I knew that.'' Simon glanced at his former co-conspirator. ''While news of the *soi-disant* betrothal was a shock, Judith and I deduced that Antonia must have acted on impulse, based on her lifelong affection for you.''

Under his calm manner, Lord Launceston was reeling, his thoughts and emotions in disarray. It had been quite obvious as soon as he entered the room that Adam and Judith were together again. He should be pleased. Wasn't this what Judith had wanted, what Simon had tried to help her attain? Forcibly reminding himself that this was a glad occasion, Simon smiled and laid an affectionate hand on his friend's shoulder. ''The important thing is that you are now fully recovered. It has been an interesting interval, though not one I would choose to repeat.''

Judith spoke up, her gray eyes unreadable. ''Antonia may still be in the summerhouse. Perhaps you should go to her.''

Of course Judith wanted time alone with Adam. Simon was glad that he had not found her a few minutes earlier; having Adam enter while Simon was proposing to Adam's affianced wife would have been a little more farce than a man could bear.

''When Antonia explained why she decided to accept me, she said that she thought you were gone for good,'' Adam offered obliquely. ''Otherwise it never would have occurred to her to consider marrying someone else.''

Adam and Judith both seemed to think that Simon and Antonia belonged together. Simon pondered that in a detached way; he himself felt too numb to have an opinion. He rallied, reminding himself that at the very least he should give his friends some privacy.

His next clear awareness came in the library. He must have taken a civil leave of Judith and Adam, though he had no recollection of doing so. Simon felt like rudderless ship, uncertain of where he wanted to go or why he should bother making any effort to move. He had known Judith Winslow for only a few weeks. How could he miss her so much when he hadn't even known that he needed her?

Without consciously making a decision to do so, Simon made his way to the summerhouse. There he found Antonia curled up on the bench like a child, her knees hugged to her chest, her face marked by tears. In fact, she looked rather like Simon felt. Antonia glanced up at his approach, then tensed warily, as if expecting a scolding.

He sat down not far from her. "Has it been difficult?"

She gave him a twisted smile. "It has, rather. I've made a horrible muddle of things. In particular, I'm afraid that Judith will never forgive me."

"She was the most injured party in our little carousel of hearts," Simon agreed, "but I saw no sign that she was angry. Judith has Adam back, and her nature is not a vindictive one." He stopped, afraid to say any more about Judith; it was self-indulgent to talk about her. "She is well, but how are you?"

Antonia hid her face against her knees. "I feel such a complete fool. I took what seemed like a minor liberty with the truth, and the repercussions were disastrous."

Tenderness touched Simon as he looked at the downcast red-gold head. "You mustn't be so hard on yourself, Antonia. No one's life or reputation was irreparably damaged. More than that, none of us were being really honest, except for Adam."

Startled, Antonia raised her head again. "What do you mean?"

"After Adam's accident, I talked to Judith before coming out to Thornleigh. She told me of her betrothal to Adam and about your alleged betrothal to him," Simon explained. "We made an educated guess about what had happened, and decided to see if we could encourage you to change your mind." Having started, he might as well make a clean breast of it. "When I called on you and said that I had accepted the fact that you and I would not suit, I wasn't telling the truth."

She eyed him curiously. "You were very convincing."

"I was surprised myself to learn what a talent for duplicity

I have,'' Simon admitted. ''Actually, I had been planning all along on returning to Thornleigh after you had had time to recover from your anger. Adam's accident just brought me back a bit sooner.''

Lord Launceston's explanation clarified a few things; if Simon and Judith were playing roles, that overseen kiss could have been simulated in an effort to make Antonia jealous. It would have worked, too, under other circumstances. ''I think I see Judith's fine strategic hand at work,'' Antonia said after reflection. ''Such plotting seems too devious to be the product of a masculine mind.''

Simon smiled. ''Perhaps women are better students of human nature and better able to predict how others will act or react.''

''There is some truth to that. Certainly Judith knows me well enough to have a fair idea of how I will behave most of the time.'' Antonia admired the harmonious planes of Simon's face; having Lord Launceston at Thornleigh would certainly have ended Antonia's engagement to Adam, had it not been for the minor fact that she had fallen in love with her cousin.

It was all very dismal to contemplate. With a lightning leap of illogic, Antonia said abruptly, ''I've always wondered how you can be so exquisitely dressed when you obviously haven't the least interest in fashion.'' At Simon's startled glance, she colored and his her face. ''I'm sorry. My mind isn't working too well just now.''

His voice held amusement, not perturbation. ''One of the best things about you, Antonia, is your unexpectedness.''

She looked up with a lopsided smile. ''It is also one of the worst things about me.''

Simon considered her words gravely. ''I wouldn't disagree with that,'' he said at length, but with humor in his deep-blue eyes.

Antonia's smile became genuine; she wouldn't have thought it possible a few minutes ago. After Adam, Simon really was her favorite man in the world.

''To answer your sartorial question,'' he said, ''when I returned to England, my older sister said that she had no hope that I would ever be a man of fashion, but that she would not permit the head of the family to look like an underpaid country curate. She then informed me that she had found the perfect valet, if Stinson could be persuaded to work for me.''

Curious, Antonia asked, ''What makes him the perfect valet?'' Conversation with Simon was starting to leaven her black depression of guilt and loss.

''The fact that he is a true artist,'' he explained. ''Almost all first-class valets want their masters to be seen and admired as a reflection of their own skills. My sister knew that I was unlikely to spend much time in fashionable circles, so most good valets would not deign to waste their time on me. Stinson, however, believes in art for its own sake.''

Antonia puzzled that out. ''So as long as you look wonderful,'' she guessed, ''his sense of satisfaction is so profound that he does not need the admiration of others?''

''Exactly. Of course, he had to interview me.'' Simon smiled reminiscently. ''My sister brought him to my hotel in London. He circled me two or three times, muttering very personal remarks. Then he went through my wardrobe, fingering my coats as if they had just been fished out of the Thames and sneering at my linen.''

Antonia began to chuckle. ''Oh, Lord, I wish I had been there. And you permitted this?''

''You don't know my sister,'' he said. ''Besides, I must admit that I was amused. At any rate, after making me swear that I would buy only from the merchants he approved of, wear only the garments he allowed, and generally follow his orders precisely, he consented to take me on. Within two hours, he had me at Weston's and was ordering a complete new wardrobe.''

''One can see why he decided that you were worthy of his efforts,'' Antonia agreed, scanning Simon's lean, elegant frame, from beautifully shaped head to perfectly formed calves.

''Whatever,'' Simon said indifferently. ''I wear what he hands me. He seems happy, and in return I never have to waste a moment's thought on clothing. It's an ideal arrangement.''

Antonia gave him a affectionate look. "Thank you for cheering me up. I feel a little less villainous now.'' Belatedly becoming aware of her unladylike posture, she set her feet back on the ground and made a token gesture toward straightening her rumpled muslin dress.

"You don't look villainous. You look quite enchanting.''

Antonia gave him a look compounded of shyness and uncertainty. "Simon, are you courting me?''

He looked blank. "I'm really not sure.'' Long silence. "You seemed very happy with Adam.''

"I was. But that Adam doesn't exist anymore. Divine retribution of some sort, I imagine.'' Antonia brushed her hair back with a tired hand. "Do you think that you and I could rub along comfortably?'' She halted and smiled faintly. "I shouldn't be asking you that. If there were to be problems, they would be my fault. Your disposition is much better than mine.''

"You really are much too critical of yourself,'' Simon said gently. Antonia looked so vulnerable in her loveliness that he felt an impulse to take her in his arms. On further consideration, he did so.

Antonia nestled gratefully into his familiar embrace; it felt very good to be held and cared for. It also helped her lacerated emotions to know that when Simon left Thornleigh it had not been because he despised her. Instead, it was just another example of their dissimilar approaches to problems.

"I've learned a lot in the last few weeks," she said in a small voice. "I wouldn't plague you anywhere near as much.''

Simon chuckled. "That is a very unromantic sort of declaration, if declaration it is.''

"I have given up on romance.'' Antonia leaned back in his embrace, her cinnamon-brown eyes meeting his. Adam and Simon were different in many ways, but one thing they had in common was a deep and abiding kindness. Next to love, she wanted kindness more than anything. "Shall we try again, older and wiser?"

Why not? They had come full circle. Simon was no longer dazzled by infatuation, but the mixture of tenderness and desire that he felt was very potent. While no other woman could fit his mind and spirit as well as Judith did, Antonia would come closer than any other. And he did care for her, a great deal.

"I still have the telescope, and I don't know anyone else who would appreciate it as much as you." Antonia's flawless countenance was a study in contradictions, with both doubt and longing visible.

Simon had to laugh. "What astronomer could possibly resist a woman with a dowry like that?" He dropped a kiss on top of her bright head. "It seems that we are meant to marry."

"Thank you, Simon," Antonia said, resting her head on his shoulder. It was an odd way to reach an agreement to marry, but then, it had been a very odd day.

When he had talked with Judith long enough for civility's sake, Adam went riding, needing to stretch his mind and muscles alone among the hills. He felt brittle, as if a hard knock might shatter him. After a mad gallop had burned off the worst of his restless energy, he pulled back to a canter, thinking that it was the worst irony of his life that he should briefly obtain the one thing he desired above all others, yet not remember a single moment of it.

To marry Antonia was more than a dream; it had been his lifelong obsession, though he had known that the chances of achieving his goal were almost nonexistent. Then, by an absurd set of circumstances, Antonia had decided to accept him. More than that, she appeared to have been content; the one recollection he did have was waking up to the sight of her face smiling down into his, the feel of her lips lingering on his forehead, her body soft and welcoming.

But he had been confused and disoriented, and the incident was over before he had had time to savor it. Adam had felt more than confusion; a lifetime's hard experience had taught him just how dangerous it was to be near his cousin. Had he understood what was happening, he would not have been so quick to stand and move away from her. It would have been easy to reach up and pull her head down for a kiss, and she would have welcomed it. . . . His stomach knotted from the devastating knowledge that he had wasted the opportunity of a lifetime.

Inevitably, Adam made his way to the Aerie. Too restless to sit and contemplate the sky, he paced the length of the small ledge, thinking of the many times he had been here with Antonia, most recently to comfort her on the loss of Simon. Then she had been racked with grief, yet when he looked down at the grass, what he imagined was making love to her. With heart-stopping clarity he saw her laughing up at him, her exquisite face shining with love and framed with the red-gold richness of her hair.

The image was so realistic that he could taste her lips, feel the silken warmth of her skin beneath his hand, and he turned away, aching. While more vivid, it was the same dream he had experienced countless times during the years of exile. During bouts with alien fevers, in tropical hellholes where tormenting heat prevented sleep, Adam had always dreamed of Antonia . . . and of England.

It was better to be moving, so he returned to his horse and made his way along the narrow trails he had known in childhood. He was unalterably committed to Judith, a woman he esteemed and cared for, and he would never betray her. More than that, by now Antonia would have reconciled with Simon, a man who had a thousand times more to offer than Adam did, including legitimate birth, a title, and a face like a young god, as well as the more enduring assets of intelligence and character.

Antonia's happiness meant more to Adam than his own, and if Simon would make her happy, the couple would have Adam's sincere blessing. Yet surely as a reward for painfully difficult and honorable behavior, Adam should be allowed to remember a few more moments of Antonia looking at him as if they were truly lovers?

* * *

It was late afternoon when Adam returned to the house, and he entered the hall just as the butler was greeting a visitor, an energetic man with prematurely white hair and a Scots burr. The newcomer recognized Adam, though recognition was not mutual; a few sentences established the conditions under which they had met, and that Antonia had asked Dr. Kinlock to visit Thornleigh on his return trip to London. Within a few more moments, the physician was cheerfully taking stock of his erstwhile patient in the drawing room.

The examination involved a cursory look at Adam's head ("Healing well. You must have a skull like an elephant, Mr. Yorke,") and a much more lengthy set of questions about his amnesia and memory recovery. When the doctor began to take notes, Adam asked in an edged voice, "Now can I ask you some questions and get some answers?"

"Of course." Kinlock grinned disarmingly. "Sorry to be taking so much intellectual pleasure in what has been a dangerous and harrowing experience for you, but amnesia is a rare condition, and a fascinating one. It raises so many questions about the role of memory in personality and identity." He set his notebook aside. "At any rate, ask away, and I'll do my best to answer."

"Will there be any long-term effects of the head injury, and will I ever remember the three weeks between the injury and full memory recovery?"

"Given the completeness of your recovery, I think you are unlikely to have serious physical problems in the future. Headaches for a while perhaps, but that would be the worst." Kinlock paused for a drink of the tea that had been brought for his travel-weary throat. "As for the three weeks you lost, there is an excellent chance that you will remember at least some of that time. Eventually, you might recollect almost everything except the time directly before and after the accident, but I can't guarantee that."

Adam nodded, satisfied. After convincing the physician that it was too late in the day to continue his journey and that Lady Antonia would take it as a personal insult if Kinlock didn't spend the night, Adam summoned the butler to escort the guest to a bedchamber, then retired to his own room.

It eased some of the ache to be able to hope that in time he might remember some of what he had lost.

Judith had gone to her room to rest when Adam went riding, and she did not see Antonia until just before dinner. Judith had just finished applying a subtle rouge to her pale face when a knock on the door heralded Antonia's arrival. Her employer was wearing the sari that Adam had brought back from India, and her apricot hair was dressed high on her head with a gold chain woven through. She looked quite staggeringly beautiful.

Antonia halted just inside the door, her back braced tensely and her face reflecting uncertainty. "Judith, I owe you the most profound apology. Can you ever forgive me?"

Judith didn't speak for a moment, and her fingers tightened on her hare's foot. A month ago, she had been content with the thought of marrying Adam Yorke. More than content, she had been awestruck at how lucky she was to have won the regard of so fine a man. The explosion and Antonia's careless actions had brought about a result that tarnished that happiness; for the rest of Judith's life, she would live with a secret regret born of these last three weeks.

Yet, if it hadn't been for Antonia, Judith would never have met either Adam or Simon; she would be a governess, locked in the bleak life of a permanent outsider in some great house. The gracious chamber in which they stood, the very gown on Judith's back, came from Antonia. And her employer had given freely, asking only honest friendship in return. "As the bible says, we reap what we have sowed. You have sowed love and generosity. How could I return less than that?" she said in an even voice. "There is nothing to forgive."

Antonia whispered, "Thank you." There was a shine of tears in her wide brown eyes.

"Have you and Simon reconciled?" Judith girded herself to hear the answer that she was sure must come.

Antonia nodded. "Yes. He is the most incredible man. Amazingly enough, he is willing to overlook my mad starts and to begin again. I'm not quite sure why."

Looking at Antonia's lush, provocative loveliness, Judith

knew why. What man could resist that combination of beauty and spirit? Glancing at her mantel clock, Judith said, "It is time we went downstairs." With effort, she made herself add, "Dinner should be something of a celebration. After all, aren't we both getting the man we wanted?"

Antonia's face was very still for a moment. "Yes," she agreed softly as she turned to go out of the door, "we are both getting what we wanted."

Champagne was served that night, wedding plans discussed. As honored guest, Ian Kinlock had an enjoyable evening, though his ever-lively curiosity wondered at the current alignment of lovers. Why had the beautiful Lady Antonia gone from her cousin to the equally beautiful Lord Launceston? Did Adam Yorke's injury have anything to do with the switch from Lady Antonia to her sweetly pretty companion? Though he had never been known for tact, the doctor did not quite have the temerity to ask.

As he continued his journey to London, Kinlock mulled over the difference between what he saw and what he sensed under the surface. Thornleigh held four very attractive and appealing young people, and it was easy to feel the currents of affection running between them. That being the case, why did he have such a strong, visceral belief that all four of them were miserably unhappy?

13

Life at Thornleigh settled into a new pattern. Simon worked on plans for converting an outbuilding into an observatory. Judith and Adam visited an estate that was for sale on the far side of Buxton, discussing its pluses and minuses as a future home. Wedding plans were finalized. Both couples would be married from Thornleigh, Adam and Judith in four weeks, Simon and Antonia a few days later. Since the Continent was effectively closed to English travel, no exotic honeymoons were planned; after the Launceston wedding, Adam and his wife would journey to the Lake District, while Simon would take his bride to visit his own family seat in Kent.

On the surface, everything was mirror-smooth. Underneath, Judith felt a growing sense of utter wrongness. She tried to deny it, but the feeling expanded until it occupied her thoughts every hour of the day and interfered with her sleep at night. Her nerves stretched tighter and tighter, until a fortnight before the wedding, they snapped.

Antonia and Simon had gone on an overnight trip to introduce him to her aunt, Lady Forrester, leaving Judith and Adam alone at Thornleigh. The situation was somewhat lacking in propriety, but Judith was a widow, not a young girl, and the couple was so close to marriage that even a high stickler could not have gotten too exercised.

After a leisurely dinner, they had withdrawn to the music room, where Judith played her harp at Adam's request. The melodies rippled forth from her fingers, expressing the longings of her heart and bringing her buried emotions to the surface. By the time she stopped playing, she felt fragile, on the verge of inexplicable tears.

When the last note had faded, Adam rose and crossed to where she sat by the harp, pulling a small box from his pocket as he did so. "This is for you, Judith. I had sent the stone to London to be set before my accident." As Judith accepted the box, he explained, "It was intended as a betrothal gift, though with everything that happened, I'm afraid the matter had slipped my mind until it was delivered today."

Inside the box was a ring, a blue cabochon in an elegantly simple silver setting. When Judith lifted the ring out, the gem caught the candlelight and a shimmering pattern of radiance flickered deep inside. She made a soft admiring sound and tilted the ring, watching the play of light in the heart of the jewel.

"It's called a star sapphire. I bought it in Ceylon, mixed in with a number of other unset gems," Adam said. "I thought you would like it."

Judith glanced up into Adam's tanned, pleasant face, thinking how ruggedly attractive he was in his evening dress and how fortunate she was. Since he had recovered his memory, their interactions had been superficial, but she hoped that in time they would regain the ease they had known before his accident. That hope died with shattering suddenness when her gaze caught and held Adam's, forcing her to acknowledge a grimly unwelcome truth: while his desire to please her was sincere, in the changeable depths of Adam's gray-green eyes was soul-deep sorrow. Recognition was instantaneous and undeniable, because it echoed the corresponding sorrow in herself.

The charade that she had been living collapsed around her, all her doubts and fears and rationalizations disintegrating beneath the knowledge of what she must do. Her fingers had tightened around the ring, but now she held it out to him, her voice breaking. "I'm sorry, Adam. I can't marry you. It was wrong of me to accept your offer in the first place."

Through the tears that were starting in her eyes, she saw him stiffen with shock as she dropped the sapphire ring in his hand.

"Why, Judith? Is it something I have done?"

Her resolution wavered at the sight of his bewilderment. She could still change her mind, accept the warmth and kindness between them, the security of marrying a wealthy man. The only price for that would be to hate herself for the rest of her life. Judith slid sideways on her stool and stood, needing to be farther away from him; if Adam touched her, she would cling to his kindness and never have the strength to carry through.

A safe distance away, she said, "No, it is nothing you have done." Judith spread her hands helplessly. A hard life had taught her to do difficult things, but never more difficult than this. "Can't you feel how wrong things are here at Thornleigh? We are all being so careful with one another, as if we are mourners after a death.

"No one is really talking or listening to anyone else, except in the most superficial way. Antonia and Simon are watching every word to avoid any more rows, but you and she never look at each other. Simon never speaks to me, while you are being so kind to me that I can't bear it." Her gaze was beseeching as she tried to will Adam to understand her inchoate thoughts. "Everyone is being kind and honorable, and no one is being honest. It's wrong!"

Adam put the ring back in its box and set it on a table, his movements mechanically precise. "I'm sorry, I must be very thick-witted. I still don't understand your meaning." His deep voice was as stiff as his movements, his face a numb mask.

Judith hid her face in her hands for a moment, trying to define her thoughts. "Adam, you and I have agreed to marry each other, made plans for a future, without ever once mentioning the word 'love.' I know that there is kindness between us, respect, and caring." She raised her head and looked at him. "But the real reason that we agreed to marry was because we decided to settle for what we could get rather than that we wanted."

When Adam made an involuntary movement toward her, Judith lifted her hand to stop him. "Please, let me finish. You loved Antonia and thought you couldn't have her. I gave you sympathy and understanding when you needed it badly, and in gratitude you offered me a life better than I had dreamed possible. I have neither beauty, nor youth, nor fortune to offer a man, and was greatly honored and gratified that a man like you could want me.

"Our reasons were not bad ones. Though neither of us was in love, at the beginning there was honesty between us. Now that is gone, and with neither love nor honesty, it would be horribly wrong to marry."

Rubbing the heel of her hand across her eyes, she added in a husky whisper, "I married once because I thought I could do no better, and I accepted you for essentially the same reason. You are a kinder and more honest man than Edwin Winslow was, and I care for you much more than I cared for him. Perhaps I do love you, but not enough, not in the right way."

Adam sat down carefully, leaning back in his chair and unconsciously massaging the scar on his head, his face drawn. Judith ached at the expression on his face.

"Is it such a bad thing to settle for what is possible?" he asked finally. "Is it really better to cry for the moon? I have wasted half a lifetime yearning for what I can't have, and I wish to be done with that. Perhaps I can't offer you the romantic love a woman craves, but I swear I will give you everything I am capable of."

At his words, Judith folded onto the bench in front of the harpsichord and buried her face, giving way to wrenching tears. This was even more painful than she could have guessed, but she knew to the marrow of her bones that she was right. "Adam, why should you settle for less?" She looked up at him, wanting him to believe her. "If you love Antonia, fight for her! You demean yourself by giving up without trying."

His darkly shadowed eyes met hers. "Why should Antonia marry her bastard cousin? Granted, I'm a rich bastard, but that is the most that can be said, and Antonia doesn't need riches." He sighed and glanced away. "She regards me as a brother, and I am grateful to have that much."

Judith felt like swearing. "Adam, the greatest barrier

between you and Antonia is your own self-judgment. Have you ever tried—really, truly, heart-and-soul tried—to win her? From what I have seen, you surrendered without even making the attempt. And by not being brave enough to risk losing, I think you are hurting not only yourself, but Antonia.''

His face froze, and she wondered if she had gone too far. His voice bitterly edged, he answered. ''You seem to forget that Antonia is in love with Simon. Apollo himself would have trouble winning over competition like that.''

Judith shook her head in negation. ''In the beginning, she was infatuated with Simon. As handsome as he is, any woman will fall a little bit in love with him at first sight.'' Thinking of Simon caused her throat to close for a moment. Doggedly she made herself continue. ''Certainly she cares a great deal for him now, enough to marry him.'' She sought Adam's eyes, wanting him to believe her next words. ''But I doubt that she loves him more than she does you. You may not remember those three weeks when you were betrothed, but I do. And I swear, Antonia did not behave as if you were her brother.''

For a moment he was still. Then he leaned forward, his posture strained. ''What did you see? I have scoured my mind, but don't know if what I find are memories or dreams.''

''Antonia was content as I had never seen her before,'' Judith said slowly, trying to define the subtle differences she has sensed at the time. ''And you were not apologetic about yourself. As soon as you awoke after the accident, Antonia told you that the two of you were to marry. Because of that knowledge, you had a kind of confidence with Antonia that was not there before or since. Perhaps the amnesia freed you of the ingrained belief that to be illegitimate is to be inferior.''

He rose and paced across the room, his muscular body taut with barely contained energy as he struggled with what Judith had told him. She watched in silence, knowing how difficult and painful it must be for him to evaluate her words.

''Even a bastard should have some honor, and Simon is my best friend,'' Adam said, his voice strained. ''Trying to steal the woman he loves is hardly the action of an honorable man, and it will certainly destroy our friendship, whether I am successful or not.''

Judith replied even though his question was more for himself than for her. ''The tragedy of a lovers' triangle is that it cannot be resolved without someone being hurt. At worst, everyone suffers. If Antonia loves you but marries Simon, only he will be happy, and in the long run he may be miserable because she doesn't care for him as much as he cares for her.'' She sighed. ''At least if Antonia loves and accepts you, two out of three people have a chance for happiness.''

Adam was in the shadows at the far end of the room, but she could see his faint, humorless smile. ''Does honor come down to a simple matter of numbers? If more people benefit, does that make an action right?''

Judith shook her head, drained. Only Adam could decide whether to act on the information she had offered him. ''Honor can be defined in many ways. Remember your Shakespeare? 'To thine own self be true, And it must follow, as the night the day, Thou canst not then be false to any man.' '' She stood and made her way to the door. ''Be true to yourself, Adam. Please.''

Her hand was on the doorknob when his voice came softly, the deep tones dark with grief. ''You say that I demean myself by not daring to fight for what I want. You equally demean yourself by saying that you have nothing to offer a man.''

She turned, and her eyes met his for an endless moment as painfully real affection and respect pulsed between them. Anguished, she whispered, ''I wish it could be different.'' Then she left, before her resolve could crumble.

It was time to leave Thornleigh; Judith did not belong here anymore. One way or another the triangle would be resolved, but she could not bear to stay and witness the inevitable. Judith's own guess was that Antonia would chose Adam over Simon, if her cousin dared try to win her. If that happened, it meant that Simon, whom Judith loved, would be the one left suffering. His pain was agonizing to contemplate; only the fact that she cared deeply for Antonia and Adam could justify her interference. She prayed that eventually Simon would find someone else who would make him happy, even if he could never love another woman as he loved Antonia.

Shuddering, Judith broke her mind from the painful circle of thoughts by forcing herself to concentrate on what needed to be done. First, before the evening was too advanced, she ordered a carriage for five o'clock in the morning. She received a surprised look but no questions; her orders were accepted as readily as Antonia's.

Then she packed. The abigail whom she and Antonia shared had gone on the overnight trip, but no matter; for this journey, Judith herself must make the decisions of what to keep and what to leave behind. Amazing how many possessions she had accumulated in two years of security. Choices were hard but not impossible; she would hire a post chaise in Macclesfield to take her to Liverpool, so a reasonable amount of baggage could be carried.

She worked swiftly; most of her books must go, but her more elaborate gowns were not likely to be needed in the colonies. Judith reminded herself to think of her destination as the United States, or the natives might take it amiss.

Because she had been contemplating leaving off and on for several months, she had a substantial amount of money at hand, and the remainder of her account could be transferred when she had decided where she would settle. Antonia had paid her companion very generously over the years, and Judith had saved a large proportion of her salary, enough so that she could go for a long time without another situation.

The most difficult part was writing her farewells. Judith had already said more than enough to Adam. She considered leaving a note for Simon, but what could she say? That she felt privileged to have known him, that the days of their conspiracy had been the happiest of her life, and that she would love him forever? Unthinkable. Worse than unthinkable, pathetic.

In the end, she wrote only to Antonia, explaining that she

had broken her betrothal to Adam and was leaving immediately to prevent awkwardness. It was time to pursue her long-time ambition to visit the New World; she would write eventually. In the meantime, Judith gave her sincerest thanks for everything Antonia had done for her, and wished her all joy in her marriage.

She did not specify which man Antonia would be marrying, since that issue was still in doubt.

Adam sat alone in the music room long after Judith had left him, thinking of what she had said, eventually moving to the library, where a glass of brandy could be found to aid his deliberations. Over the last fortnight Adam had been too absorbed in his own unhappy thoughts to pay much attention to what the others were doing; in particular, he had avoided watching Antonia and Simon together. But Judith was quite right: they had all been walking on eggs. Adam could not remember having a single significant conversation with anyone since he had regained his memory: not with Antonia, his cousin; not with Simon, his friend; not even with Judith, his betrothed. They had been avoiding interaction like an assembly of polite ghosts.

Judith's words about his cowardice were painful, but he could not deny their harsh reality; it was indeed his own fears that had stopped him from ever declaring himself to Antonia. To do so would have been impossible before he left England, and when he returned, he had lacked the courage. At first, he had rationalized that it was too soon, that they needed time to become reacquainted. Then, with appalling suddenness, it had been too late.

Yet, if Judith was to be believed, for a few short weeks he had been different, freed of the shackles of the past. Vaguely he recalled that Antonia had told him of his illegitimacy in her attempts to reacquaint him with his history. But the simple knowledge of bastardy was not the same as recollection of the thousand small slights that he had suffered because of his birth, nor of that one enormous, life-changing rebuff. It was easy to believe that he had behaved differently

without the bar sinister graven on his soul. And it was undeniable that since recovering his memory he had slipped
back into the old hesitant patterns when he was around his
cousin, acting the insecure bastard rather than the successful
man of affairs.

With fierce deliberation Adam invoked the images of
Antonia that had been haunting him since he had regained
his memory. Discarding the recurring dreams that he had
experienced over the years, he examined what was left in
an attempt to decide what was a true memory. Could he and
Antonia really have picnicked at the Aerie and discovered
a passion as intense as what he had dreamed of? In the
summerhouse, had she sworn that she loved him without
limits or qualifications and that she wanted—most desperately—to marry him?

He could not be certain. But if those events were real, not
figments of his imagination or battered brain, then perhaps
Antonia did love him as more than a brother, possibly even
more than she loved Simon. If by some miracle she did, he
owed it to both of them to act rather than to let her drift into
marriage with the wrong man, but there were a hundred ways
of losing, and the consequences of failure could be
devastating.

Even if Antonia loved him, her own sense of honor might
prevent her from breaking her betrothal to Simon a second
time. The best Adam could hope for was winning Antonia
at the price of betraying his best friend. At worst, he would
sacrifice Antonia's regard forever, no longer have the
closeness of friend and brother, and he would lose Simon's
friendship as well. He could not believe that he and Simon
would end up facing each other over cold steel at dawn, but
that was one possible result.

Adam was not a gambler by nature; he had forced himself to become one in the lonely years in Asia, when only
continual risk-taking offered any hope of winning what he
wanted. Ironically, it had not been hard to risk his life and
growing fortune when the possibility of winning Antonia was
the prize. It was only where Antonia herself was concerned

that he was a coward, because he cared more for her than
for life and fortune. Yet now he must risk everything on one
colossal gamble; he might have only one chance to plead his
case, and God help him if he did it badly.

For the rest of the night Adam sat alone thinking, about
Judith, about himself, but most of all, about Antonia.

Having reached her sanctuary, Antonia glanced around the
stillroom with a sigh of pleasure. She found the place very
soothing, which was why she had retreated here shortly after
her return to Thornleigh. Visits to Lady Forrester were
always something of a strain, especially to introduce a future
husband. Not that there had been any major problems; Aunt
Lettie was delighted that her wayward niece was finally
marrying, and had been more than a little charmed by Lord
Launceston. In fact, Antonia would not hesitate to say that
the old beldame had flirted with him. Fortunately, Simon
was not of a womanizing disposition; it was bad enough that
every female in sight melted at his entrance, but it would
be far worse if he encouraged them.

Still, Antonia had been uncomfortable in the role of
blossoming bride-to-be; it seemed fraudulent to be accepting
good wishes when she was secretly pining for Adam. But
at least she and Simon were getting along well; ever since
they had become rebetrothed there had been no harsh words
or rows. Regrettably, there was also little relaxation or casual
companionship, but no doubt matters would improve in time.

The stillroom was the most remote corner of the kitchen
and storeroom complex, and in midafternoon on a quiet
summer day it was delightfully private. When Antonia was
a child, she had thought of the stillroom as an enchanted
Oriental cavern of rich colors, scents, and tastes. This was
the oldest part of the house, with a flagstone floor, a beamed
ceiling, and small-paned windows high on the walls.

The chamber was completely lined with cupboards and
open shelves of pickles, brandied fruits, homemade cordials,
and a multitude of other preserved foodstuffs. A scrubbed
deal worktable stood in the center of the room, and one
corner sheltered a drying rack for fruit. Bunches of herbs

hung from the rafters, and a locked chest contained small jars of expensive spices.

Preserving the products of the land was satisfying in a very elemental way, and Antonia and her housekeeper, Mrs. Heaver, spent many happy hours discussing recipes, tasting, and planning what to try in the future. It was the only aspect of housekeeping that really interested Antonia. Now she made her way around the room, looking for areas where supplies were low as an excuse to linger. Opposite the door she paused to lift a bottle of raspberry vinegar: if she recalled correctly, good for coughs and sore throats as well as cooking.

Antonia was admiring the rich burgundy color of the vinegar when she heard the unexpected sound of approaching footsteps, tensing as she recognized who made them. She forced herself to relax. Though she had managed to avoid anything resembling a tête-à-tête with her cousin, she could hardly spend the rest of her life doing so.

As he entered, Antonia looked up with a bright smile. "Come to steal some crystallized peaches, Adam?" As children, they had enjoyed periodic raids on the treasures stored here, and candied fruit had been a prime favorite.

"Not today." Adam closed the door behind him. "This time I'm looking for you, and Mrs. Heaver thought she saw you sneaking in this direction."

In some subtle way Adam seemed different today, and Antonia was vividly and uneasily aware of his forceful masculinity. "How can I be sneaking when I am in my own house?" she asked with mock indignation, hoping to keep the conversation frivolous.

"It was sneaking since you were trying to avoid being seen," Adam explained. "Speaking of trying, how was Lady Forrester?"

"As trying as usual," Antonia said ruefully.

Adam's coat emphasized the breadth of his wide shoulders, and the afternoon sun found gold highlights in his light-brown hair. Wishing that she could feel as casual as her cousin appeared, Antonia shifted her feet and manufactured a smile. "She approved of Simon, but wanted to know when you would call on her. Said that you are most remiss.''

"Really? It never occurred to me that Lady Forrester expected a call. I've always thought she disapproved of my existence. But I suppose that the best thing about her is that she disapproves of everyone universally," he said after reflection. "In her way, she's a perfect democrat." In spite of his banter, Adam's gray-green eyes were fixed on Antonia in a way she found profoundly disturbing. "Do you know where Simon is?"

Antonia was relieved by the question. If Adam was just looking for Simon, he would leave soon. "Checking progress at his future observatory. He hopes to start assembling the telescope today or tomorrow."

"Good. That should keep him occupied for a time. I need to talk to you, and I don't want any interruptions." Adam crossed the stillroom with light deliberate steps, like a lion prowling the plains in search of supper. "But before I talk, there is something that I must do to refresh my memory."

Adam deftly removed the bottle of raspberry vinegar from Antonia's nerveless fingers and set it back on a shelf, then drew her into his arms. Startled and indignant, she turned her face up, only to have her confused protest checked by a kiss.

Antonia gasped with shock. There was nothing casual or cousinly about Adam's embrace; it was deep and sexual and demanding. While her mind reeled at her cousin's outrageous behavior, her body responded with shattering urgency to his knowing mouth and hands. Ever since Adam had recovered his memory, she had kept as far away from him as possible, trying without success to forget the intimacy and passion that had been between them. Now every fiber of her being pulsed with desire and the erotic awareness of being surrounded by great strength barely restrained.

Even as her better judgment screamed that this was wrong and dangerous, Antonia kissed Adam back, twining her arms around his neck and pressing against him, craving his touch and the hard warmth of his body. She wanted to melt onto the cool stone floor and pull him down with her, complete what had been tantalizingly unfinished during that brief idyll when they had thought that a lifetime of fulfillment lay ahead of them.

In another few moments she would pass the point of no return, and it took every fraying shred of Antonia's self-control to break away. Her breasts heaving with agitation and desire, she retreated until her back was flattened against the vinegar cupboard. "Adam, have you run mad?" she asked weakly, too shaken even for righteous outrage.

"No. I just needed to confirm my memory of what happened during the time I had amnesia." Though Adam's breathing was ragged, he made no attempt to pursue or persuade her, for which Antonia was profoundly grateful.

She stared incredulously. "Just what were you trying to determine?"

"Whether you might be in love with me." Adam leaned back against the deal table, one knee bent and his hands resting casually on the edge, as if preparing for a lengthy discussion. "Judith seemed to think so, but I needed to find out for myself."

"You are mad," Antonia said with conviction. "Why would Judith say something like that?"

He smiled humorlessly. "It was one of her principal reasons for ending our betrothal."

"Judith ended your engagement?" Antonia's senses were still disordered from the impact of Adam's closeness, and it took a moment to absorb the sense of his statement. "Adam, I'm so sorry. But really"—she gave a shaky laugh—"I don't think Simon would appreciate your using his future wife for solace."

Adam's thick brows arched. "That was hardly my intention. I was just confirming my facts before asking you to marry me."

"If you aren't mad, you're drunk," Antonia said, perilously close to tears. "Or else you are teasing me in a way I do not find amusing." To her horror, there was a crack in her voice. He wanted to marry her. He actually wanted to marry her! Why did he have to ask her now, when it was far too late?

"I have never been more serious in my life." Adam's

grave voice underlined his words. "Tony, look at me."

Almost against her will, she raised her eyes to meet his.

Regarding her with mesmerizing intensity, he said quietly, "I love you. I have loved you since I was seven years old, and that fact has shaped my entire life. For too long I have been silent, but I am speaking now, and I pray it isn't too late."

His words were an eerie echo of her own thoughts, and Antonia felt a knot of pain deep in her chest. She had thought he looked different, and now she understood why. Today it was as if the two Adams had merged—the familiar beloved cousin and the dynamic, unpredictable stranger were now one. "I don't know what to say," she said helplessly.

His lips quirked with amusement. "I believe it is customary to say, 'This is such a surprise.' Perhaps it is, although it shouldn't be. Am I misremembering what happened up at the Aerie?" He halted and watched her face as Antonia blushed at the memory of the first discovery of passion. Then Adam continued, "And the time in the summerhouse, it must have been just before my memory came back. I think you said something about loving me without limitation and wanting most desperately to marry. Did that really happen or did I imagine it?"

Antonia felt as if she was in quicksand, and sinking fast. "You didn't imagine it," she whispered, her gaze shifting away.

"Did you mean what you said?" he asked, his voice mild but insistent. "Or were those words only for the Adam with amnesia?"

"I—I meant it." With explosive suddenness, his probing questions cracked her defenses, exposing the pain and anger that she had buried so deeply eight years earlier. Antonia lifted her head to glare at her cousin. "If you have loved me forever, how come you ran away to India the way you did, without a word, not even good-bye?" she asked furiously. "It was a shabby way to treat a friend or a sister. If you really loved me, as you claim, it was unspeakable."

Adam's mouth twisted with bitter regret. "I did not have

any choice, and the reason that I didn't was a direct result of the fact that I loved you.''

"Then why didn't you offer for me then, instead of going to India?'' she cried. "The whole time that we were growing up, I assumed that someday we would marry. It seemed unnecessary to speak of it, because marrying you was as natural and inevitable as the rain and the hills.''

Antonia's voice broke and it was a long moment before she could continue. "Then you just ran away, as if you couldn't get away from England fast enough. That was when I realized how much I had misjudged your feelings.''

"You thought that we would marry someday?'' Adam was looking at her with wonder, a glow deep in his eyes. "I assumed the same when we were young, but later, when I understood the difference in our stations, I came to believe that marriage was impossible, that you had regarded me in the light of a brother only.''

"After you left, I had to think of you as a brother so I could get on with my life.'' Antonia brushed at her eyes angrily. "Did you think I would patiently wait here like Penelope? At least she was married to Odysseus, but you never made a declaration, never offered so much as a single word of love, either in person or in your letters after you left. A pretty fool I would have been to wait and hope! Since you treated me as a sister, I responded in kind.''

"It was impossible to speak,'' Adam said flatly, struggling to maintain his own composure. Though he ached to kiss away the tears in Antonia's beautiful cinnamon-brown eyes, there was still much that needed to be said. He had confirmed that there was fire between them; now he must persuade her mind before he could win her heart. Restlessly he shifted his weight against the deal table, his fingers gripping the edge hard. "You remember that your father was going to buy me a commission?''

When she nodded, he continued, "Just before I finished at Cambridge, some busybody relative told Spenston you and I were behaving with disgraceful impropriety, that you were far too free in your ways and risked damaging your chances of a suitable match, and that I had ideas far above my station. So Spenston called me in to find out if there was any truth to the rumor.''

Arrested, Antonia stared at him. ''Why didn't you declare yourself and ask his permission to court me then?''

''I did,'' Adam said, a hard edge in his voice. ''Oh, I knew better than to ask him if we could marry soon. You were only seventeen and needed to see more of the world before making a decision, and I knew that I must do something to prove myself. That's one reason I thought the army was a good choice: it seemed the best avenue available for a young man with no expectations. If I managed to distinguish myself without getting killed in the process, it would narrow the disparities in our station a little.''

''Father never told me that you had offered for me,'' Antonia said with puzzlement. ''Yet surely he agreed. You two always got on so well—why, you were like a son to him.''

''No!'' Adam tasted bitterness harsh on his tongue. ''Spenston rescued me from the gutter for the sake of his connection with my father and for his image of himself as a charitable and generous man. He let me live in your household for your sake, and perhaps to assuage his own guilt for the unpardonable way he neglected you. But I was never a son to him, and he was never a father to me.''

Even now, it was painful to discuss that interview with Antonia's father. ''The earl asked me if there was any substance to the rumor that I aspired to your hand. When I said that it was true, he gave me the worst dressing down of my life. He was shocked and appalled that I had the effrontery to set my sights on someone so far above me in birth and fortune.''

Antonia sprang to her father's defense. ''Father would be the last man on earth to condemn you for your birth! He believed that all men were equal in the eyes of God, and he spent his life fighting for reforms to help the common people.''

''Spenston may have worked for the common people, but

he certainly never thought that he was one of them," Adam answered acidly. "On the contrary, the great Whig liberal spelled out in excruciating detail how scandalized he was at my ingratitude, how pathetic and inappropriate my aspirations were. He made it very clear that the only child of the ninth Earl of Spenston would never be permitted to waste herself on a penniless bastard."

Antonia stared at Adam with horror. "No, he couldn't possibly have been so cruel as to say that."

"He did say it. And worse." It took Adam a moment to collect himself enough to continue. "Not that I could blame him." He made a sweeping gesture with his hand. "It is natural for a father to want his child to marry well, and you were not just any daughter—you were one of the greatest heiresses and most beautiful girls in England. A royal duke would scarcely be good enough for you."

Antonia's eyes were drowned in tears. "It must have been ghastly for you," she whispered. "Why didn't you tell me?"

"How could I?" Adam asked bleakly. "Spenston was right: my aspirations were pathetic, but I had been too naive and too much in love to see what a fool I was. I had adored you since the day we met, when you accepted me as a valued cousin even though I was a soot-covered urchin. But after your father finished with me, I realized just how unworthy I was to marry you."

"By any reasonable standard, you are far worthier than I," she said, her hands clenching into fists. "You were wiser and kinder and more generous than anyone else I knew."

"You were the only one who believed that," Adam replied bluntly. "Everyone else was quite clear about where I belonged on the social scale. Here at Thornleigh, at Thornton family gatherings, at Rugby and Cambridge, there were always subtle and not-so-subtle reminders that I was allowed among my superiors only on sufferance. I never told you because I knew you would come charging to my defense, and I would be damned if I would let you fight my battles for me. Besides, there was nothing you could do or say that would alter the reality of what I was."

"Stop talking as if you were a leper!" Antonia cried. "I can't bear it." It was horrifying to realize how unperceptive she had been and how Adam must have suffered. It also hurt to realize just how cruel her idolized father had been. Her cousin was far more tolerant of the earl's behavior than Antonia could be. How dare her father, who had never had time for his daughter, dismiss the one person who had always been there for her?

Adam's words were creating a whole new picture of the past, and now she could better understand what had happened. "Did my father force you to leave England to get you away from me?"

"In a way. He didn't have me kidnapped, but he demanded that I swear never to see or contact you again. Amusing, isn't it? In spite of my unworthiness, he was willing to believe that my word was good." Adam smiled humorlessly. "I proposed a bargain. I refused to promise that I would never contact you, but I told him that if he found me a post with the East India Company and gave me the money he had intended to use to buy a commission, I would go to India, and that I would say and write nothing that would interfere with your finding a suitable husband."

"I see." Antonia swallowed hard, absorbing that. "That is why your letters were always so resolutely unloverlike?"

Adam nodded. "I could have defied your father, but again he was right. Whatever his reasons for taking me in, I did owe him a great deal. It would have been very shabby to court his only daughter against his wishes."

He sighed and ran one hand through his light hair, tousling it thoroughly. "There was more to the bargain. I couldn't do anything about being illegitimate, but I could do something about being penniless. I told your father that I would never ask you to marry me unless I had a fortune equal to yours.

"Spenston found my proposal amusing, knowing that the odds of my achieving my goal before you married elsewhere were infinitesimal. He also supposed that my lowering myself to trade would quash any romantic longings that you might cherish. It was a very safe bargain for him to agree to."

Antonia voice was hushed. "That is why you worked so hard in India?"

Adam nodded again. "It was the only hope I had. To be a rich baseborn merchant was somewhat better than to be a penniless baseborn soldier. I seized every opportunity to build the small stake I began with. I took risks, always trying the long chance that might pay off spectacularly." His face tightened. "And whenever I received a letter from you, I wondered if it would contain news of your marriage."

The magnitude of what he had endured was beyond Antonia's experience and comprehension. Adam must have suffered agonies, particularly in her first few Seasons, when she was the object of considerable attention. Antonia had written him often, gay little letters about her doings and her suitors, with the unadmitted desire of showing that some men wanted her, even if her cousin didn't. She faltered. "So when I wrote you that I was betrothed to Lord Ramsay . . . ?"

"You said that you were planning an early wedding, and I thought you must already be married by the time I received the letter." Adam's face was rigid. "I went out and got blind, stinking, paralyzed drunk that night."

Antonia bit her lip as she imagined how he must have felt. "Adam, I'm so sorry. I had no idea that I was hurting you," she whispered. "I had long since accepted that there had never been anything romantic between us except for my dreams." She thought back. "It must have been almost a year until you got the letter saying that I had cried off."

"Ten months, two weeks, and three days," he said precisely. "Don't blame yourself, Tony. How could you know? I was trying very hard to keep my part of the bargain." He shrugged. "I survived by becoming philosophical. If, as I tried to believe, we were meant to be together, it would happen if I worked hard enough. The longer you stayed unmarried and the wealthier I became, the more possible it seemed. When I achieved the financial goals I had set in the beginning, I came home."

Adam gave a smile of wintry bleakness. "It seemed a bad omen to find you a baroness. The gap between us was as wide as ever. Then Simon came along, and it appeared that all my efforts were for nothing.''

Antonia gasped. In the drama of her cousin's story, she had completely forgotten about Lord Launceston's existence. "Adam, you shouldn't have said any of this. I'm betrothed to Simon.''

His gaze burned into hers. "Are you in love with him or with me?''

Antonia shrank back against the cupboard, feeling trapped. Adam's story had brought vividly alive all the love and romantic assumptions she had felt as they grew up together, plus the passion she had discovered so recently. But she had given her word to Simon; he deserved her loyalty, and she did care for him. "I love you," she said wretched, "but it would be wicked and dishonorable to cry off from Simon a second time.''

"It would be more wicked to marry him if you love me," Adam said, his voice implacable. "As Judith reminded me when she broke our betrothal, in the long run it is better to be honest than noble. Simon is my friend and I would do almost anything for him, but I will not politely stand by and let him marry you without a struggle. The decision is yours, Tony. Which one of us do you want?''

Antonia buried her face in her hands. "I don't know what I want! To marry you seems so selfish.''

"Because it is more virtuous to suffer than to do what you want? Don't forget, your virtue will condemn me to suffer as well," Adam pointed out with relentless logic. "I could bear it if you loved another man, but that isn't what you are saying.''

She began to shake with silent tears. Too much was happening: learning of Adam's love and how much he had endured for her over the years; discovering that her idealized father had had his share of hypocrisy; having to make a choice that must hurt one of the men she cared most about. Adam was right: her own guilt was inclining her to make the choice that would punish her, but doing so would punish him as well.

Adam's dark velvet voice cut through her misery. "You

may not know what you want, but I do. Look at me, Tony."
She raised her head and looked into his intense gray-green
eyes as he said, "You want a husband who will hold you
at the center of his life. You don't want a man who will put
politics, or gaming, or society, or anything else first. Simon
may love you, but he loves ideas and the challenges of the
mind as well. You will never come first with him in the same
way that you do with me. I love you, and I have spent my
life proving it." Adam stretched out his hand to her.
"Come," he said softly.

Antonia could feel the force of his will pulling her, and
she took an involuntary step toward him before halting. While
the decision was hers, Adam was exerting all his physical,
mental, and emotional power to prove why she should choose
him. She wanted him—dear God, how she wanted him! And
Adam, who knew her better than anyone else, was right. She
wanted a husband who would put her first, not push her aside
like her father and mother had. The worst thing about Simon
was his ability to withdraw into himself, excluding her; she
did not want a lifetime of frantically wondering if she had
done something wrong and must win her way back into her
husband's good graces.

The universe narrowed down to Antonia's thoughts and
Adam's beckoning gesture. His hand was broad and powerful, the long fingers capable of delicacy as well as strength.
As she stared at his hand with mesmerized longing, Antonia
realized that the true reason she had never married was
because she wanted a man she could trust to love her always,
even in the midst of the disagreements that all couples
sometimes experience, even when the years robbed her of
the youthful beauty that men so much admired. Beyond
question and doubt, she knew that Adam was offering that
kind of love.

And if she was the center of Adam's life, he was the center
of hers. It had always been her cousin whom she trusted and
turned to, who had been the touchstone of her existence even
when he was half a world away. If she had known that he
loved her as she loved him, they would never have been
separated so long. She would have defied her father, would

have gladly followed Adam to India. The honorable reasons
for standing by her betrothal to Simon were frail and
irrelevant. All that mattered was Adam, who offered love
and warmth and protection—Adam, whom she loved.

As Antonia struggled between what she wanted and what
she thought she should do, she took another step toward
Adam, then one more. Then, the inevitable decision made,
she flew the remaining distance in a rush of joyous abandon,
drawn to Adam as a compass seeks its pole. Wrapping her
arms around his solid strength, she raised her face for a kiss,
and as their lips met, all doubts disappeared. She and Adam
belonged together, two halves of the same whole, and she
had been blind not to know it sooner.

Adam's embrace was rib-bruising in its intensity. "Lord,
Tony, I love you so much," he whispered huskily. "I was
so afraid that I couldn't change your mind." Then for a wild
sweet interval they were lost in each other as memories,
promises, and words of love wove a binding spell around
them.

Reluctantly Antonia made herself think of what still lay
ahead. She leaned back in Adam's arms, tenderly brushing
a disordered lock of his oak-colored hair from his forehead.
"I had best find Simon." Her smile was unsteady. "I'm not
quite sure how to explain that I am jilting him a second time."

"One would think that you have had ample experience."
Adam's tan skin crinkled around his eyes as he tried to tease
a smile from her. "You've been betrothed to Lord Ramsay,
Simon, and me in my amnesiac stage, and broken off from
all three of us."

Antonia laughed a little, ducking her head against his chest
in embarrassment. Her voice muffled, she asked, "Does this
mean that I am about to be betrothed for the fifth time?"

"No," Adam said firmly, linking his arms around her slim
waist. "No more betrothals. We will simply get married,
and as soon as possible."

She laid her head against his chest, listening to the steady
rhythm of his heart, reluctant to leave his sheltering embrace
for the difficulties that lay outside the stillroom. The worst
would be confronting Simon. Though not as painful, there

would also be the incredulous and disapproving relatives and the members of the *ton*. Lady Antonia Thornton, Baroness Fairbourne in her own right, was going to be judged a total, fickle idiot.

Antonia didn't care. As she settled back into Adam's embrace, she knew that no amount of gossip or censure could make her regret her decision.

Then reality intruded. The door to the stillroom opened, and Antonia looked past Adam's shoulder into the startled blue eyes of Simon Launceston.

14

Antonia's gasp of alarm alerted Adam, and he turned to see Lord Launceston standing motionless in the doorway, his chiseled countenance like stone as he saw his affianced wife in the embrace of his best friend.

"Might I ask what this means?" Simon asked, his voice as expressionless as his face.

Adam slid a protective arm around Antonia's waist. "Until half an hour ago, there was nothing going on behind your back," he said steadily. "Direct your anger at me. I was the one who undertook to change my cousin's mind, and it was not attempted or accomplished lightly. Tony was about to seek you out to end your betrothal. I'm sorry that you had to find out this way."

Simon's searching blue gaze turned to Antonia. "You wish to marry Adam?"

She nodded, biting her lip. "Yes. I know that I am behaving despicably, but Adam and I belong together."

"Does Judith know yet?" Simon's soft tenor was edged.

Adam's eyes narrowed speculatively. Lord Launceston had been startled and taken aback to find Adam and Antonia together, but there were no signs of anguish or fury. In fact, he seemed far more concerned about the effect on Judith. "She cried off from our betrothal last night, saying that all of us were mired in confusion and dishonesty. Because of what she said, I realized that I must declare myself to Tony."

"That explains a great deal," Simon said slowly, his thoughts turned inward for a moment. Then he gave a self-mocking smile. "I really should make a dramatic exit now, but I had an important reason for coming here. A few minutes ago I inquired after Judith, thinking she might be interested in seeing how a telescope is assembled, and the butler said that she ordered a carriage for five o'clock this morning and left with considerable baggage. At my request, a maid went to Judith's room and found this.'' He held out a sealed envelope to Antonia. ''Mrs. Heaver said you might be in the stillroom, so I brought this down, since it is addressed to you.''

Surprised, Antonia took the envelope and tore it open. As she scanned the enclosed sheet, she sucked her breath in. ''Judith has left Thornleigh and is going to America.''

''What!'' Manners for once forgotten, Simon grabbed the note from Antonia's hand and read it himself. He looked up, his face pale, his eyes seeking Adam's. ''What happened?'' he asked tensely. ''Why would she leave so abruptly and go so far?''

''I'm not sure,'' Adam replied with puzzlement. ''Judith gave me no inkling of her plans.'' He thought back to what had happened. ''She said the reason she and I had decided to marry in the first place was because we were both settling for what we could get rather than what we really wanted. She had guessed that I loved Antonia. By implication, she may have meant that she also was in love with someone else.'' He stopped, then added with wry humor, ''You might know more about that than I.''

There was a flash of emotion in Simon's deep-blue eyes before he turned and wordlessly headed toward the door.

''Where are you going?'' Antonia asked, more than a little confused.

''After Judith, of course,'' Simon flung over his shoulder.

''Wait!'' Adam's voice commanded. When his friend stopped, Adam asked, ''Are you in love with her?''

''Yes, but I never said so because of the prior engagement between you and her.'' Simon gave Antonia a rueful glance. ''I can hardly accuse you of fickleness when I was behaving much the same way myself.''

''Thank heaven,'' Antonia said, crossing the room to throw her arms around Simon in a spontaneous hug. ''You have just done wonders for my guilty conscience. It had occurred to me more than once that you and Judith would suit admirably. Is she in love with you as well?''

Simon glanced at the letter he still had clenched in his hand. ''I have no idea,'' he said bleakly. ''Judith never gave me any reason to believe that she returned my feelings, and I don't find this promising.''

''I think you're wrong,'' Adam said. ''Judith was convinced that you and I were both in love with Tony. Believing that, she may have left because staying near you would have been too painful.''

''I hope you are right,'' Lord Launceston said, a grim cast to his handsome face. ''I'm going to ask her to marry me, even if I have to follow her to America.''

''Don't go running off blindly,'' Antonia put in. ''If we can deduce where she is going, we stand a much better chance of finding her.''

''You're right,'' Simon admitted, shaking his dark head distractedly. ''I'm not thinking clearly.''

Adam and Antonia exchanged glances. It must be love to interfere with Lord Launceston's usually admirable thinking processes.

''Adam, you're the expert on shipping. Where would she be most likely to go?'' Simon appealed.

''Liverpool,'' Adam said instantly. ''It's much closer than Bristol, and these days it handles the majority of the North Atlantic trade. But we had best hurry.''

''We?'' Simon asked, bemused.

''Of course. You're going to need help looking for her.'' Adam glanced at Antonia and got a confirming nod. ''Neither Tony nor I will be able to relax and plan for the future until this tangle is sorted out. Nothing could make either of us happier than seeing you and Judith together.''

''What if I find Judith and she refuses me?'' Simon said with another bleak glance at the letter in his hand.

''She won't,'' Antonia said with utter confidence. ''I promise you that.'' Only a woman who was loved by Adam Yorke would be fool enough to turn down Simon Launceston.

The sails unfurled, the heavy canvas snapping as it began

to catch the wind. Judith wondered if she would ever see
her native land again, her fingers tightening around the railing
until her knuckles were white. Perhaps it had been wrong
to choose to run so far away; she had never felt more English
than now, when she was leaving everything she had ever
known.

Shuddering, Judith pulled her shawl around her shoulders,
thinking how cool the wind was over the water. She had been
fortunate to catch the *Lady Liberty*. The next Boston-bound
ship wouldn't leave for over a week, and during a wait that
long she might have been mad enough to change her mind
and go back to Thornleigh. She wondered if matters had been
resolved between Antonia and her two suitors, and which
of the people Judith loved was hurting now.

Someone came to join her at the railing. "We're on our
way at last," a buoyant voice said. "I've seen enough of
the old country, let me tell you. I can't wait to get back to
Boston."

Judith glanced at Mrs. Maxwell, with whom she was
sharing a tiny cabin. The plump, rosy older woman was an
American widow returning home after a once-in-a-lifetime
visit to British relatives. She was a pleasant creature, if a
trifle overexuberant. "You'll have to see Belfast first,"
Judith remarked.

"Only for a day," her cabinmate said cheerfully. "Then
it's home again. I wonder if my youngest grandchild will
remember me. My daughter and her husband thought I was
quite mad to go so far alone, you know. But I say, seeing
another country makes you appreciate your own more."

Mrs. Maxwell said quite a lot of things, Judith thought
with amusement. Still, she was a good-natured woman and
clearly prosperous. Perhaps she could help Judith find a
situation in Boston.

"You won't regret emigrating to America, Mrs. Winslow.
It's a country for people who dare to dream," the older
woman went on. "Not like England, with so many fusty rules
to squeeze the life out of a body." She stopped abruptly,
an apologetic expression on her round face. "No offense
meant."

Judith couldn't help smiling. "None taken." It was impossible to take umbrage at such innocent criticism, though she could not help wondering if all Americans were so friendly and outspoken. If they were, she might find the New World a bit overpowering.

Her brief smile faded; the only dream she had ever had was to marry Simon Launceston. She turned her gaze back to the shore, where the bustling docks were already too distant for detail, trying to swallow the lump in her throat. It wasn't that she aspired to be Lady Launceston; it was Simon himself she wanted, not his title or comfortable fortune. But that was not a dream she could achieve in America.

The party reached Liverpool very late and spent what remained of the night at an inn near the harbor. Next morning, after Adam had consulted with the innkeeper about the shipping news, they plunged into the teeming Liverpool dockyards just as the port was waking to the day's business. A forest of masts rose in front of them, and other ships bobbed out in the harbor, waiting their turns for dock space. Sailors and stevedores yelled in incomprehensible dialects, gulls screeched overhead and fought for tidbits, and the air was filled with the pungent scents characteristic of places where the land meets the sea.

Antonia and her companions had to dodge around bales of goods and drays as they made their way along the waterfront. She was attracting huge amounts of unabashed male attention, but felt quite secure with her male escorts and would have enjoyed the new sights and sounds immensely if they hadn't been on an errand of such urgency. Simon's anxiety was contagious; it would be far better to intercept Judith before she left. One small woman could disappear very easily in a raw new nation, and if she decided not to write, they might never find her.

Though Adam had never been to Liverpool, he had been in enough ports to know how to proceed. Antonia was impressed to get a glimpse of the merchant prince in action; it gave her a whole new view of the man she loved. In an amazingly short time they were in an office where a substantial gratuity persuaded a weathered old clerk to check his passenger lists. As Antonia understood it, this office acted as local passenger agent for a number of foreign-owned ships.

With excruciating slowness, the clerk perused the list of names, finally allowing that a Mrs. J. Winslow had purchased a ticket on the *Lady Liberty*, an American ship out of Boston.

Antonia breathed a sigh of relief that it had been so simple. But then, there was no reason for Judith to conceal her identity.

"When does it leave?" Lord Launceston asked eagerly.

The clerk blinked saurian eyelids. "Left yesterday on the evening tide."

Simon began to swear with a startling fluency. Antonia would not have guessed that the calm scholar could forget himself so far in front of a lady; it was more proof of the strength of his feelings for Judith. While Simon swore and Antonia reflected, Adam asked the clerk a series of swift questions. After getting the answers, he ushered his companions out of the office. "The *Lady Liberty* will put in at Belfast before going on to Boston."

Simon's face lit up. "Will the ship be there long enough for me to catch up with her?"

"Not in the normal course of events. The *Lady Liberty* will stop for only about twenty-four hours, and there is no ship leaving for Belfast today. The mail packets go out of Port Patrick." As he spoke, Adam's eyes scanned the harbor intently.

"Would it be possible to hire a ship that could get us there in time?" Simon asked, grasping at any possibility.

"None of the small boats we could hire can catch a fast Baltimore schooner like the *Lady Liberty*, not when she has almost a day's lead." Adam shaded his eyes with his hands as he squinted to see the more distant docks.

"What are you looking for, Adam?" Antonia questioned.

"When we came in, I thought I recognized . . ." He stopped speaking, then a wide smile crossed his face and he took her arm. "Come along. I think that fortune favors our quest."

They made their way through the confusion to a dock where a trim ship named *Star of India* was moored. Antonia wondered what class of ship it was; she felt very ignorant. The only thing she was sure about was the come-hither look in the eye of the buxom black-haired figurehead gracing the prow—not at all a respectable sort of female, Antonia decided as they boarded.

A neatly dressed sailor appeared as they reached the deck. "Is Captain Langdon on board?" Adam asked. At the sailor's nod, he continued, "Tell him Adam Yorke is paying a call."

Visibly startled, the sailor bobbed his head, then turned and ducked below. In less than a minute, a tall man of unmistakable authority appeared, his broad smile very white against his dark skin. "Adam, my friend, what an unexpected pleasure! Welcome aboard." He offered his hand, adding, "My ship is yours."

"Not anymore," Adam said with a grin as he shook hands. Both of the men laughed while Antonia observed with interest. The captain had a distinctly foreign look, though his name and accent were British. Of mixed race, perhaps? Not an easy condition in a bigoted world. Of one thing she was sure: the wickedly attractive Captain Langdon was the very image of what Antonia imagined a pirate should be.

When Adam finished the introductions, the captain bowed over Antonia's hand with a flourish. "You are betrothed to Captain Yorke? A pity that one so beautiful should waste herself so," he said soulfully, unabashed admiration in his black eyes.

"On the contrary." Antonia chuckled as she retrieved her hand. "It's the wisest thing I've ever done."

The captain turned back to Adam. "Come, you and your friends must join me for morning coffee." As they went below, he asked over his shoulder, "Is this purely a social call?"

"No," Adam said. "We need to get to Belfast as quickly as possible to intercept a friend on the way to America. Would you be able to take us across immediately?" They emerged from a narrow passage into a spacious cabin. "Her ship left Liverpool last night and will spend only a day in Belfast before sailing on to Boston.''

"I'll pay your charter fee, whatever it is," Simon added, too anxious to be a good bargainer.

Captain Langdon gestured airily. "For a friend of Adam's there will be no charge." There was a gleam in his eye. "It will be a splendid diversion. I arrived ahead of schedule, and my cargo won't be ready for at least a week. In fact, I must move from the dock now I am unloaded. A quest for a fair lady—she is a fair lady, I trust?—will be a great improvement over lying at a mooring in the Mersey."

"Thank heaven," Simon said with patent relief. "How soon can we leave?"

"To catch the tide we must leave within the hour. Do you have luggage or servants to board?" the captain asked.

Antonia's maid and Simon's very superior valet were summoned from the inn with the baggage, and within half an hour they were under weigh. Fortunately the ship was equipped with several passenger cabins that were unoccupied until the next voyage, so everyone could be accommodated comfortably.

While Lord Launceston prowled the deck restlessly, Antonia found a spot at the stern railing to enjoy the sights as they sailed from the mouth of the Mersey River into the Irish Sea. To her relief, the rise and fall of the ship produced no symptoms of *mal de mer*. "I feel rather ashamed of myself, having such a good time when we are on a serious mission," she confessed to Adam, who stood next to her.

"We're doing the most we can, and brooding won't improve our chances of success," Adam pointed out. "And there is something very special and enjoyable about being at sea."

"Do you think we will reach Belfast in time?"

"We have a very good chance. The *Star of India* is fast, and we're less than a day behind."

Transferring her gaze from the sea to her true love, Antonia decided that he looked very much at home on a ship. He'd left his hat below, and the wind ruffled his sun-streaked light hair as he balanced on the rolling deck with the unconscious skill of long practice.

"You look very dashing," Antonia murmured, knowing that she sounded quite besotted, as well she should. "Are you really a ship's captain?"

"I've commanded ships," he admitted, "though I certainly haven't the skill or experience that Ramesh Langdon does."

"If you asked him to take us all the way to Boston, he would do it, wouldn't he?" Antonia had been intrigued by the obvious intimacy between the two men and was curious to learn more about her cousin's merchant life.

Adam turned his eyes seaward again. "Perhaps. He feels that he owes me more than he does."

"What happened?"

Adam shrugged. "Nothing dramatic. I offered him a ship to sail when no one else would. This ship, as it happens. He did very well, made us both quite a lot of money, and eventually bought the *Star of India* for himself. We both benefited."

Antonia smiled warmly. "I'm sure that that is an oversimplification, but doubtless you won't tell me more. Have I mentioned lately how much I love you?"

"Not in the last twenty-four hours." He laid his hand over hers on the railing. "By the way, before we left I dispatched my man Bradley to York to get two archbishop's licenses. They should be waiting when we get back to Thornleigh."

"One for us and the other for Simon and Judith?" Antonia said with delight. "Clearly a life in trade makes one marvelously efficient." Her voice dropped. "I don't want to wait a day longer than necessary."

"Nor do I, love." Adam put his arm around Antonia and she settled against him with contentment. She refused to believe that things would not work out equally well for Simon and Judith.

They made good time for the first half of the voyage, but the winds fell off west of the Isle of Man, and even the cleverest of sailors needs wind. By the time the *Star of India* entered the harbor at Belfast, they were a full day behind the *Lady Liberty*, perhaps more.

As the ship slowly made its way into port, Simon and Adam stood in the bow, Lord Launceston with grim lines in his face. "Do you think we're in time?" he asked tightly.

"It's hard to say," Adam replied, trying to combine comfort with honesty. "Even if Judith's ship has left already, it doesn't mean that she is lost forever, just that you have a voyage to the New World ahead of you. Surely there must be some interesting geology on that side of the Atlantic?"

Simon smiled reluctantly. "Yes, but I can't say that the prospect is prominent in my thinking. Do you see anything promising?"

Adam's experienced gaze was scrutinizing the mass of ships moored about the large harbor. "We're too far to read the names, but to the right of where we will be docking there is a Baltimore schooner that could be the *Lady Liberty*. Don't get your hopes too high," he cautioned as he pointed out the ship. "The class is a popular one with the Americans."

Unless Adam greatly mistook matters, the schooner was preparing to set sail. But there was no point in mentioning that to Simon when there was nothing his friend could do about it until they docked.

Based on her very limited experience, seaports were much the same, Judith decided. Belfast was smaller than Liverpool and the accents of the stevedores were different, but the overall effect was remarkably similar. She was impatient to set sail, anxious to put the British Isles behind her so that she could begin looking to the future rather than mourning the past.

Mrs. Maxwell had joined her on deck, and together they watched the final preparations for putting out to sea.

"They're about to remove the gangway. It won't be long now," the American woman said, glancing along the quay. Then she stiffened. "Would you look at that," she exclaimed in a reverent voice. "Here comes the handsomest man I have ever seen in my born days."

Judith didn't bother to look where Mrs. Maxwell was indicating; it was not easy to impress a woman who had known Simon Launceston.

Then Mrs. Maxwell elbowed her in excitement. "Look, he's coming aboard the *Lady Liberty*! I swear," she said impishly, "if he's going to be on the voyage to Boston, I'm going to disgrace myself by following him around like a puppy dog. Lucky my daughter isn't here to see her old mother making a fool of herself."

Judith said, "Women are always making fools of themselves over men. It's part of our nature." She glanced over to see the man who had impressed her cabinmate so much, then froze. No, it couldn't possibly be Simon. It couldn't be!

But it was. Lord Launceston had raced up the gangway just before it could be removed, stopping at the top to peruse the deck. Even with most of the length of the ship between them, she could see the vivid blueness of his eyes when his gaze met hers. Then he gave her a smile of such intimacy that she thought her bones would melt. Judith knew that her jaw was slack with astonishment, and she clasped the railing for support. She could not have spoken to save her life, a fact proved when Mrs. Maxwell said, "Do you know him? He's looking right at you."

Judith just shook her head dazedly as she watched the *Lady Liberty*'s captain approach Simon. The wind brought fragments of words, the captain gruffly saying that the ship was on the verge of departure and that the newcomer had better leave if he didn't want to see Boston and have to pay for the privilege.

The only part of Simon's reply that could be heard was "Ten minutes."

Something passed between the two men that elicited a respectful nod from the American captain. "Very well, ten minutes."

Before the captain had finished speaking, Simon was taking swift strides toward Judith while she watched in blank confusion.

An elbow from Mrs. Maxwell helped return her to reality. "Will you introduce me?"

Simon stopped right in front of Judith, tall, elegant, and paralyzingly handsome. But he had always been that. What was different now was the expression in his eyes, as if she was the most beautiful and desirable woman in the world.

Weakly she said, "Mrs. Maxwell, Lrod Launceston. Simon, this is Mrs. Maxwell, my cabinmate."

He turned and gave the older woman one of his devastating smiles as he bowed over her hand. "My pleasure. My I impose on you for a few moments' privacy with Mrs. Winslow? I have something very important to say to her."

Dazzled, Mrs. Maxwell returned his smile, then retreated until she was out of earshot. Barely.

"What are you doing in Belfast?" Judith made a feeble attempt to collect her scattered wits. "Did Antonia ask you to come after me? There was no need for that. I'm quite capable of managing on my own."

Simon shook his head. "I'm here on my behalf, not hers." He stopped for a moment, then said ruefully, "There is no time for roundaboutation, and I'm no good at it anyhow. Judith, will you marry me?"

That was the trouble with dreams; they turn into hallucinations if you aren't careful, Judith decided. This couldn't possibly be happening. Or if it was, it was for the wrong reason. "Are you asking me because Antonia has accepted Adam, and I'm the best available substitute because I have been close to her?" she asked tightly.

"No. Antonia has accepted Adam, but I'm asking because I want very much for you to be my wife." He smiled with self-deprecating charm. "I'm something of a slow learner in matters of the heart. I didn't suspect that I had fallen in love with you until I kissed you in the garden. In retrospect, I saw that I was just looking for a good excuse to do something I had wanted to do for a long time. Even so, the impact was so great that it took me several days to sort myself out. I was on my way to ask you to marry me when Adam's memory came back. Since I thought you preferred him, I didn't speak."

It sounded much too wonderful to be true. Judith looked searchingly into Simon's deep-blue eyes. "But what about

you and Antonia?'' she asked. ''You were so much in love
with her.''

He shook his head. ''I was infatuated, not in love. Antonia
is a glorious and splendid woman, and I suffered the sort
of calf love that I might have experienced at nineteen if I
hadn't had my nose buried in a succession of books. Since
she was feeling the same kind of infatuation for me, it was
easy to believe that it was meant to be.''

''You looked so much like you belonged together that it
seemed inevitable,'' Judith agreed. ''You are the two most
beautiful human creatures I have ever seen.''

Simon's handsome face showed self-conscious color.
''Antonia has a dramatic beauty that turns all heads when
she enters a room,'' he said softly. ''You are every bit as
lovely, but your beauty is a quieter kind, meant to be savored
close-up.'' He cupped Judith's cheek in one hand. ''I want
to spend the rest of my life as close to you as possible, not
just because you are beautiful, but because when I am with
you, I am happier and more complete than I have ever been
in my life.''

Time was running out; from the far end of the ship, the
captain began to move toward them with deliberate steps.
Simon said quickly, ''I daresay my absentmindedness is
incurable, and I will be forever coaxing you into caves and
observatories, but I'll try to be a good husband in spite of
that. Will you marry me?''

He looked so earnest that it was impossible to doubt him.
For some incomprehensible reason, Simon really did prefer
her. Feeling a joy beyond anything she had ever imagined,
Judith exclaimed, ''Yes. Yes, yes, *yes*!'' and threw her arms
around him.

She must have learned that from Antonia, Judith decided
as Simon returned her embrace with gratifying enthusiasm;
such profligate behavior was most unlike the Widow
Winslow.

Perhaps profligate behavior is contagious; as the impatient
captain arrived, a gleam of unholy mischief appeared in
Simon's eyes and he bent over and swept Judith from her
feet, cradling her easily in his arms. He gave the captain a

look of cherubic innocence. "Will you be the first to wish us happy? Mrs. Winslow has just agreed to make me the most fortunate of men."

As Judith blushed furiously and hid her face against Simon's shoulder, the captain stopped in his tracks. Then a reluctant smile began to show through his bushy beard; it is a rare person who hasn't a streak of romanticism buried somewhere. Gruffly he asked, "Are you leaving or staying?"

"Leaving."

"Very well." A semicircle of interested onlookers had gathered, and the captain signaled to the nearest sailor. "Go below and get Mrs. Winslow's gear, and be quick about it."

"I'll show him what to take," Mrs. Maxwell said helpfully. Before leaving, she turned to Judith. "Sorry I won't get to show you Boston, dear, but you'd be a fool to turn that one down," she said in a stage whisper, rolling her eyes. Then she blew Judith a kiss and led the sailor below.

With perfect gravity Simon ssaid, "Thank you for delaying your departure, Captain. Have a safe voyage." Then, with the aplomb of a man who swept females off their feet every day, he carried Judith along the deck and down the gangway.

Two dark-skinned sailors waited at the foot, and at a word from Simon they boarded the *Lady Liberty* to get Judith's baggage.

Everyone loves a parade, and Simon and Judith's progress along the quay rapidly attracted an audience of sailors, small boys, stevedores, and other assorted denizens of the port. At a guess, half of the population of Belfast was present, smiling, waving, and making graphic comments calculated to bring a blush to any cheek.

Judith herself was such a hot, bright red that she feared that her skin might never return to its normal hue. She really ought to demand that Simon put her down, but being held in his strong arms was too wonderful to end. She felt foolish, conspicuous, and quite absurdly in love.

As they reached a ship called the *Star of India* and Simon carried her up the gangway, the crowd on the quay broke into a roar of applause and whistles that must have been audible in Dublin. Once they reached the deck, Simon set

Judith on her feet, then turned and waved to the crowd before whisking her out of sight belowdecks.

Breathless with laughter, Judith said, "I will never dare set foot in Belfast again."

Simon smiled with impish tenderness. "I daresay I won't be very good at romantic gestures, so I wanted to make at least one that you will always remember."

"I will certainly never forget that!" Judith said fervently.

Simon guided her to a sizable cabin where Adam and Antonia waited. While Adam watched with warm approval, her former employer flew across the cabin to give Judith a hug.

"Thank heaven everything has worked out," Antonia said joyously. "We were all being so noble and self-sacrificing that we would never have gotten sorted out properly if it hadn't been for you, Judith. I don't know how I can ever repay you."

Her friend looked up at Simon. "I have my reward," she said softly, her gray eyes glowing with happiness.

While Simon presented Judith to Captain Langdon, Antonia returned to her cousin and twined her arm in his. "Adam, is it true that sea captains can perform marriages?"

He looked thoughtful. "I'm really not sure. The ship would have to be on the open sea. Even then, since large amounts of property are involved, it would be wiser to have a ceremony performed by a regular vicar, so there would never be a question about the legality."

"We could have a second ceremony, just to be on the safe side. After all, the special licenses will be waiting at Thornleigh." Her voice dropped, husky with promise. "But since we have a perfectly good ship and sea captain available, why don't we have him marry us on the voyage to Liverpool? The present sleeping arrangements leave a great deal to be desired."

Adam's gray-green eyes met hers, and the rest of the world faded into insignificance as laughter and desire blazed between them. "You're right, Tony, we've waited quite long enough," he agreed, his voice husky with intimate promise.

He glanced up at Captain Langdon. "Shall we be off? The sooner we're on the open sea, the better."

With a marvelous disregard for decorum, Adam bent to kiss his intended. As Antonia returned his kiss, she thought it strange that the perfect lover she had dreamed of had been there all the time, as playmate, friend, and refuge. Had it not been for his near-fatal accident and amnesia, she might never have come to see Adam as the passionate, devoted man she had longed for. Truly God worked in mysterious ways.

Captain Langdon found the voyage back to Liverpool rather tedious, but he accepted it philosophically. One could hardly expect two pairs of newlyweds to be good company.

In White's, the long-standing wagers on who would wed the scrumptious and unattainable Lady Fairbourne were all canceled because no one had bet on the man who actually won her. Very bad of the fellow to spoil their sport, it was agreed.

News of the marriage of Lord Launceston caused massive weeping and wailing among those unmarried female members of the *ton* who had had the good fortune to meet him. While his lordship's interests were admittedly eccentric, it was universally acknowledged that Lord Byron couldn't hold a candle to him.

James Malcolm was shocked speechless when he received the letter saying that Adam Yorke had decided to invest in his company; the engineer had never really expected the nabob to be so tolerant over the fact that the steam engine had almost killed him. Yorke was a real gent, and no mistake. The letter of intent included a line saying that the accident had paid unexpected dividends, whatever that meant.

Ian Kinlock was not a man to follow society news, and it was purest chance that he spotted familiar names in the newspaper that had been used to wrap the dinner his landlady had put up for him. Flattening the greasy sheet, he saw that Lady Fairbourne of Thornleigh had lately wed Adam Yorke. The item below that informed the world that Lord Launceston of Abbotsden had married Mrs. Judith Winslow, and the couple would be residing in Kent and London. Kinlock threw back his head and roared with laughter, releasing the tension of a hard day's work at St. Bartholomew's Hospital. A pity he would never know exactly what had happened, but he had a feeling that when the music had stopped, everyone had ended up with the right partner.

Antonia's aunt, Lady Forrester, read the news of her niece's marriage with initial shock, followed by a thoughtful silence. Over the years, she had sometimes wondered if she had done the right thing to tell Lord Spenston about his daughter's youthful involvement with her cousin. Certainly it had looked like a most unsuitable match at the time, but Adam Yorke had been a decent lad, for all his birth and lack of fortune, and Antonia had never been the same after her cousin went to India. Still, Adam Yorke had come back a nabob and far more eligible than when he left, so everything had turned out for the best. Lady Forrester took full credit for the satisfactory outcome.

Antonia gave the telescope to Simon and Judith as a wedding present. As she pointed out with invincible logic, it wasn't the sort of thing you could give just anyone.